CW00840121

First published in 2018 by Sharpe Books.

ISBN: 9781718034167

CONTENTS

THE KING'S KNIGHT

BOOK TWO OF A TRILOGY BASED UPON THE LIFE OF WILLIAM MARSHAL

AUTHOR'S NOTE

Insert Readers familiar with the first volume of this trilogy - and the long Author's Note with which I prefaced it - will recall that I make no claims for the work being one of historical fact. As with *The Knight Banneret*, *The King's Knight*, is an attempt to tell a story of one remarkable man who lived through an age of incredible instability. To this end the torrent of historical events, all of which interplay and interrelate, have of necessity to be pared down and while I have passed over much of the detail outside the immediate purview of William Marshal, I have followed the causal chain in the interest of seeking out the extraordinary life he led.

I hope historical purists will forgive me this presumption, but a novelist has no business writing history unless he is prepared to wear a different hat, in which case he will not write a novel. The purpose of a novel is to entertain not to educate, though a historical novel – if well-done – may spark an interest in its subject such that the reader is led on to make enquiries of her or his own. To achieve this must be the historical novelist's highest aspiration – but that is a matter beyond my control.

However, almost everything he accomplishes in the pages that follow – even his advice to King John to abandon his hereditary lands in France – seems to be backed-up by the original sources. What I can say with a degree of confidence is that William Marshal, who lies buried somewhere in the Temple Church, just off the Strand in central London, continues to fascinate. Like another hero of mine, George Monck, Duke of Albemarle, (see my *Sword of State* trilogy), he rose from relative obscurity to become a King-maker and a great peer, yet his dynasty did not last. Unlike Monck, however, although embodied in statuary both in the Temple Church and in the Palace of Westminster (neither of which image is more than a representation), we know even less about William Marshal himself, or what really formed the basis of his reputation as 'the Perfect Knight,' a man held to be peerless by his contemporaries in an age where such plaudits did not rule out the use of casual brutality when it served. Like Monck, Marshal not only lived in a time of constantly shifting politics, but he could be ruthless; like Monck he turned his coat, and the question I set out to answer in this series was: why – despite all this - he nevertheless left an enduring reputation for loyalty.

To expose the essence of the man seemed to demand the imaginative freedom of the novelist, rather than the dry rigor of the historian for whom the sources are, in so many respects, unclear or conflicting.

THE KING'S KNIGHT

PROLOGUE: THE WESTERN
MEDITERRANEAN 1185

'You are sad, William,' Robert de Salignac said, breaking into his companion's thoughts.

William Marshal turned from the flaming glory of the sunset and stared at the amused countenance of De Salignac. His sun-burned and weather-beaten face was further ensanguined by the blood and fire blazing on the western horizon. They had been through much together and knew each other's minds, or thought they did.

'Do you not find this hour induces contemplation?' William said, seeing behind the familiar face the high and jagged peaks of Corsica aflame before the diurnally revolving sun plunged them into night.

'Not as much as those I spend at night sleepless in this accursed vessel,' responded Robert as the ship rose and fell to a low swell, compelling him to grasp a rope stay. 'I am sick of rats.'

William chuckled and looked aft to where the watch stood at the tiller. Poor Robert had never quite conquered sea-sickness. He looked up. There was barely enough wind to fill the single sail, but the pennon at the masthead, made of lighter woollen cloth, lifted languidly to a faint breeze.

'There'll be a wind afore midnight,' one of the seamen remarked familiarly, reading William's mind as ably as De Salignac as he coiled down the tail end of the lee sheet he had been easing at the behest of the mariner in charge of the deck.

'How do you know that, fellow?' asked De Salignac sharply, as if reproving the man for his apparent lack of respect in addressing his superiors without invitation.

The seaman straightened up, rubbing his hands together and shrugged. It was clear the man did not much care for rank; why should he, belonging as he did to a fraternity without whose expertise these gilded fools could not accomplish their 'Holy' doings in Outremer? He spat to leeward. 'Why, 'tis always the way at this season, my Lords,' he said simply before, looking round to see that all was secure, he made his way forward and took his night-station as lookout.

William grinned at his friend as they two men settled on the hatchway just abaft the mast to enjoy the twilight, delaying the moment they must seek the discomfort of their palliasses and attempt to sleep amid a tumult of rodents in the foetid stench of the hold.

'The Master expects to make land the day after tomorrow if all goes well, but this bight, or whatever they call it, is known for the mistral, a contrary wind for us,' De Salignac remarked. 'We should have disembarked in Sicily...'

'What do you intend to do, Robert?' William asked, cutting across De Salignac's argument.

'You know well what I intend to do, for you have asked the question often enough and my response now will be no different. We shall meet our fortunes jointly...' Then it struck De Salignac that perhaps William's persistence in asking the question indicated he had something else in mind, something brought to the fore as they approached the end of their voyage from

Acre. 'Unless of course you have no need of me. What shall you do? I see something troubles you.'

William sighed. 'You have some land, Robert…'

''Tis but a small parcel. Not much larger in value than your own rents in St Omer.'

'Pah! To hold rents is not the same. I am landless and I…'

De Salignac studied his friend, noting the change that two years in the Holy Land had wrought; that and the death of his patron and friend, the Young King Henry who had died prematurely and laid upon William Marshal the obligation of taking his cloak to the Holy Sepulchre at Jerusalem. De Salignac had long ago sensed William's desire to detach himself from the service of the Young King's father, King Henry II, known as Curtmantle. It was only now that he realised the depth of William's desire not to return to the turmoil of the Angevin Court.

'Why then did you not stay in the Holy Land?' he asked, the question direct, like a lance point to William's heart. 'We rendered the Templars knightly service and the offers of…'

'I know,' William broke in, as if unwilling to admit he had made a mistake in embarking upon this voyage that would return him to the hatred, division, factionalism and sheer folly of the familial disruptions between Henry and his turbulent sons. 'But after the death of Young Henry I owe allegiance to Queen Eleanor and, whatever I am to make of what remains of my life, must either serve her or obtain from her permission to return to the Holy Land and join the Templars.'

'When we departed no man knew where Henry

Curtmantle kept his Queen mewed up.'

'Someone will,' William said shortly. 'Her Grace will be in southern England. De Salignac said nothing. England, south or north was unknown territory to him, a reputedly wet and miserable land whose barons were in constant quarrel. 'After recovering my destriers from Henry Curtmantle, if they live, I must seek her out, that is why I ask what you will do, for I cannot ask you to accompany me into England.'

'If once the King divines your intention he will thwart you.'

William shook his head. 'He has no interest in me, a landless knight banneret. Two years and time has moved on. There will be others who have claims on the King, younger men. We are no longer young, you and I,' he concluded wistfully.

De Salignac stared at William. It was almost dark now and the shadows about his face showed his strong features in an oddly fascinating beauty. 'The matter of a lack of land troubles you deeply, does it not.' It was a statement not question and William shrugged, staring over the ship's rail to where the sea began to ripple with the first stirrings of the predicted wind.

'With it I might be one thing; without it I am compelled to be something else.' William looked up at De Salignac, dropping his voice. 'Would it not be better to serve God in the Holy Land, than return to military servitude to the feckless House of Anjou? God knows the Kingdom of Jerusalem is in grave danger and Gerard de Ridefort made it clear to both of us that, should we wish it, we would be welcome in the order.

De Salignac nodded. He had been less enthusiastic

than William to accept the honour bestowed upon them by the Grand Master of the Order of the Temple, but he appreciated the crisis of conscience that now beset his friend. A twinge of guilt that his reluctance might have dissuaded William from staying led him to temporise. 'Is not the Kingdom in better hands now that the younger Baldwin is on the throne? Surely he is better than the Leper, his uncle?'

But William was not listening. He shook his head and suddenly looked at De Salignac, whose face was little more than a pale oval in the encroaching darkness. 'I could not in all honour stay, Robert, not after Baldwin's mother remarried following the death of her first husband. Guy of Lusignan has long been an enemy since the ambush that killed my own Uncle, Earl Patrick of Salisbury, and he stands now high in the favour of Baldwin the Fifth.'

'Ah, I had forgot, though you have told me the story often enough.'

'So, I must come back, ransom my war-horses from the King and then seek-out Her Grace, Queen Eleanor.'

'He will not let you, Will. The old fox will attach you to his mesnie, mark my words.' De Salignac rose, stretched and yawned. 'I fear that, like any other lump of cargo aboard this creaking nightmare, I must consign myself to my bed, such as it is. I am no natural channel-crosser like you Englishmen.'

'I shall wait awhile, Robert, but thank you for your counsel.'

'I have given you none but more thought to ponder gloomily upon, I fear,' remarked De Salignac, patting William on the shoulder. 'But it will bear a different look in the morning.' William made no response and De Salignac paused a moment, and then said quietly. 'We are redeemed by our pilgrimage, Will. What is past, is past.'

After his friend had gone below William Marshal remained on deck. There was something quite mystical about this crepuscular hour which he had come to love and revere. It compelled a man to take stock and he suddenly envied the common seaman who stood at his post at the bow, a dark shape against the last of the sunset. Such men, mused William, inhabited a world of extremes: danger to be sure – they had endured a tempestuous outward voyage – but also moments like this and the thought conjured up such evenings in Outremer when it was possible to think one walked directly in the footsteps of the Apostles, if not the Christ himself. God forbid that the Kingdom of Jerusalem fell to the forces of the Turk; the soldier in him told him that it was likely; the believer said it was impossible. It had been God's will that the forces of Christendom had ousted the unbelievers and established Charlemagne's line in the Holy City; it would be God's will that the Frankish Kingdom would endure until the Second Coming. No-one of faith could doubt this.

Where then should he follow the Master? In the ranks of the Templars, where a novitiate had been offered him, or in Normandy; or England, the land of his birth? During his years in Outremer, he had found his thoughts ran often upon England.

'An old man's thoughts,' he muttered to himself. 'I shall be, what? Forty soon enough.' And rising to go below he knew he must first go back to Henry

Curtmantle. 'Without land, I have only my horses,' he murmured.

PART ONE: HENRY CURTMANTLE 1186 - 1189

CHAPTER ONE: THE LOYAL KNIGHT 1186 - 1187

'FitzMarshal, you are welcome.'

'My Lord King...' William bent over the extended hand of King Henry II and kissed the heavy bejewelled ring.

'Stand and let me see you.' William straightened up and returned the King's scrutiny. Henry Curtmantle was sixty-three years of age; even seated, his powerful, thick-set frame showed something of its former glory but he was now marked by age and, William suspected, the onset of disease, for there was a curious pallor upon him and his hair was thin and grey.

'You did your duty by my son, FitzMarshal?'

'Aye, my good Lord. Mass was said for his soul at the Holy Sepulchre and his cloak laid there as he instructed me.'

Henry nodded gravely. 'That is well done William,' he said, his tone softening into intimacy. 'And now you shall join my mesnie for there is much to be done and to honour thy return and seal our bargain I return to you your destriers. No man has ridden them save for exercise.'

'My Lord...' Despite his conflicting emotions William was touched. He had no desire to rejoin the King's household, though the only alternative was a return to an impoverished life in England, but this was a different Henry; a man diminished by age. William felt the strange tug of loyalty and duty, a refinement of his sensibilities formed by his experience in the Holy Land.

'You are much changed,' the King remarked. 'Is the experience of the Holy Places such as to effect a change of heart?' The King's tone was almost one of awe and in an intuitive flash William realised Henry was thinking of his own mortality. At the same time he recalled the curious world of Outremer: the great Frankish castles, the imposition of feudal authority by a shaky regime for which the teeming population of the *bazaars* and *souks* gave not a thought. He thought too of the near barren hills rising from the lush green of the river valleys, of the mystery of the Holy Places which had once seemed so secure under Christian rule but which were now under an ever-present threat of the Turk and the new faith.

'One is touched by God, Sire, almost as much as by the sun.'

'Give me your hand, William. I would touch one who had prayed at the tomb of the Christ.'

***

After a long ride north during which Robert de Salignac had left him at Cahors, William had found the King hunting at Lyons-la-Forêt in Normandy in March 1186. Despite the emotion of that first encounter he quickly found out that matters, though different in detail, remained much the same in substance. The King's rages were as notorious as his surviving sons were disobedient. Among the knights of the King's retinue he found old friends in Robert de Tresgoz, Peter FitzGuy, Gerard Talbot and Baldwin de Béthune and in the days which followed they acquainted him with the turmoil engulfing the House of Anjou.

'Truly they are the Devil's spawn,' William, Baldwin de Béthune confided in him one night as they lingered over their wine, referring to Henry's three surviving sons. 'The Count of Poitou is a born rebel, Geoffrey of Brittany is as cunning as his father, while the Lord of Ireland, huh,' Baldwin harrumphed and raised his eyebrows at the grandeur of the title, 'is a born incompetent. They used to call him Lackland but I think of him as lacking *bone*.'

'John is what? Not yet twenty?' William remarked.

'Think of yourself at twenty, William,' Baldwin riposted. 'No-one would have called you spineless.'

'Perhaps not,' William laughed, 'though Richard should know better being ten years his brother's senior,' he added seriously, 'and he stands as heir to Henry.'

'Only if Geoffrey does not rob him of his inheritance.'

'How could that be? He has proved himself able and ferocious in the field.'

'Aye, but how long do you think Richard could tolerate being shorn of the powers he presently enjoys? Remember how Curtmantle kept the Young King dallying in constant expectation and what it did to that noble Prince.' Baldwin sighed and went on: 'And recall too, how often Richard has been in rebellion against his father...' Baldwin de Béthune raised his hand for silence as William made to speak. 'Oh, I know that you will say that he always acted in the interests of his mother and the steward-ship of Aquitaine but you know too that that is only part of the whole. The Lord Richard is a man of great lusts: for women, for blood, for power and yes, I know some fools say, for men or boys too, though I think that a canard.' He paused, before saying: 'I think your sword will be much employed for as Henry grows older and, God help me for saying so, weaker, so much does Philippe of France grow in stature and puissance. He has too great a hold over the King's progeny for any good to come of it all, for the moment they fall-out with their father, Philippe offers them sanctuary and understanding, Richard worst of all…'

'*Understanding?*'

'Aye, William, *understanding*. Incredible though it must seem to you, and probably to Philippe who can pursue his policy of aggrandisement at so cheap a price, they are like curs when whipped, John especially, curs that bite the hand that would feed them.'

William shook his head. 'That is something I profoundly *misunderstand*,' he said ruefully.

'So do many of us,' responded Baldwin draining his glass, rising and yawning. 'You know, in the King's private chamber in Winchester His Grace has had a fresco executed which shows an eagle being torn to pieces by its own eyasses. What can one make of that, eh? And all will be the same in the morning.'

William sat on, staring at the dying embers of the fire in the ante-chamber until the cold of the northern night made him shiver. 'Jesu Christ,' he murmured, crossing himself, 'I am unused to this.' Though whether he referred to the chill after the warmth of the Outremer or the intrigues of the House of Anjou he was himself not entirely sure.

***

But if the internal wrangles of the Angevins seemed unchanged William found himself in a new milieu. For all his age and creeping infirmity, Henry retained the

15

most splendid Court in Europe. Since he was King of
England, Duke of Normandy and overlord of the western
half of most of France, Henry's was an itinerant Court,
constantly on the move, constantly prey to supplicants
and place-seekers, intrigue and the importunate
tradesmen who pursued the sums of money owed them.
When static the King's Court resembled the worst
aspects of a grand tourney, being populated by as many
whores as courtiers such that the King's household
included two whore-masters to control them. Sundry
other odd posts included entertainers, troubadours and
jesters, and a *petomane* called Roland the Farter who
could simultaneously whistle, leap in the air and break
wind with a noise like a trumpet.

Falconry, stag-hunting and intermittent warfare now
occupied William, for the ambitions of Philippe II of
France kept up a near-constant bush-war burning along
the land-borders and in the marches such as Berri and
the Vexin, the latter land separating Normandy and the
lands Philippe directly ruled himself. Faced with such a
powerful vassal as Henry, a King in his own right in
England, the younger French King was determined to
destroy the House of Anjou and draw under his own
royal hand the vast tracts of land of which Henry held
the fief. Chief among Philippe's grievances was the
unmarried state of his half-sister the Lady Alice who
had, some seventeen years earlier, been delivered up into
Angevin custody and betrothed to Richard of Poitou and
Aquitaine, Henry's second son. But Henry had denied
Richard his intended wife and debauched the lady
himself and thereby rendered any attempt of Philippe's
to secure a dynastic claim on Angevin lands as useless

since, even if Richard did marry his father's cast-off mistress, the union could and would be declared incestuous by Holy Church.

For all the fulsomeness of William's welcome back to Curtmantle's mesnie, amid Henry's seething yet extravagant Court, William Marshal found himself – just as he had feared – a landless knight. True, provision was made for him to maintain his status as a knight banneret, but it was plain that he was but one of many. Nevertheless, his establishment as an independent knight, with his own small mesnie that formed but part of the King's own, brought William some advantages. Near illiterate himself, his acquaintanceship with one of the King's confidential clerks, justices and administrators, Geoffrey FitzPeter quickly ripened into friendship for no better reason that both men possessed what the other lacked. This, instead of exciting jealousy, conjured up a form of dependence in which the kind of candour William had enjoyed with De Salignac rapidly matured. A quiet, genteel and scholarly man, FitzPeter seamlessly polished William so that the burgeoning courtier who had graced the Courts of both Eleanor of Aquitaine, the King's estranged wife, and that of their son, the 'Young King' Henry, acquired the graces required of a *preudhomme*, a virtuous knight deserving of respect at every level of the social hierarchy jostling for position amid the splendour of the Angevin Court. Most specifically, FitzPeter taught him the absolute necessity of self-control, of never provoking an argument with anyone hostile to his own advancement. William had never been a true hot-head but if not a man of letters, he had a ready enough wit and a tongue to match it. Fortunately his prowess in the field had conferred upon him a soundness of judgement and a coolness of execution that matched FitzPeter's expectation and gave the lay-lawyer a powerful protection in the counselling of the King and his closest advisers.

That August a great tournament was held and William sought to enrol his mesnie but was directly forbidden to do so by the King himself. It was FitzPeter who told him of the injunction and at board that evening Henry beckoned William to the high table and indicated that he should pour his wine. It was the first time Curtmantle had taken any notice of William since their encounter on William's return and, mindful of FitzPeter's advice, he kept his own counsel. It did not deceive the King.

'You are troubled that I barred you from the tournament, FitzMarshal,' the King said after drawing a great draught from his goblet that, William noted, seemed accompanied by a wince of pain. The King extended his arm and William refilled the vessel. 'Well? I am not a fool, man. I can see thunder on a man's brow even when he bites his tongue.'

'My Lord I would support my mesnie and my honour by any means at your service but the chance at the tourney is a means of...'

'Of making money, eh?' The King chuckled. 'Oh, you were ever good at that, FitzMarshal,' Henry said, setting down his drink, leaning forward and lowering his voice. 'As for your honour, that is a matter that rests with me. I do not wish you to tourney because I wish to keep you close. You are no longer young; the tourney is a young man's occupation and I take you for a man of parts who may be of greater use to me than obliging me to pay for your ransom and release. Go back to your place at board and leave me to find a way of rewarding you that is better than the hazard of the tourney.'

Henry dismissed William and he bowed his head. On the one hand the King had distinctly rebuked him, using an old jibe about his desire for money that stung him deeply and that night he sought out FitzPeter and vented his spleen. When he had finished his friend smiled.

'What in the name of God's bones do you find amusing in all this?' William demanded.

'Henry's days may be numbered, William, but they are not yet out and he plays the game of policy right well and with great cunning. You did well not to rile him for not only is he easily angered – more so now than ever with his distemper – but he still holds what is his own in a grip as firm as when the Young Henry challenged him and he forgets neither that you were an adherent of the Young King, nor that you were a loyal one. Forget the tournament and bide your time…'

'For what?'

FitzPeter shrugged. 'Who knows, but something will come of it in due course.'

But neither man forgot the grand tournament that year for in the mêlée the King's third son, Geoffrey, Count of Brittany, was dragged from his horse, fell and was trampled by the high-bred destriers of his own retinue. Grievously hurt, he was rushed to Paris where he died, leaving his wife gravid.

The loss of a second son sent King Henry into intermittent fits of rage and anguish. Beset by doubts and the pain of a condition that would kill him, Henry thought himself still laid under a curse after the death of Becket. Although he had atoned for the instigation of the Archbishop's death and received the Church's absolution, his off-hand remark – an off-hand remark made by a King and taken as a command by the four murdering knights of his mesnie – rebuked the very nature of his kingship. The death of the Count of Brittany caused the King to order the removal of the Court and amid the turmoil William was left bereft of any hope of advancement, notwithstanding FitzPeter's encouragement.

But then, the following summer, FitzPeter's quiet influence led directly to his prophecy coming true when the King granted William a parcel of much-longed-for land and two ward-ships. The land-grant of Cartmel in Lancashire was not large but it would yield William a handsome thirty-two pounds per annum, money enough for him to hold his head up at Court, though he must needs ask FitzPeter to show upon a parchment map where it lay.

As for the ward-ships, one was that of John de Earley, the son of a minor baron, with lands in England, in Somerset and Berkshire. De Earley's father had been Royal Chamberlain, much as William's had been Marshal of King Stephen's horse, a post which had conferred upon his sons a form of surname. The appointment of the young John as William's ward and squire was an honour, since it granted William the right to marry the sixteen year-old lad off to whom he pleased and in patronising William thus, the King enabled William to dispense a modest form of patronage himself.

The two got on well, John de Earley reminding

William of himself as a young boy, hostage to King Stephen against his father's good behaviour. As for John, his duties as squire quickly led him to revere the man in whose service he found himself. To John, William Marshal was no landless knight, but a hero of the tourney, a man who had a military reputation at home, who bore his own device – a red lion rampant upon a ground of green and yellow – who had his own mesnie and who had broken his lance in the Holy Land against the Turk.

And with that of John de Earley came a second wardship, that of the orphaned Heloise of Lancaster, heiress to the barony of Kendal in Westmoreland which lay close to the borders of the royal lands of Cartmel in Lancashire which effectively increased William's fiefdom.

With two ward-ships and his lands of Cartmel came two English knights, summoned by the King and ordered to join William's mesnie at the latter's expense. Geoffrey FitzRobert and William Waleran were both from Wiltshire, William's own natal county and they brought news of an England William, growing older had not forgotten and for which he found he suddenly felt an attachment.

'I had not much cared for the place since I left it,' he confided to FitzPeter, provoking his friend to laughter.

'That is because you had title to no land there, William. Matters are different now, as I predicted.'

'Aye,' acknowledged William ruefully, rubbing his jaw. 'You are right.'

'You should marry the Lady Heloise, William,' Geoffrey FitzPeter advised. 'The transfer of one of His

Grace's wards to yourself is a mark of considerable esteem and your lands – both Kendal and Cartmel - would be extensive.'

Yet William havered; although the grant of land was exactly what he most desired, it was, of course, conditional. As for the lady herself, though her looks were 'pleasing' and she possessed 'great elegance,' he experienced no strong attraction. And while he dithered King Henry was warned by agents of Richard of the possibility of hostile action by the French monarch and William was ordered by the King to take a force towards the Vexin. But the duplicitous Richard had served his father disinformation, for instead of the Vexin, Philippe of France launched an attack on Berri, quickly laying siege to the Angevin fortress of Châteauroux.

Unaware of his son's treachery Henry ordered his forces under immediate arms and, with Richard by his side, rode south, through Le Mans, Tours and Loches, to the relief of the castle. From Le Mans he sent a courier hot-foot to William to join him as quickly as possible with the greatest force at his disposal.

***

The army of King Philippe of France that lay about the ramparts of Châteauroux was immense. Among his own, Philippe was being called 'Augustus,' an acknowledgment of his rising star. Henry, with an inferior force but with the murderous and experienced Richard at his side, cut the French king's direct communication with Paris. When William rode into camp and bent his knee to Henry Curtmantle, Count Richard was absent.

'Ride the lines with me, FitzMarshal,' the King

ordered without offering William the chance of refreshment and William quickly called for John de Earley to bring up his second destrier. While he waited he observed that the King not only required assistance to mount but seemed to sit uneasily in his saddle. A light rain had begun to fall and the day was drawing to a close as the King and a small escort passed through the Angevin encampment. The soldiers had lit their bivouac fires and the damp pressed the smoke low so that it drifted over the undulating countryside, catching in their nostrils as they passed.

Mounted, William caught-up with the King and took post behind him until, half-turning, Henry beckoned him forward.

'Should we seek a pitched battle here, William?' he asked in a surprising display of candour. Such a thing posed great risk, such affairs usually being settled by sieges and negotiation once both sides had sufficient of the enemy's strong-points, or held for ransom the nobility of the other.

'I have sent Duke Richard to open a conference with that bastard Philippe, but if we could destroy him with a bold stroke I would die happier...' The King spoke in a low tone, kicking his mount forward so that he and William detached themselves slightly from their escort which, as it caught-up, Henry waved back.

'My Lord,' William began, but the King waved him to silence and drew rein alongside a large scrub of gorse. The French lines lay in full view, the great fortress beyond, the twin leopards of Anjou just visible lifting languidly above the dongeon in the dank twilight. For a long moment Henry contemplated the scene that lay before them, leaving William somewhat non-plussed. It was unusual for Henry to call Richard 'Duke,' a courtesy title for his lordship of Aquitaine which he held in right of his still-living mother and which rightfully resided with her estranged husband, Henry Curtmantle. Richard was usually called the Count of Poitou and William thought there had been more than a hint of sarcasm in the King's tone.

Henry leaned from his saddle and broke off a sprig of the yellow flower and, leaning forward, stuck it between the metal rosette and the leather strap of his horse's head-gear. 'A pretty thing, *la plante genet*, do you not think, eh?' he remarked inconsequentially.

'Pretty enough, Sire,' a puzzled William responded.

'I am dying, William,' the King went on, 'and I have been tricked too many times by my sons to rely upon their word any longer. Philippe has the twisting of their tails and by theirs mine. For all Richard's talents in the field, he is a fool and no match for that French turd. Jesu Christ...' The King's voice dropped as he uttered these last words and William realised that he was positively squirming in his saddle.

'My Lord King, you should return to your quarters...'

The King turned upon him. Even in the encroaching twilight William could see the ice in Henry's eye. 'You presume too much, FitzMarshal!' he snarled.

'Then I beg Your Grace's pardon and will confine myself to answering Your Grace's question as to whether we should seek a battle.' William's response was cool and Henry grunted his assent. 'I think,' William went on, 'that neither the ground nor the relative weakness of our force would enable us to entertain the slightest hope of success. Had you struck the moment you arrived, then surprise might have yielded something...'

'Richard dissuaded me,' replied the King. 'Think you that odd?'

'May I speak frankly, Sire?'

'Why do you think I brought you here?'

'Then yes, Sire. Duke Richard and I have discussed such matters, before Neufchâtel-en-Bray to be specific. He seemed inclined to my view then and to prevaricate now seems odd enough. My Lord,' William went on, articulating a concern that he had pondered since being sent to defend the Vexin. 'what was your source of the intelligence that led you to believe that King Philippe would attack the Vexin?'

The King swivelled his head with the speed of an old eagle, regarding William through narrowed eyes. 'By the Holy Rood, it was *him*!' Henry jerked his horse's head round and was about to dig spurs to its flanks when William put out his hand.

'Stay my Lord, I think the Duke comes now.'

Henry followed William's pointing arm. A small cavalcade was riding towards the main Angevin encampment. Even in the twilight Richard's huge white destrier was conspicuous.

'Come, we shall meet him at my tent.'

Ten minutes later, almost simultaneously, father and son reached the entrance to the King's pavilion.

'My Gracious Lord,' said Richard, his handsome face flushed with wine or wind, or both, thought William as he slid from his horse and followed the King, who beckoned him into his great tent. 'I bring good news.'

Richard glanced at William, then ignored his presence as the two met and stood eyeing each other. 'In your behalf I have negotiated the terms of a two-year truce and treaty. The expense of a campaign is avoided…'

'When did the expense of a campaign ever trouble you?' the King asked curtly.

'Perhaps never,' riposted Richard smiling calmly in the lamplight as they entered the tent, 'but it is a feature of your own rule and that I respect.'

'How very good of you.' Henry's tone was deeply sarcastic.

'Besides,' Richard ran on with a smooth candour that William found profoundly suspicious, 'I would not have Aquitaine bled dry to support Normandy.'

The barb had an almost physical impact upon Henry. He had half-turned away from Richard, in the act of handing his gauntlets to a waiting squire, and seemed to freeze. Then William saw his broad shoulders sag and he turned, his features like stone.

'No, of course. Aquitaine is sacrosanct.' Henry took the goblet of wine proffered by one of his squires.

Richard said nothing but made a little bow as if to acknowledge and agree with his father's apparent concession. Observing this curious exchange William felt a creeping sense of prescience but any analysis was dashed from his mind as Richard turned and regarded him.

'Why Marshal, you have come at last.'

'My Lord Duke.' William made his obeisance.

'Then the Vexin is quiet, hmm?'

'My Lord the King summoned me hither, my Lord Duke, as I am sure you know.'

'Well,' replied Richard with the air of one who considered all troubles laid aside, 'the Vexin and Berri are safe enough now...' he turned to the King, 'provided, of course, His Grace my father ratifies the terms...' And with a half-smile, half-sneer upon his handsome features Richard made his bow and withdrew.

William made to do the same but Henry stopped him. 'Stay a while, FitzMarshal...' The King indicated that wine should be offered to William and a stool was placed for him. He awaited the slow and obviously painful seating of the King then, as Henry expelled his breath and nodded, William too sat down.

'Draw close. I would have counsel of you, William,' the King said when they were alone. William pulled the stool closer to the King's chair so that he sat adjacent to but lower than Henry.

'Your Grace?'

'I am not long for this world,' the King began, 'and when I am gone my work is like to be all undone by the fools I have bred of the Lady Eleanor.' William was acutely aware that this confidence of Henry's was a mark of huge esteem and he met the King's cool gaze of appraisal. 'I have trusted few men and those that I have, have usually turned treacherously against me so you may lay it upon your own soul if you betray this, my faith, that I this night invest in thee, William Marshal.'

'My Lord, I am not the man...'

'Do you think that?'

'Aye, my Lord...'

'Then that is why I judge you to be just the man.' Henry paused, allowing William a moment to digest the importance of the charge. 'Now hist me well for the

27

burden I intend for you makes my son's charge light. When I am dead and Richard dissipates my power and treasure in endless war, as he is bound to do, being of the blood that he is, do you always think beyond tomorrow. Men say my son has the heart of a lion, but he has not always the judgement of a King. I would have thee act this part as best you may. I cannot advise you of the particular, since I may be a King but am no necromancer, and you must needs employ wisdom in how to proceed, but you have years yet and may serve the good of my cause long after the years of my body.'

'My Lord, I am an unlettered man…'

'You are not a fool and I see you have made a friend of FitzPeter, guard that and other friendships among such men as he is.' Henry paused, adding wistfully: 'Becket was such a one until… but that is no matter now.' The King cleared his throat. Such men will serve you well if they find you protect them and you are a warrior, perhaps the only knight in my mesnie that might match Richard.'

'How should I *match* Duke Richard, Your Grace, unless you have named Count John…'

'No, no,' the king said testily, 'Richard will succeed me and you must serve him well with the wisdom of your counsel, having always the things that matter to the Kingdom in your heart.' The King paused, then asked, 'do you understand of what I speak?'

'In part, my Lord, but…' William paused, the thoughts rushing into his head like a torrent as he scratched his beard. Never, in all his wildest dreams, had he expected to receive such a confidence from Henry Curtmantle, the most puissant Prince in Europe.

'Come, speak your mind.'

'I conceive the King of France a man of vaunting ambition…'

'Huh! You are right there!' exclaimed Henry with an almost light-headed acknowledgement of William's perspicacity.

'What if the choice must be made between Normandy and England, my Lord?'

The shrewdness of the question drew a sudden intake of breath and a darkening of Henry's mood. Even in the feeble lamplight his blue eyes clouded. 'Aye,' said the King, nodding, 'you see the future William and prove the sense of my entrusting these matter to you. Always hold Normandy in my memory; Normandy, Anjou and all my ancestral lands are where my heart must ever lie but,' and here the King lent forward and placed his hand upon William's shoulder. 'But,' he repeated, emphasising the conjunction with a second buff that reminded William of the rough punch of a knight's dubbing, 'ever hold England for the power of my Crown…and Richard's,' he added, almost as an afterthought, as if the very idea of relinquishing the Crown with the natural termination of his life was physically painful to him. The King sat back regarding William for a moment before saying, 'I know you for a man of ambition, William, but I know you also for a man of moderation and good sense. You did not seize the hand of Heloise of Lancaster like a drowning man might have done, but bided your time. That was wise and, God grant that I live a little longer, you shall not be disappointed, though I would have you use the lady well.'

'Of course, my Lord.'

'Promise me then just one thing, that you will keep always the good of the English Crown before you? 'Tis the burden of a King that I lay upon your shoulders...' Henry winced again as he moved uneasily. The audience had lasted too long for his comfort and William, for all the misgivings that tumbled about in his head, was unwilling to try the king's patience beyond his enduring.

'If it be in my power, my Lord King,' William said firmly, rising and making his obeisance.

'Shall I have you swear to this? I have FitzPeter waiting without?' Henry asked, looking up at William.

'If it pleases Your Grace, but you have my word...'

Henry sighed. 'Aye, William and I have laid the matter to your immortal soul.'

It was then that the full import of Henry's charge fell upon William: the duty laid upon him came from God's anointed. As if to mark his realisation Henry thrust out his right hand; William kneeled and kissed the King's great ring.

As he rose, the King's tone changed. The moments of confidence were over; William was no more than a knight banneret in the mesnie of Henry Curtmantle.

'Send FitzPeter to me. I have work for him this night,' he commanded.

***

That night the clerks drew up the documents necessary to conclude the agreement between Duke Richard and King Philippe Augustus and the following noon, with sundry flourishes and the trumpeting of the heralds, the exchange of the copies of the treaty took place. The next day the two armies broke their respective camps and began to withdraw, Philippe's north towards Orléans, Henry's north-west towards Tours. It had rained hard all night and the going was hard, especially for William's mesnie and the troops he commanded, for he had been assigned the rear-guard and the track was churned to a mire.

They had been one hour on the march when he was aware of a commotion in the column that snaked ahead, towards woodland. For a moment he feared some ambush and then he saw a large party of horsemen coming back from the head of the column led by the gonfalon of Richard. The Duke rode at its head and he drew rein briefly alongside William, who checked his horse accordingly. Richard waved his mesnie on, back the way they had come.

'My Lord, what means this?' William asked, frowning.

Richard was smiling, his golden beard catching the first sunshine since the night's downpour. 'You will have to make your mind up soon, Marshal,' he said enigmatically.

'Loyalty binds me,' William responded sententiously, his mind still preoccupied by his audience with King Henry. 'Whither does my Lord go?' And then the thought struck him: 'Surely not to join King Philippe?'

'Philippe guarantees me Aquitaine, Marshal,' Richard snarled, gathering up his reins, 'which is more than my noble father ever did.' The Duke drove his spurs into his mount's flank and the great horse moved off at a gallop.

'Aye, but for how long?' William murmured to himself as he watched Richard ride off, clods of mud flying up from the hooves of his horse. Then he turned to Geoffrey FitzRobert and William Waleran, the two

31

English knights whom he most favoured and trusted, turning over the command of the rear-guard to them. Waving John de Earley to follow with his own banner, William spurred his own palfrey towards the head of the column. A few minutes later he drew rein alongside the King who rode in a litter, such was the pain of riding on his charger.

'My Lord, Duke Richard...'

'So I have just been told,' snarled the King, his teeth working on his lower lip with such vigour that William feared the onset of one of his terrible rages. 'Stay close, FitzMarshal,' he growled after a moment, then asked 'who commands the rear?'

'Waleran and FitzRobert, my Lord.'

Henry nodded and resumed chewing his lower lip. 'God's bones, but I thought a week or two of peace...' he said to himself then, banging the side of the litter with such violence that the contraption rocked, roared: 'by the Christ, can I trust no-one?'

'My Lord!' William responded, as if half reminding Henry of their conversation.

Henry looked at him sharply. 'So soon?'

'If not, when, my Lord?'

Henry beckoned William to draw close and William leaned from his saddle so that the King suddenly shot out his right hand and grabbed William's surtout at the shoulder. 'Bring the bastard back, William that I may put the jesses back on the dog's turd.'

The King's breath was hot and foul in William's face and he shot in response, 'perhaps 'twould be better to offer him Aquitaine,' he said boldly.

For a moment he thought he had over-shot the mark,

then Henry shook his surtout with such violence that William heard the seam tear.

'Promise heaven itself but get the spawn of Satan back in my camp.' The King thrust him away then called after him: 'Wait! Take my herald and leopards and leave your banner with me.'

Thus William rode off on his first mission of diplomacy leaving John de Earley to stand surety for him. Clearly for all his fine words the King did not yet trust him, a situation that truly puzzled William until, an hour later, he bethought himself of what he would say when in the presence of Duke Richard.

Three hours later that June day he caught up with the marching column of the French army and, covered by Henry's herald, was escorted to the head of the column where King Philippe Augustus of France and Duke Richard rode side-by-side, bosom friends.

'And what,' asked Philippe,' does this fellow want?'

'This is William FitzMarshal, my Lord,' replied Richard. 'A retainer of my father's,' he explained dismissively.

Philippe looked William up and down and was clearly unimpressed, though William's stature more closely matched the magnificent physique of the Duke than the unprepossessing, lank-haired appearance of the King.

'He wishes to persuade me to return thither, I have no doubt,' remarked the King, his mouth curling into a smile. 'Is that not so, FitzMarshal?'

Bare-headed, William bowed in the saddle. 'Craving your pardon, Your Grace, but my embassage is for my Lord Richard.'

'Naturally,' replied Philippe, continuing to regard

William with an expression of faint amusement but making no move to facilitate any exchange between Henry's messenger and his new ally. Then Philippe turned away and began to talk to Richard, leaving William looking a fool in front of Philippe's immediate escort who chuckled merrily behind him at the discomfiture of Henry Curtmantle's emissary. They rode thus for some minutes before a French herald rode alongside William and leaned forward and grasped William's reins.

As was customary on the march, he was not riding either of his destriers and the palfrey did not react, but William did.

'Your Grace!' he shouted. Convention forbade him from striking a herald, but he could claim the protection of Henry's. 'Your Grace!' he shouted again, Philippe having ignored his first remonstration. 'I came here under the protection of King Henry of England.'

Without turning round Philippe held up his hand and the column came to an awkward halt. Then the French King beckoned and his herald led William forward until his horse was halted alongside the hind quarters of the King's palfrey. Only Duke Richard turned, grinning from ear-to-ear.

Still with his back to William, Philippe threw his words back over his shoulder so that William stared at Duke Richard. 'If, FitzMarshal, you claim to come hither under the protection of the King of England, pray tell me what the King of England does here? If you mean the Count of Anjou, kindly return to him and thank him for his duty in sending his heir as a hostage to me.'

William did not miss the flash of uncertainty that

crossed Richard's face, nor did he miss the reassuring hand that Philippe extended to Richard indicating that it was a jest. Meanwhile, the knights closest to this pretty farce all laughed at Philippe's wit. After that second of misgiving Richard joined in, though his humour faltered when Philippe added, 'And tell the Count of Anjou that I am his liege lord and he is mine to command.'

At this point Philippe swung his horse round and confronted William. 'Go now FitzWilliam, back to the Count of Anjou and deliver my message.'

William bowed his head and looked from the King to Duke Richard. 'Your Grace,' he said respectfully, then raising his head he fixed Richard with his gaze and added, 'with Your Grace's permission I am charged with conveying my Lord's felicitations to the Duke of Aquitaine.' And here he bowed to Richard before turning his horse about.

It was late when he returned to the Angevin camp but, it not being long after mid-summer, there was yet some light as he reported to Henry all that had transpired. Henry listened in silence and held his peace for some moments after William had finished. William was acutely aware that he had not brought Richard back, but Henry was not foolish enough to think he could have done so and, looking up at William, nodded grimly.

'You have done well, FitzMarshal. We may expect an emissary from the Duke in a day or so and he will return to the fold within the month.'

King Henry misjudged the matter by three weeks, but by the end of August Duke Richard had re-joined his father at Tours where the Angevin Court lay when the news from Outremer tore Christendom wide open.

RICHARD WOODMAN

CHAPTER TWO: *AUDITA TREMENDI* 1187 - 1188

It was at Tours that they first learned of the disaster in Outremer. Like hundreds of others, William was profoundly shocked by the news from the Holy Land. The Saracenic Turks had been revivified by a charismatic new leader. He was said to possess demonic powers, to be the anti-Christ and Satan's arch-angel on earth. More to the point he was everywhere victorious and his name was soon upon the lips of every military man in the West. They called him 'Saladin'.

This Saladin was an Ayubite Kurd and he had fought the forces of the Christian King of Jerusalem under the twin peaks known as the Horns of Hattin near the city of Tiberias and had thrown them into an utter rout. The King of Jerusalem, none other than Guy de Lusignan, had fallen a prisoner to Saladin who soon afterwards entered the Holy City of Jerusalem as a conqueror. How could any knight banneret, any *preudhomme*, any baptised gentleman in Christendom even begin to think of his own ambition when the most Holy territory in the world was occupied by the infidel?

The Court was filled with rumour and expectation. Robert de Tresgoz gave vent to the feelings of many when he punned that the Horns of Hattin had placed the Kingdoms, Duchies and Counties of the West on the horns of a dilemma, though few were amused by the sophistry. Most were more inclined to lend their ears to the Pope, Gregory VIII, who had issued a Bull, *Audita Tremendi*, preaching a new crusade to recapture the Holy Places and most of the young gallants and the more sober knights on the Angevin Court expected to be taking the cross within weeks. After his own experiences in the Holy Land William was powerfully drawn to the cause; Cartmel could wait, the Lady Heloise could wait, he was half obligated to the Order of the Temple and he had FitzPeter write on his behalf to De Salignac in the Dordogne for his opinion. All now waited upon the King's sense of Christian duty.

But for all his dewy-eyed reverence for the pilgrim William Marshal and the disastrous news that followed hard on the heels of his return, Henry Curtmantle was absorbed playing his endless games with his rebellious elder son, Richard, taking from him what delegated powers he had enjoyed during the life of the Young Henry and, just as he had done with his first heir, denying Richard any taste of the government that must, William thought, fall to him in due course.

At first it seemed that Richard would himself neutralise the situation, for that November Richard had taken the cross and vowed to go on crusade to wrest the Holy Places from the infidel. But then Richard learned of a rumour that Henry intended cutting him out of the succession and passing the Crown of England and his lordships in France directly to his younger son John.

When William heard this he was aghast until FitzPeter quelled his anxiety.

''Tis a canard raised in Paris,' the lawyer explained. 'Trust it not.'

'Philippe did not invent this,' William said

dismissively. 'I am not that easily duped.'

'No, you are not duped, but Philippe is cunning and fosters the wind of credulity hereabouts.' FitzPeter waved his hand to encompass the Angevin Court.

'You may be right, Geoffrey, but men believe what they wish to believe and my own eyes and ears tell me that something more than straw is in the wind.'

And indeed events seemed to lend credence to what had first circulated as mere gossip, for Henry increasingly gave every indication of favouring Prince John. Although his distemper was not known, Henry's physical state was now of real concern. All knew he was ailing and his marks of preference for young John took on a sinister significance. The young man was handsome and, when he had a mind to be, personable enough. He had even proved himself in the field – once or twice, as Robert de Tresgoz was fond of remarking – but he lacked his older brother's talent for ruthless war.

Matters rested for some months until the January following when Richard, still intent upon going on crusade but not until he had secured his succession, persuaded Henry to again meet his own ally, Philippe Augustus, in an attempt to settle their differences and underwrite the Papal guarantee that no advantages should be taken of any lord absent on crusade. Confirmation of this came from the Archbishop of Tyre who thereafter distracted both Henry and Philippe from their internecine wranglings by an account of the extent of the destruction of the Frankish Kingdom of Jerusalem by the Turks, under the charismatic Ayubite Emir Salah ed-Din.

'This heathen devil,' the Archbishop thundered,

raising his Cross, 'took Aleppo, laid siege to Krak des Chevaliers, captured Tiberias, defeated King Guy under the Horns of Hattin, thereafter taking Ascalon, Acre and then…' The Archbishop threw his eyes up to heaven and brought them back to earth to glare at Philippe and Henry, lowering his voice to a menacing and reproachful growl, 'he seized Jerusalem.' He paused as the two Kings and their assembled lords, knights and gentlemen all but quailed under his withering glower, shifting uneasily upon their feet. 'Put away your childish quibblings, my sons,' the Archbishop cried, raising his voice. 'God calls you to redemption! Take back the Holy Places! God places this charge in *your* hands for *your* glory! Let not Christendom stir without *you*, the great Kings of the West!'

William looked about him as the entire company stirred as one man to pledge their swords to the retaking of the Holy city of Jerusalem. Richard was chief among these, and even the King of England, ill and feeble as he was, joined the general enthusiasm. While William's private desire was to himself go on crusade, he perceived in those about him an almost childish enthusiasm too febrile to last. He judged well; within days it had begun to falter, almost as soon as Geoffrey de Lusignan gave clear evidence of his own determined intention to sail east to liberate his brother, King Guy of Jerusalem. It was as though Geoffrey could stand surrogate, at least for the time being. In William's eyes, the two Lusignans had so treacherously ambushed Queen Eleanor and killed William's uncle, Patrick, Earl of Salisbury, that he felt no compulsion to join Geoffrey's banner. Besides, his obligations were to await the pleasure of King Henry, in the meanwhile maintaining his mesnie for any forthcoming eventuality.

For months after the great meeting with the Archbishop an uneasy peace lay over the land. Desultory preparations were made for a crusade, money was raised by the enforcement of taxation but the mutual suspicions that underlay the relationship between Henry, Richard and his powerful ally, Philippe Augustus, prevented any firm orders for departure being given by any of the three principals involved. To force a rapprochement, that August Philippe sought another meeting under the great elm at Gisors.

Once again William found himself among the waiting nobles and knights attending the two Kings and their most powerful lords. All knew the agenda: Henry must renounce that portion of the Vexin – the march between Normandy and Philippe's ancestral land of the Île de France – that lay within Normandy. Philippe would in turn relinquish his claims on Henry's French lands if Henry recognised Richard as his heir and Richard married Philippe's sister, the Lady Alice, as had long been proposed.

''Tis but a warming up of old chestnuts,' FitzPeter had confided in him the night before, 'and is likely to produce the same answer.'

William, dreaming over his wine of Outremer, had asked rhetorically, 'Are we never to have peace?'

FitzPeter had scoffed. 'What would such men do with peace, William? They thrive on war, as long as it enriches them.'

'But it is bleeding them white,' William had responded, sitting up and taking the conversation seriously.

'And even then it will not stop them.'

'If they must fight, there is a greater war to be fought in Outremer,' William had said after a pause.

FitzPeter had shrugged and the two had sunk into a depressively contemplative silence. Recalling the conversation with FitzPeter, William watched as, within half an hour, the conference reached its inevitable conclusion. Fatally for any hope of peace, Henry, who could neither sit nor stand in comfort, was - in such a condition - in no mood for compromise. He was rumoured to be suffering from open ulcers and the pain further shortened his fiery temper. Even at a discreet distance William heard him roar: 'Never! You have my son in your breeches and if I confirm him my heir I give all to you. Normandy, Anjou, the Vexin are mine! Mine!'

Then, to a stirring of the French nobles, Philippe strode away, followed by his entourage.

The following day, as the encampments broke-up, William received a visitor.

'Robert! In the name of God 'tis good to see you!' The two men clasped their hands and forearms in friendship then William drew back and looked into De Salignac's eyes. 'You are troubled?'

'Aye, William. I am but late arrived, summoned by Count Richard who tells me there will be war if your master does not give ground.'

'Why does he not marry the Lady Alice?'

De Salignac shrugged. 'God alone knows, but he will do nothing until Henry pledges to renounce the Vexin.'

'Which he will not do,' William added, 'for he knows

that Philippe's design is upon Henry's ancestral lands through Richard. Surely we should be advancing our force towards the Holy Land,' he said despairingly.

'Aye, if our masters sought forgiveness and did God's will,' De Salignac responded, crossing himself. 'But should we go to war here, you and I shall find ourselves upon opposing sides, my lands being in fief from Philippe.'

William nodded. 'Let us pray it does not come to that.'

'God damn the six peers of France who thought it a good idea to elect the Duke of France to Kingship,' Robert growled darkly.

'Should it come to blows between us, Robert, I should not raise my arm against you so wear your device conspicuously as I shall mine.'

'God help us, William, and may He go with us both.'

And upon that unhappy note the two men parted again, William withdrawing with the King's entourage towards the western Vexin, while De Salignac re-joined Philippe and Richard as they fell back towards the River Oise. Two days later a courier caught-up with Henry's slow-moving column. It moved sluggishly across the country for out of his opponents' eyes the King was carried in a litter. The messenger brought news that, upon the orders of the King of France, the ancient elm of Gisors - the traditional meeting-place of the Capetian Kings and their powerful vassal Dukes of Normandy - had been felled.

'Christ have mercy,' FitzPeter murmured when he heard of it. Crossing himself he turned to William with whose mesnie he rode. 'We are at war again.'

***

And so it proved. Calling his Norman nobles to their

duty, Henry ordered his household to arms and summoned Welsh mercenaries from England. With Richard's loyalty uncertain, Henry determined to stop Philippe in his tracks.

To William fell the task of organising the King's army and he was in daily conference with the King, amazed at Henry's recovery as he summoned his vassals to Rouen. Whatever salves had been recently applied to his open ulcers they had so far eased his pain that he seemed to be the old Henry, brim-full of energy and spoiling for a fight.

'But I need time, Marshal, time for the ships to arrive from Southampton. Go you with Archbishop Walter de Coutances and buy me time.'

'But your forces, Your Grace…'

'Can do without you for a week and when you return the Welsh will be here. Buy me just a week, ten days. You have already proved yourself a diplomat in regard to my son. Go! Go!'

The embassy bought Henry his week, and although the Archbishop of Rouen pleaded the case for a more general and long lasting peace he added demands: the restoration of fortresses, reparations, the evacuation of Berri. Philippe spurned all such notions, demanding instead that Henry relinquished all claims to the Norman Vexin.

William and Archbishop Walter rode back to Rouen empty-handed, but secure in the knowledge that the Welsh troops had arrived in great numbers, news with which Henry greeted them as they made their report to the King. Henry swept the news aside and turned to William, a gleam in his eyes all too rarely seen of late.

'Well, Marshal, while they think we lick our wounded pride we shall attack. Where lies their weakness?'

'My Lord, perhaps a strike south of the Vexin? Philippe will expect you to hold your lands there but a chevauchée into King Philippe's…'

'By God's eyes! Truly you have the matter to heart. Two columns and raid in depth…'

'Taking tar from the ships in the port, my Lord King,' suggested William, 'the more readily to burn and destroy.'

'Give orders to that effect.' The King called for wine, rubbing his hands with satisfaction and that August the Angevin war host, moving up the line of the River Eure, crossed into French territory near Ivry and began to lay waste King Philippe's lands between the Eure and the Seine, sacking Bréval and taking great amounts of booty.

Then, as the King fell back into his own lands, he detached William with the second column to strike south, away from pursuing French forces, towards Montmirail before retiring himself into Touraine.

'Leave nothing behind you, William,' the King ordered. 'Nothing so much as a rat could live on.'

Leaving only a light rear-guard, William broke up his column under his chief knights and, sending out parties of scouts, detached marauding groups of incendiaries who burnt crops, villages, vineyards and harried the peasantry off their lands, spreading terror wherever his men went.'

'By God, but these Welshmen know their business,' William remarked to John de Earley, feeling the satisfaction of war as they sat their horses and watched a village burn. It had been long deserted by its population who had fled at the news of the approach of the enemies of their King. 'This is how Richard wages war and by Heaven 'twill wound Philippe!'

But it was Henry who was most wounded when the fighting petered-out with the onset of winter and, once again, a conference was called in mid-November at Bonsmoulins. Despite the rape of his ancestral lands, attacks that were said to have entirely shaken Philippe and disrupted his own military plans, he rode to the rendezvous in full state, accompanied by Count Richard. The two men were in high good spirits and on obvious terms of great intimacy, so-much-so that, almost within sight of King Henry and the Angevin nobles, Richard went down upon his knees to do homage to Philippe for Normandy, Anjou, Aquitaine, Maine, Touraine and Berri.

'He has no *right*..!' Henry raged tempestuously, giving orders to withdraw. A few days later Henry received news that Richard, again a firm ally of the tendentious Philippe, had ridden into Poitou to raise an army. Again the King gave way to his furious temper while William, hearing the intelligence, thought of Robert de Salignac and the pledge they had made between them.

Later that day, by which time the King had exhausted himself of his anger, Henry called William to his side.

The physical deterioration of the King was increasingly obvious. His difficulty in sitting and the foul stench from his undergarments could no longer be ignored. He received William standing, leaning against a window place as if in contemplation of the view but William could see all too well his pallor and the beads of sweat that stood out on his forehead like rain-drops.

'Marshal,' the King ordered abruptly, 'ride to the Count of Poitou at Amboise and use all your skills to end this madness. Pray him to come hither that we might settle our differences...' Then Henry waved William out as an expression of agony passed over his features. Calling upon Geoffrey FitzRobert and William Waleran to ready the mesnie, William had John de Earley saddle-up and the small column of armed knights and their squires rode south and west, ready to defend themselves if attacked. Reaching Amboise, William was ushered into the Count's presence.

Richard sat before a fire while about him clerks busily scribbled to his dictation. He had been at it for hours and made no attempt to conceal his actions from William, keeping him standing idly by until he had completed his business which was, quite obviously, the organisation of his military train.

'You are wasting your breath, FitzMarshal,' Richard replied when William had pleaded his master's cause. 'You see how I am placed here,' he gestured round as messengers came in and the clerks passed them the Count's orders.

'My Lord, the King your father is in ill-health...'

'The King my father has been in ill-health for some time,' Richard responded laconically, picking a fig from a silver salver and peeling it.

'This time is different,' William ventured, dropping his voice. 'There are good reasons why your Lordship would be wise...'

'You are not the man to teach me my business, FitzMarshal,' Richard responded sharply, staring at

William who lowered his head.

'I speak as an emissary and counsellor of the King, my Lord.'

For some moments a silence hung in the air and then Richard replied. 'Get you gone back to the old man, FitzMarshal. Had you an inheritance you would fight for it.' He turned away.

Masking his fury at the insult and mindful of Henry's injunction, William refused to budge, so that Richard looked up again. 'I said begone!' Richard roared.

'My Lord the King exhorted me to use my best endeavours…'

'Then you have failed!'

'Perhaps, my Lord, but I have yet one more thing to say.' William's tone was such as to brook no abrupt dismissal. Richard stared at him in silence which William broke. 'Your Lordship has taken the cross by a solemn oath, yet you remain here. The Holy places are in the hands of the infidel. Do you not think that as the foremost warrior in Christendom…'

'You are bold, sir! I will not tolerate such false flattery, FitzMarshal,' Richard snarled, gesturing the clerks to leave their presence. 'I am not fool enough to know that the minute I have left for the Holy Land my Father will settle the succession on Count John, Papal injunction or not! You are one of the King's counsellors; for all I know you are party to such a plot…' William was stung a second time and just for a moment thought to interject intemperately but as Richard went on an idea struck him. 'Mayhap,' Richard was saying, 'you placed it in the mind of the King, though God knows he needs not you to poison him against me.'

'Do not dishonour me, my Lord,' William said with slow and deliberate menace, throwing the words in Richard's face. 'I may have no land, but as counsellor to His Grace I am but one of several and hold my trust as sacred.'

The two men stood glaring at one another. It was as well that William's physique matched Richard's and while he was but a landless knight, his own reputation for prowess combined with his age and sincerity to compel Richard's grudging respect.

Richard grunted. 'You know well that if I leave for Outremer and my father dies, John, who has made no move to take the cross, will succeed…'

'No, my Lord, I do not.' William said firmly, then dropped to one knee. 'I for one should uphold your claim as better than your brother's.'

For some moments Richard stood stock-still, staring at the kneeling William who held his gaze, then Richard asked: 'On the bones of Christ?'

William swallowed. 'I am the King's man until he departs this life,' he said with slow deliberation. 'Thereafter I am yours.'

'Get up!' Richard commanded and turned to stare into the fire. William rose and waited, his heart thumping in his breast, intuitively aware that he had just done some great and consequential thing in his life, though whether for better or worse it was impossible to tell with this devil's brood. Then, without looking at William, Richard remarked, 'You have been to the Holy Land upon my late brother's command.'

'Aye, I have.'

'And would you go again?'

'As you remind me, my Lord, I have no land to hold me here and unless some great matter stayed my inclination, as at present it does, I should return thither.'

Richard continued to stare into the fire before, at last, turning back to William. He nodded. 'Very well. I shall think upon your words, FitzMarshal, but God and His angels have mercy upon you should you break your word to me.'

***

'Well?' The King was a-bed, propped up on wolf-skins with a priest and two clerks in attendance when William returned from Amboise. He wore a night-shirt agape at the neck where a crucifix rose and fell upon his breast.

William made his obeisance. 'I had discourse with my Lord Richard, Your Grace. At first he was unwilling to entertain hearing any message but I prevailed upon him to hear me.' Here William faltered, well aware that he had far exceeded his diplomatic brief by promising Richard his fealty in the event of the death of the formidable man before him. Ill though he was, Henry was far from being a man to cross.

'Well?'

'He remains of the opinion that John is favoured, Your Grace, and although he promised to give my words his further consideration, I am not hopeful.'

Henry swore and turned away. 'Shit!' William heard him growl as he clenched his right fist with his supressed anger. Then the King turned again to William. 'My son can see no further than the nose upon his face,' he said. 'Philippe has entrapped him and will use him to his own ends.'

'My Lord King I did everything in my power to

persuade him to make his peace with you,' William added, suddenly sorry for the old man whose life's work was unravelling before his dying eyes.

The King lay back with a sigh and nodded. 'You have done your best Marshal and I thank you for it.'

'Your Grace.' William began to back away and had reached the door to the King's chamber when Henry called him back. Motioning him to kneel so that only William could hear his words, Henry whispered, 'promise me this William, that you will serve my House to the end of your days…' Henry's right hand rose to his breast and he fumbled with the crucifix on its plain leather thong, holding it out to William to kiss. 'Give me your oath,' the King commanded and William, moved almost to tears, did as he was bid.

'Good,' the King murmured as William rose. 'You may go.'

CHAPTER THREE: THE BROKEN LANCE 1188 - 1189

Isolated and increasingly bed-ridden, Henry held his Christmas Court at Saumur where the absence of several of his senior vassals was an ominous augury of the future. There followed a restless progress through the heartland of the King's ancestral domain of Anjou, from Saumur to Chinon. By Easter he lay at Angers, prostrated again by his illness, attended by his son John, a diminishing number of his nobles and William Marshal. At the end of Lent he summoned a number of his courtiers and knights to his bedside, William among them. It seemed that Henry was close to death and that he was attempting to secure the position of his successor by binding to his line a number of powerful nobles and to this end he requested that William relinquish his ward-ship of Heloise of Kendal in order for the King to bestow it upon another. Disappointed, William grimly acceded, witnessing the charter that partially wounded him.

'You shall retain Cartmel,' Henry said, his voice weak. 'It is time that you married, Marshal. You lack sufficient land. A man without land is nothing.' William bit his tongue, thinking to have stood higher in the King's esteem. 'But you spurned the Lady of Kendal…'

William was about to protest but Henry was smiling wanly.

'But I have a match for you Marshal, a great heiress,

the Lady Isabelle, daughter of Richard de Clare, Lord of Striguil on the southern Welsh march, astride the River Wye. She should better please you.'

The King held out his hand and William knelt and kissed the great ring, murmuring his gratitude.

''Tis but a promise,' William muttered when that evening FitzPeter congratulated him upon the ward-ship. 'And, moreover, that of a dying King. Let us see...'

'But Isabelle de Clare, William, daughter of Richard Strongbow, now there *is* a match. Do not neglect it, I beg you. It is more than a promise, for the Clerks have been ordered to draw up the charter in your favour, William,' FitzPeter said with the authority of a lawyer, but William merely grunted. The prevailing gloom of the Court could not be denied and an English marriage seemed at that moment to be as elusive as catching moonbeams.

'There is nothing remaining of even that little certainty that prevailed formerly,' William growled as he called for wine and greeted Geoffrey FitzRobert and William Waleran who had joined him for their evening meal which they took in their lodgings now that the King was a-bed with his distemper. And it was of that upon which the conversation now turned.

'At least a-bed he smells less of shit,' remarked Waleran. 'His women being handy to keep him clean.'

'D'you know what ails him, my Lord?'

William shrugged. 'They say he is covered in ulcers and hath a great growth in his bowels...'

'He has an anal fistula,' put in FitzPeter knowledgably. 'They say it will poison the blood in due course...'

'A what?' asked Waleran, a man of rough manners.

'A fistula,' responded FitzPeter, adding for the better information of the ignorant, 'a hole in his arse.'

'Well, we all have that,' snapped Waleran, looking about him uncomprehending.

'He has an unnatural and extra orifice,' explained FitzPeter further.

'May the Lord have mercy,' said William and they all crossed themselves, appalled by the horror to which even a King must submit if it be God's will.

'They say it is where the Devil goes in and out of him,' added FitzPeter, reminding them all of the old stories about the supposedly Satanic origins of the House of Anjou. 'And through which, when his time comes, his soul will be dragged down into Hell.'

'Jesu Christ!' said FitzRobert, crossing himself again. The three knights sat bolt upright, their faces pale with the horror of the thing.

'I thought you all knew,' remarked FitzPeter looking from one to another, half amused by the effect his explanation had had upon such fearless warriors. 'God knows His Grace has smelt of excrement for months now.'

'I merely thought him…unable to contain himself owing to a growth,' said William, whose own birthmark had persuaded his parents he was Satan's imp.

'Cancerously incontinent, you mean,' FitzPeter said, pedantically. 'No, no, this is far worse than a mere consequent loosening of the bowel. This is a rotting of the body.'

Geoffrey FitzRobert laid aside his knife and put down the chicken leg he had been holding for some moments. He motioned for more wine and his squire, who had been listening attentively, refilled their goblets with a shaking hand.

'Then it is fatal?'

'Oh yes, my Lord. In time. They put salves into it which I understand eases the King's pain, and pledgets that divert the anal canal, and he is advised not to over-indulge himself but,' FitzPeter shrugged, 'he is Henry, Count of Anjou and King of England and does not take instruction, even from learned men.'

**

By May Henry had rallied sufficiently to leave his bed as news came in of the renewed offensive of Philippe and Richard. The latter, who men now frequently called Coeur de Lion – the Lionheart – began his own pitiless and brutal war across a great swathe of Maine and down into Aquitaine. News came in of the fall of castle after castle, including Chateauroux, enraging Henry who suspected, rightly, that their constables and castellans had surrendered their keys knowing their own master was close to death and that they would soon enough serve another.

But despite the King's miraculous recovery, few of Henry's Norman vassals mustered their mesnies at Le Mans and in early June Henry learned they had instead combined and awaited the outcome of events at Alençon.

'I am betrayed,' snarled Henry, as intelligence also arrived that a huge army led by Richard and Philippe was rapidly advancing towards Le Mans. But at Le Mans Henry received a Papal-Legate, come from Rome to remind the King, along with King Philippe and Count Richard, that they had all taken the cross and sworn to deliver the Holy Land from the Turk. Touched by his own mortality and moved by the new Pope's appeal, the King sullenly agreed to once again meet Philippe and Richard, this time at La Ferté-Bernard, a day's ride north-east of Le Mans.

Thither went William, in the train of Henry, who rode his palfrey with difficulty and great courage, behind which his squire drew after him his destrier caparisoned for war. This was to be a show of splendour, reminding the world that Henry of England, Normandy, Anjou and Maine was not yet dead and a warrior capable of a crusade. The knights of Henry's own mesnie, and the accompanying entourages of his vassals like William Marshal, had all been ordered to ride armed and accoutred for war. But they did not come in great force and at La Ferté-Bernard they found the huge entourages of Philippe and Richard not only similarly equipped, but backed by a war-host of immense size, a fact that profoundly affected the outcome. Having listened for some two hours as the emissary of Pope Clement III harangued the two Kings as if chastening children, lecturing them that it was not seemly for Christian Kings and Princes to make war upon one another when the Holy Places were lost to the King of Jerusalem, Henry could no longer contain himself.

'Why, in all good faith, dost thou come hither with a war-host?' he asked Philippe, turning to the Papal-Legate with an expression of despair. 'Do you not see how here, upon my own land, this perfidious King,' and here Henry pointed a shaking but accusing finger at Philippe, 'and a treacherous son, bring an army? What hope have I of doing the bidding of the Holy Father faced with such constant perfidy?'

It was a *tour de force* of sorts, Henry playing the part of the faithful Christian, thwarted by deceit, but it did no good. The meeting broke up in disorder with threats and curses being thrown by each party and only the Legate's presence of mind in raising his crozier, prevented the drawing of swords. Then, abruptly, Philippe withdrew and Henry was left to plead further with the Legate until Robert de Tresgoz, who had sniffed a rat in this sudden departure and followed the French party, came hurrying in with the news that, rather than retiring east into the French lands, Philippe's knights were ordering an advance on Le Mans.

'Jesu Christ!' roared Henry, tearing at his hair. 'See! See!' he spat in the face of the Legate who, thoroughly alarmed, passed word for his own hasty departure.

'Your Grace!' called William, recalling the King to the nature of the moment, 'we have not a moment to lose. We must to Le Mans.'

'Aye, by God, you are right!'

***

Henry and his entourage rode into the city of Le Mans towards sunset on the 10th June. The city stood proudly behind its sturdy walls at the confluence of the River Sarthe and its narrower tributary, the Huisne, the latter crossed by a single bridge. To the south-east of the ramparts lay rough country seamed by a marshy ravine. The defences had been further strengthened earlier that summer, stakes having been driven into the beds of the rivers at any fording places and a number of hovels close to the city walls that might give cover to an attacker had been destroyed.

As Henry entered the southern gate he was met, as

was customary, by the city fathers, answering their anxious enquiries about the situation with the assertion that Le Mans was the city of his birth and the burial-place of his father, Geoffrey of Anjou, who lay at peace in the cathedral of St Julien.

'I shall never give up this place, messieurs, never!'

But that evening Henry summoned William and ordered him to conduct a survey of the city's outer defences the following morning.

'Divine the point of attack, Marshal,' the King said, confidentially, 'for this place, strong though it seems, is unlikely to hold-up my bastard of a son for long. I may have been born here, but I am not minded to die here also.'

Shortly after daybreak, lightly armed and with only a handful of knights in attendance, William rode out into a thick mist that rose over the two rivers and spread out over the flood plain of the Huisne. It was from here that the enemy could be expected and they had hardly crossed the Huisne when they were suddenly in sight of a party of French knights.

'Come away, my Lord,' one of William's knights advised. 'We are but lightly armed.'

'Wait!' ordered William, aware that the warmth of the rising sun was swiftly dispelling the mist. Rather than retreat he spurred his horse and took post on a low knoll from where he could observe the surrounding countryside for some distance. With a palpably uneasy air his knights followed and as they halted their mounts and regarded the vista William saw first the sunlight twinkling upon the bobbing lance-heads of the enemy. Slowly the great host emerged from the mist.

'Holy Christ!' someone behind him blasphemed and without looking round William heard the rustle as his companions crossed themselves. Then William turned his horse and caught the eye of Robert de Tresgoz.

'As soon as we are across, hold the bridge. John, ride back into the city and bring out combustibles and axes! Ride for your life! The rest of you, retire to Le Mans.'

For a moment he hesitated, Tresgoz by his side, watching the advancing front at the head of which he could see the leopards of Anjou.

'Philippe, the cunning bastard, has Richard doing all his dirty work for him while Richard, revelling in the business he knows best, acts like the Capet's favourite hound, God rot him.' Robert de Tresgoz turned his horse. 'D'you follow, my Lord?'

William nodded, leaving Tresgoz at the bridge with a handful of followers and riding hard for the city main, southern gate. As he arrived John de Earley was emerging with two mounted men-at-arms leading mules with firewood, cans of oil and large axes.

'Hurry, John. They will reach the bridge 'ere long.'

But the enemy did not press the attack that day. As they awaited the arrival of the full war-host they left the defenders free to retire from the wreckage of the bridge and set fire to the remaining dwellings, barns and byres that might afford the enemy shelter.

In the city the defenders spent an uneasy night but at dawn William roused his mesnie, ordering it under arms before making a tour of the ramparts and seeking the King's presence.

'Well, Marshal, what news d'you bring?' The King was at stool, a page holding cloth in front of him and

William heard the grunts of unnatural defecation. The stench was appalling.

'We should make the city ready for a siege, Your Grace. They will not delay an attack.'

'You mean Richard will not delay an attack,' the King said ruminatively as he emerged. As William stood in attendance he ordered his leather hauberk. 'We will delay them at the Huisne,' Henry said. I will conduct a reconnaissance myself and you will hold the southern gate, to be open in my absence. Call the men to arms and let us have the ramparts manned. A show of force will not hurt.'

With some misgivings William made his obeisance and left, but his anxiety only increased when, shortly thereafter, he pulled his horse aside to let the King pass under the portcullis at the southern gate and noted Henry had not donned mail. The unwisdom of this struck William forcibly so that he checked the King.

'Your Grace…'

'Well?'

'You eschew your armour, my Lord. Is that wise?'

'Perhaps not,' snapped the King, jostling William aside and leading a number of knights out. 'We have rendered the Huisne impassable, have we not, Marshal?'

'But they have archers…'

'They did not hit me at Limoges, Marshal…' the King replied, kicking his horse into motion. William watched him go, followed by his youngest son, Count John, Baldwin of Béthune and Robert de Trsegoz. Tresgoz had heard the exchange and lifted his shoulders, as if to imply it was the King's affair if he chose to risk his life, leaving William to recall the narrow escape Henry had

had when reconnoitring the defences of Limoges several years earlier. That had occurred when confronting a rebellion by his eldest son, the late Prince Henry, the Young King; now he was threatened by his second son, Richard. Then it struck William that perhaps Henry sought death, and a death in the field at the hands of his treacherous offspring rather than from a – what did FitzPeter call it? A fistula? Patricide would lay an ineradicable mark upon Richard's soul.

William advanced his horse clear of the gate; he had an uneasy feeling gnawing at his guts. Behind him mounted sergeants, men-at-arms and foot soldiers clustered reassuringly, and above, on the ramparts, archers had been stood-to, but he was unable to throw off the sense that all was not well. As on the previous morning a low mist hung over the rivers, lighter but – oddly – more persistent. The King and his retinue had passed beyond his line of sight, and William rode some way out of the city so that he could see the broken bridge over the Huisne. A party of French knights were milling around it, then trailing off to either side, as if prospecting along the river bank. He could see that from time-to-time, one would drive his horse into the river, leaning forward to test the bed with his lance. But they had impeded all the fords... or had they?

William felt his vague anxiety form a ball in the pit of his stomach. It was one thing to experience the heart-thumping exhilaration of waiting a well-planned ambush in the tourney, or the sudden lust for blood and triumph that carried one through the execution of a *coup d'épée*, but he disliked awaiting something amorphous over which he had no control.

Above his head someone cried out. He looked up. They were pointing south and east, to something hidden by undulating ground. Then he heard shouts go up: 'The King! The King!'

Christ! Had Henry found his death? William strained to see what was going on above his head but could make nothing out. Then someone - William thought he recognised the voice of a knight of the king's household - shouted, 'hold your discharge!' So the archers could not fire for fear of hitting the King, William concluded, turning to pass back to the gate and await events.

He did not have long, nor did he understand until Tresgoz told him much later what had happened, that Henry riding along the Huisne had encountered some of Richard or Philippe's knights on the opposite bank. They had traded insults, Henry amused that they were prospecting for a ford, secure in the knowledge that they had all been spiked. The two parties, moving in opposite directions had passed out of sight of each other in the mist when the enemy discovered a perfectly serviceable ford, one previously unknown to anyone and within minutes had sent word for reinforcements.

Within minutes first a handful and then a flood of the enemy knights was across the river and rapidly overtook the King who was compelled to ride for his life, all thoughts of a glorious death tossed aside. The pursuing enemy caught the rear of Henry's escort and butchered it, but the head-most few of the French rode on, intent upon over-taking the King before he could find refuge inside the city.

'And now, just as the sun had burned off the mist the day before,' Tresgoz had explained afterwards, 'a breeze picked up…'

The first William knew of all this was shouting, shouting from the ramparts and, carried on the rising wind, shouting from somewhere beyond his line-of-sight. Then Henry himself rode pell-mell up to the gate, followed immediately by a great press of men and horses wearing the devices of Anjou, Normandy and France, a wild and moving mêlée. Sword in hand, William found himself driven back by the weight of men and beasts, unable to defend the narrow gateway as a fierce tussle took place.

'Lower the portcullis!' Henry roared as he wheeled his horse and slashed about him. They could despatch a handful of pursuers within the walls if they could drop the portcullis, and William added his own voice to the commands to do so, but suddenly he realised they were too late. They were no longer under the shadow of the great stone gateway, but had been forced back into the narrow street leading to it. The gate and the first few adjacent houses were already in the hands of the enemy. Townsfolk, drawn by curiosity to see what was going on were caught up and impeded the fighting; women and children were screaming and as William tried to drag one of Richard's knights from his horse, his own destrier slithered in the blood and guts of some fool who had got trampled underfoot.

William too was fighting for his life now, his breath coming in gasps stung by the sharp stink of smoke. Christ! But they had entered the first houses and turned over the cooking fires and William could see, as more and more of the enemy forced their way into the city, the flicker of flames. Suddenly a great lick of fire shot out from an adjacent bakery; William's well-schooled destrier baulked at the sudden, almost explosive inferno that followed. William was driven back as he felt the scorch of heat and the destrier screamed and tugged at the bit.

But the ferocity of the attack was easing as the Angevins fell back and the French drew breath, or so it seemed. William found the King's standard in the square, and Henry standing in his stirrups, Count John beside him, looking decidedly scared.

'The citadel, my Lord?'

'The citadel is lost, Marshal,' the King snarled. 'Having cleared us from the gate they made directly for the citadel. We were too slow. Le Mans is lost. By the Christ we must get out! *Now!*'

William looked about him. God knows where his mesnie were; everything was in a riot of complete disorder, towns-people, archers and foot-soldiers – most of them Henry's Welsh mercenaries – milled about or ran, panic-stricken, from place to place, though mostly towards the sanctuary of the cathedral. Above the crowded streets a dense and growing pall of smoke rose slowly, only to be torn away by the steady summer breeze. William Waleran rode up to him, his shield indented, his mail coat seeping blood.

'Get you to the north gate, Will,' William ordered. 'But stay; have you seen FitzRobert?'

Waleran shook his head. 'Get you gone then,' said William curtly, his voice all but lost under the King's. Henry was roaring orders: 'Tresgoz to me! Béthune to me! Raise your standards, damn you, that you may summon your men! Des Roches to the Marshal! And you, Marshal, shall cover my retreat! God grant that they have not yet taken the north gate!'

'I have sent to see it secured. But where to?' William asked abruptly.

'You north to Alençon,' Henry said, drawing up his reins, 'draw them off and when you get there bring those cowardly bastards that think Henry of Anjou and England is done to join me at Chinon!'

'My Lord!' It was the ever vigilant Tresgoz, shouting a warning. On the far corner side of the square, above the mass of seething humanity a brace of knights could be seen clearing the way. Their intent was obvious and with them came the leopards of Anjou – Richard's men.

'Come away!' and the knot of mounted knights about King Henry moved as one in a swirl of harness and horse-hair, making for the northern gate, their duty to secure the person of Henry Curtmantle from capture, or to die in the process. William watched them go, then turned his attention to the group of enemy knights. Des Roches was alongside him. He did not know the man but he took his advice.

'Time to go, Marshal.' The two were the last to leave the square and within a few seconds the enemy were in hot pursuit. Only then did William realise that his destrier was wounded.

At the south gate William found Waleran with three wagons full of straw and firewood; as soon as William and Des Roches had passed, the wagons were drawn across the passage of the northern gate and set on fire. Waleran, with an axe, broke their wheels that they might not easily be rolled away.

'That was well done!' William shouted.

And then all that was left for a rear-guard, Des Roches, Waleran, John de Earley and William himself, were riding north, leaving Le Mans in flames.

**

For a mile they rode through the cultivated fields of the demesne lands dotted with burnt peasant hovels. William looked back: the burning wagons had delayed any pursuit. He was swept by the sensation of reaction to the exertions and anxieties of the past hours, overwhelmed with a sense of disgrace at having to abandon the city and the troops, especially the Welsh mercenaries, who would be massacred by Richard and Philippe. But he had little time for remorse. They had hardly cleared two or three miles before John de Earley called out a warning and William turned in his saddle.

Without a word all four men spurred their horses to a gallop for, over the brow of a low eminence came a troop of armed knights and well ahead of them rode two who had all but gained upon them. Upon the instant William threw caution to the winds, risking everything upon a foolhardy toss of the dice. Without slackening his pace he shouted: 'William! John! Ride on! Des Roches, if you're minded to, stand with me!'

For perhaps three heart-beats William continued his headlong gallop, then he drew rein and, as the pace of his destrier slowed to a halt, he swung round and couched his lance. For a further moment he was alone as the two advanced pursuers rapidly closed the distance, then he was conscious of Des Roches reining in alongside him.

'By the Christ, Marshal, you are either bold or mad! 'Tis the Lionheart!'

There was less than fifty yards between them when William too recognised the leading horseman. Des Roches was right. Richard in a hauberk with only the glint of sunlight on a steel helm: no coif; no coat of mail; no lance; no shield, riding like the impetuous wind. Just as his father had been that very morning. 'The fool,' breathed William, gathering his reins. 'He's mine!' he called, digging his spurs viciously into the destrier's flanks so that the great stallion leapt forward.

The distance between them closed as Richard, lugging out his sword shouted: 'Don't be a fool! I am unarmed!'

William's lance was levelled at Richard but as the Count threw his weight upon his reins and drew-up the destrier, William lowered his weapon's point and drove it hard into the breast of Richard's rearing charger. He held it tight, feeling it dig into his back and slow his own horse, wheeling him inwards with such violence that the lance bent, forcing Richard's magnificent destrier to twist then rear and fall over, onto its back. At that point the lance broke.

William wheeled round, threw away the haft of his shattered lance and drew his sword, Richard's charger gave a terrible whinny of pain and fear, its hooves kicked wildly in its death throes as Richard attempted to throw himself clear. As Richard attempted to stagger to his feet, casting about for his sword, he was flecked with the foam that flew from William's own wounded destrier as William rode round about him, his sword-point at the unarmed Richard's throat.

The knights of Richard's escort were no more than seventy yards away as William worked his charger round to place Richard between himself and them. Des

Roches and his opponent had not yet settled matters between them, though William sensed they were evenly matched.

'FitzMarshal, 'tis indeed you, by Christ! Remember your oath to me.'

'Aye my Lord, but I am as yet still the King's man.' William's eyes flickered from Richard to the knights who now, seeing Richard's plight, drew rein for a moment, taking stock.

'You cannot kill me. See...' the kneeling Richard, kicking himself free of the death throes of his destrier, spread his hands. 'I am unarmed and unarmoured...'

'A hasty and foolish thing to be, My Lord. Call off your men...'

'You cannot kill me Marshal, it would be a dishonourable thing to do in cold blood.'

'Call off your men! I have bested you in fair fight and shall not do murder as you would do me...'

The two men glared at each other until Richard turned his head slowly and shook it, gesturing with one hand for his men to remain where they were. William's destrier moved restlessly, the smell of blood from Richard's dead horse filling its nostrils but William kept it under control, his sword-point still at Richard's throat.

'What would you do now, FitzMarshal?'

'Leave you to the disposal of the Devil, my Lord, and have you turnabout for Le Mans...'

Then, very slowly, William backed his horse away as Richard, picking up his dropped sword, rose to his feet.

'No treachery, my Lord,' William called. 'You have no horse and your father is long gone...'

'I would have had my father but for you,' Richard

snarled.

'I should be poor recompense for your father, and you have Le Mans.'

Still Richard hesitated. A few yards distant from Richard, William reined-in again and offered Richard an alternative. 'Then to the death, my Lord? As you are, unsuited in mail but in single combat? Or honourable withdrawal? The matter lies upon your own soul…'

The two men continued to stare at each other and, without taking his eyes off Richard, William called out: 'Des Roches, give ground! Now call off your men, my Lord and give me *your* word for free passage.'

Out of the corner of his eye William saw Des Roches and his opponent detach from their duel and Des Roches backed his charger to range alongside William. For a further moment the two lone knights sat their horses, confronting some thirty or forty, between which stood Richard alongside the mounted knight who had engaged Des Roches.

Then Richard gave a brief nod to William, laughed and waved his men back. 'Get out of my sight Marshal! That was no fair fight, God damn you, but you have my word. It shall stand today, but thereafter…' Richard left the threat implicit.

Then William did something he afterwards had no explanation for; he backed his horse a further few yards and as he did so, keeping his eyes locked upon Richard, he raised his sword hilt to his lips and bowed his head.

'Until we meet again, my Lord,' William said. For a further ten seconds Richard stared at him, then his face cracked into a smile.

'The Devil will have you sooner than me, Marshal!' he

called out, motioning the knight with whom Des Roches had been engaged. The man helped hoist Richard up behind him and pulled his horse's head round to re-join their restless companions and William felt his guts twist.

'Come,' he said, backing his horse for a further ten yards before swinging round. Then, at a canter, he continued his journey north with Des Roches at his side.

'By the Holy Rood, my Lord Marshal, but I shall ne'er forget this day,' remarked Des Roches, looking nervously back over his shoulder. William grunted; under his surtout, coat of mail and hauberk, he was sweating with relieved tension. Des Roches seemed inclined to work his own nerves off with conversation.

'You will pay for that effrontery,' Des Roches said.

'Aye, I fear so,' William replied curtly.

'But 'twas well done,' added Des Roches, chuckling to himself. 'To have unseated the Lionheart! Why, that was very well done indeed!' Again William grunted. He felt over-whelmed by thirst, for the summer's day was hot. 'Dost know the device of the knight with whom I fought?' Des Roches asked.

'Aye. 'Twas Robert de Salignac.'

PART TWO: RICHARD COEUR DE LION 1189 - 1199

CHAPTER FOUR: THE STENCH OF DEATH
1189

William Marshal stood at the chamber door appalled by what he saw. Covering his nose against the stench of piss and excrement he advanced into the room.

Henry lay uncovered, dead upon a tousled couch of shit and blood stained linen. His head was drawn to one side, his right arm out-flung, his legs splayed. He wore a shirt torn to reveal his powerful torso, and a breech-clout that could not conceal the horror of what lay beneath it. His mouth was open, clogged with clotted sordes and crusted blood; his eyes too stared up at the low roof timbers and his once golden hair, now thin and grey, was plastered across his forehead by dried sweat. The Lion of England, of Normandy, Anjou and Aquitaine lay in death as low as any villein; no bejewelled rings adorned the fingers of his right hand; no cross lay upon his breast. A heavily bound chest that stood at the foot of the King's couch had been forced; its lid stood open: it was empty save for two gold marks.

William looked about him. The chamber was as bereft of any evidence of kingly status as the corpse that lay stinking before him. The King's body had been looted, his effects stolen. The chamber window had not even been opened to allow the escape of his soul.

William trembled; had the King been shriven? Or had his soul been carried to Hell as many predicted it would – and should – be? Did William stand close to the portal of that fearful place? He crossed himself with sudden fervour.

'Christ have mercy,' he murmured, 'God have mercy...'

No-one had stopped the body's natural orifices, let alone the unnatural one. The Devil had had a free hand with the King, William thought in horror. He crossed himself again then searched the chamber. There was nothing. With trembling hands William laid hands upon the King's body and, closing its eyes, straightened it. Taking up the two gold marks he laid them upon the King's eyelids then tore a strip from his bedding and bound-up the jaw, removed his cloak and covered the remains of the mightiest King in Christendom. He was no longer so, and William knelt in prayer against the couch, the sharp stench of urine released from Henry's bladder even stronger in his nostrils that that of ordure.

That was how John de Earley found him an hour later when he dared to investigate. William, Des Roches and a handful of knights had ridden hard from Alençon in response to the King's summons and it was clear, as they clattered into the mighty fortress of Chinon, that all was not well. The handful of foot-soldiers and men at arms at the gate were commanded by few knights, though in the great hall milled the greater part of the King's mesnie, which included those of his own men who had escaped from Le Mans in Henry's train. All that remained of the King's personal household were a few indecisive servants who had failed to profit from the King's death. The rest had pillaged the corpse and slipped away before anyone knew of the manner of the King's demise and once the event had occurred, not one among the combined mesnie had dared approach the corrupted body of their anointed Sovereign.

Only one person remained who had actually witnessed the King's last moments, a poor-woman whose task had been to empty the King's piss-pot. She had been kept by chance in the death chamber in fear of her life. When brought shaking with fear before William she fell on her knees and told of the King's delirium, of his sudden blindness and then the end: 'A gr...reat b...bursting of the heart, my Lord,' she stammered.

'Was there a priest present?' William asked, not unkindly.

The woman shook her head. 'I saw no p...priest, my Lord...only...'

'Only what?'

'Only a great spewing of b...blood, my Lord, and then his Grace gave up the ghost...'

The men about William shuddered and crossed themselves.

'You did not open the casement,' William said.

'No, my Lord. All was disorder... I...I...'

'Go on,' William commanded gently.

'I was told the Devil had his soul...' She crossed herself.

'Did you feel you were in the presence of the Devil?' William asked.

The woman hesitated, terrified of her ordeal and of this great man who interrogated her. 'I am not a witch, my Lord...'

'No, no, of course not,' William soothed, turning to De Earley. 'Give me silver, John.'

De Earley produced some coins and handed them to

William. 'Canst though stop the orifices and wash the body? These would be for your pains, woman.' She eyed the money, hesitating. 'If the Devil has his soul,' William reassured her, 'then he has long since taken it and I have prayed by his side. Go and open the chamber casement. This man here will stand with you until your work is done. Find clean linen for a shroud.'

The woman slowly took the coins and William nodded, saying, 'get you gone.' He looked at De Earley. 'Go with her John, stand guard within the chamber and bring me word when she is done.

De Earley withdrew obediently in the wake of the woman and William rose to gather round him the few knights that he had in attendance. Most of his mesnie were assembled, FitzRobert and Tresgoz among them, and he looked about him seeking some explanation. In the hour that followed he pieced together a little more of the events of the night of the 6th July, discovering why the knights of the King's mesnie had failed their Lord, the King.

'They had already departed, my Lord Marshal,' explained Geoffrey FitzRobert, 'ridden out with Count John when he so nobly abandoned his father to join his brother and Philippe of France.'

At first William was incredulous. That John had defected to the enemy was almost as shocking as the state in which he had found the Prince's dead father, given the standing he had in Henry's eyes. Then William learned that its impact upon the ailing Henry had proved fatal.

'At the news of John's disappearance, His Grace fell into one of his towering rages,' FitzRobert continued sadly. 'He had an apoplexy, falling into a fit and then a raving of nonsense such that no man knew what he said.'

'Why was no-one with him when he died, but that pathetic creature and his body-servants?'

'My Lord, it was night…' FitzRobert began.

'And one Odo de Caux slept outside the King's chamber,' put in Tresgoz, 'but without our knowing he was of Count John's party and slipped the leash during the hours of darkness, the bastard.'

'They opened the gates for him?' queried William.

'There was gold loose enough to buy the moon that night,' said Tresgoz contemptuously, 'though some of us,' he gestured at the knightly assembly surrounding William, 'were too far in our slumbers to know until morning.'

'*Some* of you…? And then? The King was not attended… No priest sent for to give him Holy Unction… Why was that?'

There was an awkward silence and William looked from one face to another; some were flushed, others pale, while some stood with down-cast eyes.

'Tresgoz?'

'My Lord,' Tresgoz coughed with embarrassment, looking about him as if to seek permission to justify their neglect of the King. 'Most of us had ridden after Count John, to bring him back. We would have done battle to do so,' he added, as if to add emphasis to their commitment.

'But…' put in William witheringly.

'But he had given us the slip, my Lord. No-one quite knew when he had left, nor which road he had taken.' Tresgoz fell silent.

'We might have guessed, My Lord Marshal,' added FitzRobert, 'but we knew His Grace had sent word for you to come hither urgently and by the time we had returned here the King was dead and...' his voice trailed off, intimidated by the look in William's eyes.

William stared from face to face and then it came to him in a flash. Henry had so closely kept these men under his control, just as he had kept the Young Henry, and afterwards his brother Richard, that none had the capacity to use their initiative. Except Richard, of course, and even Richard's intelligence took him no further than to King Philippe in search of *understanding*. As for the knights ranked about him, the flower of Angevin chivalry, they were but great boys, the armed might of Henry's puissance, to be sure, but that was all. It was like a revelation, yet quite unconsciously they had awaited William – the almost unlanded knight banneret – to guide them in this crisis. He expelled a great sigh and rose, the men about him almost subconsciously falling back in a circle.

'You, Tresgoz, will organise a guard upon the late King's chamber. I want a priest, better still a bishop, sent for and a Requiem Mass sang for the King's soul before another sun has set. Where is the Seneschal of this place?'

'Here, my Lord.' The man was of venerable years and wore a plain gown with a fine gilded belt but was otherwise unwarlike.

You, master Seneschal, will open the treasury and distribute alms to the poor of Chinon in the King's name.'

'That I cannot do.'

'Cannot or will not?'

'Cannot.'

'Pray why is that?'

'Because, my Lord, it is empty. Count John looted the treasury before he departed.' There was a sharp intake of breath at this effrontery.

'And did you nothing to prevent it?'

'I had not the authority, nor the means to prevent it.'

William guessed had he made motion, several of his mesnie would have taken the old man and slit his gizzard for failing in his duty.

'Go then, and consult your conscience and determine if our late Lord King would have smiled upon thee, or whether, were he alive he would have you damned.'

The old man shrunk away and was jostled by several of the knights. Someone remarked crudely that 'Curtmantle is looking up your arse from Hell, Master Seneschal,' and a ripple of amusement followed William as he left the great hall of the castle and went to tend his destrier.

***

In the days that followed William acted as he had done after the death of Henry Curtmantle's heir, Henry the Young King. In due course, the old woman having washed and straightened the corpse, and it having been dressed in clothes purchased from a rich merchant of Chinon, a High Mass was sung for the King's soul. This effected, William called Guillaume des Roches to his side.

'You are of the late King's mesnie, Guillaume,' William said, adding ruefully, 'and Count Richard will not have forgotten you.'

'No, by God, he will probably hang me as soon as look at me!'

'He will not do that, but I would have you go to him and inform him that the King his father is dead. Can you write?'

'Aye.'

'I cannot, but find pen, ink and parchment and I will dictate you a safe-conduct.'

These materials having been assembled, Des Roches - protesting feebly that he was not a clerk but that in the absence of such a personage he was prepared to assist the Marshal as he had in the matter of holding up the King's pursuers – bent to his task.

'I, William Marshal, to Richard, King of England, Duke of Aquitaine, Count of Anjou, Maine, Touraine and Berri, greeting,' William began. 'Know you that it hath pleased Almighty God to call to his bosom that High and Mighty Prince, Henry, lately King of England, Duke of Normandy, Aquitaine, Count of Anjou, Maine, Touraine and Berri.

'Know you that I, William Marshal, do Your Grace homage as my Liege Lord and that I shall bring the mortal remains of the King, your father, to Fontevrault where I shall await such orders and instructions as you shall be pleased to give me.'

When he had finished scratching in his rough hand, Des Roches looked up. 'Is that all?'

'What more would you have me say?'

'There is no mention of a laisser passer…'

'Do you write again… no, no, on a separate sheet… Er: To whom it may concern…'

When Des Roches had finished William awkwardly

scrawled his name, practically his only literate achievement, and sent Guillaume des Roches off with an escort of what remained of Henry's own mesnie.

Then William called for a river barge and laid the bier upon it, ordering all the knights remaining at his command to escort the cadaver down the Vienne to Fontevrault. The solemn procession descended the river, William and his senior knights standing armed upon the barge, the escort riding along the river's bank.

At Fontevrault the King's body was handed over to the Abbot and monks of the great abbey church who prepared it for burial, eviscerating and embalming it before dressing it in mail and surtout and laying it in state in the abbey nave. Thereafter William's mesnie stood guard over it, night and day until word came that Richard advanced upon the city. When he head of the Lionheart's approach William called John de Earley to his side to don his full coat of mail and his cleanest surtout.

'Call hither Tresgoz and FitzRobert, fully armed,' he ordered his squire, 'and come yourself, though clean yourself up.'

Half an hour later William, Robert de Tresgoz, Geoffrey FitzRobert and John de Earley relieved the knights then on duty and took up their posts, quartering the dead Henry as he lay upon his bier in his mail, a gold circlet about his head and his sword by his side. Fittingly, he no longer smelt of excrement, merely the sweet scent of embalming oil. About them rose the chant of the choir while the Abbot, fully adorned in cope and mitre, his crozier in his hand, led the clerical assembly of Fontevrault in a continuous round of devotion.

Full of apprehension William and the men of his mesnie awaited their new Lord.

CHAPTER FIVE: RICHARD, COEUR DE LION
1189

When Richard strode into the great church at the head of a small retinue he paused a moment and regarded the four armed men who stood guard upon his father. Their eyes were downcast but Richard had no need to enquire, for catching the westering sunbeams that lanced in through the abbey windows, was a tall figure who leaned upon a shield of gold and green, emblazoned with a red lion rampant.

Without a word Richard stepped up to the bier and bent over his father, then he stood back and for several moments stood respectfully beside the corpse before walking out into the sunshine of the late July afternoon.

After some time a knight approached the four motionless guards. It was Robert de Salignac. With no show of recognition he asked that 'William Marshal' should lay aside his sword and shield and follow him. Outside De Salignac had two horses saddled and waiting. De Salignac motioned for William to mount up. Fearing the worst from De Salignac's silence William did as he bid and followed as De Salignac led him out of the city into open countryside. Sensing this meant immediate banishment, William contemplated breaking the silence between them. But De Salignac could not have relished his duty and it was perhaps best for William to hold his tongue. Instead he quickly resolved to ride north, asking De Salignac to order John de Earley to follow with sufficient arms and treasure to fund their return to England. He was on the point of asking this one boon of his old friend when De Salignac drew rein.

'Wait here,' he said curtly and then put spurs to his horse.

'Robert!' William called, intending to pass the message to De Earley, but De Salignac was gone. Surprised, hurt even, and certainly thwarted, William turned in his saddle. What he saw set his heart a-tremble; De Salignac had drawn up alongside a knight who had been following at a distance: it was Richard. Then De Salignac rode back towards the distant spire of Fontevrault, leaving William to the tender mercies of the Lionheart.

Richard came on at a smart canter. He rode a bay mare, a reminder, perhaps that William had killed his favourite war-horse. Drawing himself up in the saddle William awaited the new King, noting that Richard bore no conspicuous weapon and lowering his head as Richard drew rein beside him.

'So, we meet again, Marshal.'

'My Lord King,' William made to dismount and do obeisance but Richard had other ideas.

'Stay! Come, you shall ride with me.' Richard turned his horse off the road and began to walk it across the water-meadows of the Vienne in silence. William fell into station on Richard's right-hind quarter, holding back to a respectful distance. At the river's bank the King swung south, upstream and motioned William alongside him. William was now between Richard and the river and the King eased his reins, allowing his horse to pick its way round the overhanging willows and through the tussocks of grass of the river-side. William, his heart still thumping with apprehension, did likewise.

'At Le Mans you would have killed me had I not thrust aside your lance with my hand,' Richard said at last.

It was palpably untrue and William bridled at the falsehood. Had Richard been thus explaining the event to diminish William's achievement and limit the damage to his own reputation? He might concede the point for Richard's benefit and his own oblation, but to agree to this implied his intention had been to kill Richard. He chose not to fall in with this face-saving exercise, realising that Richard had allowed his knights no closer that afternoon so that they largely missed the dialogue between the two protagonists. William's hesitation caused Richard to look at him askance.

'Well?'

William shook his head. 'It is not true, my Lord, and you know it…'

'By God's bones you would contradict me!'

'Your hand did not touch my lance, my Lord,' William said quietly.

'You lie!'

'No, my Lord King, I do not lie. *You* lie!'

Richard drew his mare to a standstill and swung her so that the beast all but forced William's backwards into the Vienne, but William jabbed his spurs to prevent his own mount giving ground. He had never ridden the animal before but it did not give way to the King's.

'By Christ, Marshal, for a man with but a hand-span of land and dark, wet English land to boot, you are damned high and mighty.'

Sensing Richard was testing him William said, 'My

Lord, I had no intention of killing you, though I might have done easily enough. Instead of your breast, I deliberately chose that of your horse…'

'Upon your honour?'

'Upon my honour, Your Grace.'

There was a long silence, so long that William, whose ears had been shut to it, heard the rustling of the willows, the lapping of the Vienne and the song of a sky-lark rising to heaven in the hot air. Then Richard chuckled and held out his hand. Even now William hesitated uncertainly, until Richard added: 'Come, I have need of trusted allies and would have you as a friend before I insist upon you respecting the oath you have already made to me and the protestation of fealty Des Roches brought me… By the way, that was not your hand on that parchment, was it?'

'No, my Lord, it was Des Roches… My sign manual…'

'Well it was execrable.' Richard went on so that William fell prudently silent. His illiteracy had not been a problem until now.

'Come, let us ride back,' Richard turned his horse's head. 'Stay with me,' he ordered as William dropped back. 'As you well know that I have taken the cross. It is my most earnest desire to recapture Jerusalem and I am persuaded that God has chosen me as His instrument. After I am crowned King I intend going upon a crusade and I shall need Counsellors, Governors and Justiciars to rule my lands in my absence.' Richard looked at William. 'I should wish you to be one of them, Marshal.'

The shock of the immensity of what Richard was asking after the event of the afternoon felt like a blow.

He was reminded of Henry's great confidence in him and felt himself at a loss to explain either, but where Henry's had been conjectural, Richard's was to be real, practical.

'Your Grace, you do me great honour, but as you yourself said, I am a man of little land. How may I command respect among greater lords than myself?'

'I intend you for England and I shall raise you, William,' Richard said with a sudden intimacy. 'My father promised you the ward-ship of Isabelle de Clare, but I grant it in my own name. You shall go to England, marry the Lady and take charge of my lands and interests as Lord of Striguil.'

'But what of Count John, Your Grace?'

'What of him, William? Surely you will treat him no more roughly than you did me under the walls of Le Mans.' Richard's expression was one of sarcasm and William glimpsed the ruthlessness below the easy charm, a charm that now sought to smooth over the affair outside Le Mans. 'You were lucky then,' he went on, 'had I been fully accoutred it would have been you rolling in the dust.'

'Aye, my Lord,' conceded William wisely, 'very probably, though I am not yet too old to grasp a lance firmly.'

Richard chuckled. They had regained the road and turned towards the city. 'D'you know why I was so ill-equipped?'

'Nay.'

'I had word they had found a new ford across the Huisne when I was breaking my fast. But ten minutes earlier I had been told my father with a mere handful of his mesnie was scouting the far bank, so I leapt into the saddle and rode pell-mell, right through Le Mans, hot on the old fox's heels and by God I should have caught him but for you.'

William bit his tongue. 'Did you know, Your Grace, that your father had gone out on that reconnaissance that morning similarly ill-equipped.'

Richard jerked his horse to a standstill and stared at William. 'No, I did not. The old fool,' he added, seemingly oblivious to the irony. ''Twas a fault of his to be so precipitate,' he remarked casually, kicking his mount forwards again.

They rode on in silence, not a quarter of a mile from the city when William coughed. Richard turned. 'You have something more to say, Marshal?' he asked, dropping the informality as they approached the gate.

'I would ask a boon.'

'Is the Lordship of Striguil not enough for you?'

'It is not for me, Your Grace.'

'Who then?'

'If you give me Striguil as a public proof of your trust, may I ask for the dubbing of John de Earley as a knight?'

'De Earley? He that my father gave you ward-ship of?'

'The same, My Lord King.'

'Who stood guard on my father this afternoon with Tresgoz and Fitz…'

'FitzRobert, yes.'

Richard kicked his horse ahead, dropping William behind. 'If you wish, Marshal,' he called back over his shoulder.

***

87

With the Court in mourning William ate that night in his lodging and he had hardly sat down to board with Tresgoz, FitzRobert and the other senior knights of his mesnie when De Salignac was announced.

'Robert!' William rose and clasped his old friends' right forearm, calling for meat and wine. 'By God, but I was wondering how matters stood between us after the affair of Le Mans, let alone that business this afternoon.

'Did you not recognise my device at Le Mans?'

'No, I fear not, at least not immediately. I was only aware of the Lionheart and another and I could not, in all honour, leave Richard to poor Des Roches.'

''Twas as well it fell out that way for I durst not despatch Des Roches for fear of having to run to Richard's aid and,' De Salignac shrugged, 'well, that is past considering.' De Salignac laughed. 'The Lionheart has taken Des Roches into his mesnie for his gallantry and loyalty to Henry Curtmantle. He has done honour to others loyal to the Old King, among them Baldwin de Béthune, who is become Lord of Aumale.' Des Salignac smiled. 'And I am sorry for my silence this afternoon.'

William brushed aside his friend's apologies and introduced him to the others at board.

'I am come only in part as a friend, I am also a messenger.'

'Richard's?'

'Aye.' De Salignac looked at William's squire. 'You John de Earley must do vigil this night and the King will dub you in the morning when he also commands your presence, William. You know he intends you for England.'

'Aye, he told me so...and you, Robert, what doth he

intend for you?'

'The Holy Land. I shall go with him but first I am to accompany you to England, then attend the Coronation before leaving with the King for Outremer.'

'The Holy Land eh?' William paused, recalling that last night at sea on their return voyage. He felt a faint envy of his friend but the moment passed in contemplation of the immediate future. 'Well then, we shall have some time together. By heaven, that pleases me.'

''Tis perpetually wet in England, Sir Robert,' Tresgoz put in, wearing a mock doleful expression.

'Perhaps, but no more so than your native Brittany,' and with that they fell to a convivial evening of drinking and recalling recent events.

John de Earley was dubbed and belted knight the following morning, after which King Richard drew William aside and addressed him in a low voice.

'You shall go to Winchester, Marshal, where lies the Lady Eleanor my mother. The Clerks are even now preparing the necessary papers. There are matters contained therein closely touching yourself which, if you please her, she will attend to. See that you do please her.'

'Your Grace?' William looked puzzled.

'The matter will fall out as it may, Marshal, but if I have my man aright, you will not object,' Richard said with a faint air of mystery before going on with his instructions. 'You shall leave tomorrow and ready her for my coronation which I intend to be in September. I must first settle matters with Philippe and buy him off by bribing him for the Vexin. Count John will not be of nomination to the Council ruling England in my absence but you do not know my brother well, Marshal. Watch him and keep him loyal; as you well know, he is easily swayed according to the wind. I entrust this duty as sacred to you. D'you understand?'

'Aye, Your Grace. At least regarding Count John.'

'Shall I lay you under oath?'

'No, Your Grace, that will not be necessary.'

Richard smiled. 'Good. Entrust your hopes with me as to the other matter. Now, FitzPeter shall go with you, for the moment he is mine and he shall have precedence over you until after he has delivered that which I wish my mother, the Lady Eleanor to be acquainted with. You may take with you those of your mesnie you wish to accompany you and who do not wish to take the cross, for I would have your arms upheld as one of my Justiciars in England. Choose wisely; men loyal only to you. I have enemies in England and there are those who would seek to profit from my absence. Use the velvet glove for the most part, but do not scruple to enforce matters by the mailed fist should you think it fit in my interest. For that you shall answer to me.'

William was dismissed and went to pass his orders for an early departure, calling William Waleran and Geoffrey FitzRobert to join him in England, along with John de Earley. It was only later that day, as he took stock of the morrow that he recalled Richard's words: 'Entrust your hopes with me as to the other matter.' William had little choice; his entire future and fortune rested upon this new arrangement. He was Richard's man now and must do as he was bid; did Richard mean something related to the proposition of marriage to

Isabelle de Clare?

He had little time to consider the matter further being joined first by FitzPeter, who laid the King's instructions before him, and then by De Salignac, Tresgoz and the other knights of his mesnie from whom he was taking imminent departure. Again, and in spite of the officially sombre mood of the Court, they dined again in mild and muted riot, saddened by the break-up of the mesnie of William Marshal.

CHAPTER SIX: THE LADY OF STRIGUIL 1189

'Rise, William Marshal. I thought never to see you again.'

William kissed the ring on the Dowager Queen's right hand and rose. 'God has preserved us both, Your Grace.'

She regarded him with the cool grey eyes he remembered well. Nor were her features much damaged by age. The straight nose and the well-formed mouth nestled somewhat in furrows but she wore her years well and she remained every inch a Queen.

'FitzPeter has been sent away upon an errand in my name. He will return hither within a few days. He tells me that you were not present at the death of the King my husband's death.'

'Not at the actual moment, Your Grace...' William began to explain.

'Why, pray, was that?' the Queen asked sharply.

'In the rout of Le Mans, Your Grace, I drew off to the north, to Alençon where the majority of the late King's mesnie awaited the outcome of events...'

'They had deserted him?' she asked, her voice quiet.

'Yes, my Lady.'

'The perfidy,' she whispered, half to herself. William held his tongue as Eleanor appeared to contemplate the ruin of her husband's ambition. 'You did not go to join them?'

'No, Your Grace, I did not. I went thither on the King's orders and found the place full of rumour and dissent. The late King summoned me then to Chinon, whither he had gone from Le Mans but before I had arrived Count John went over to Count Richard and the King of France which brought about your husband's apoplexy.'

'From which he died?'

'Aye, Madam, and most unkindly too.'

'Tell me.'

''Twas not pretty, my Lady.'

'Tell me, FitzMarshal. All of it.'

'All, my Lady?'

'All. So that I might know of it.'

William related the condition in which he had found Henry and the circumstances leading up to the King's death that he had discovered by his investigation. He told her also of the manner in which he had brought the King's body to Fontevrault. Eleanor listened, her face expressionless and when he had finished, she crossed herself and said, 'I am sorry that you had to do for the father what you did for the son, there were others whose duty should have attended to these matters.' She sighed, then added after a moment's reflection, 'it seems from the papers the man FitzPeter carried from my son, the Lord Richard, that you are destined to serve our family.' She gave him a wan smile. 'You may go now. Your lodgings are prepared and I shall send for you when FitzPeter returns.'

'Your Grace, there is one matter…'

'Go on.'

'The Lord Richard's Coronation…'

'FitzPeter has the commission for it. I shall see it sent to the Archbishop of Canterbury tomorrow. You may go.'

'And you shall attend?' William asked, making his obeisance.

'Is that what my son sent you hither to determine?'

'Aye, my Lady.'

The Queen smiled enigmatically but returned no response, only repeating her dismissal.

In the few days that followed, William kicked his heels in a quiet fury, aware that something touching himself was up and not daring to ask for fear of seeming presumptuous. On his way north from Fontevrault he had diverted his route sufficiently to visit several of the estates belonging to Isabelle de Clare, to inspect them and make his face known to their various stewards and chief villeins, but they were not his by right of demesne until he had married the Lady of Striguil and he was conscious that, should his actions be seen as importunate, the lands he so coveted might yet be snatched from him. On the journey, FitzPeter had let slip sufficient hints that he should just be patient, which was all very well when travelling, but when idle in Winchester, it ate into his soul. The only action William took during that brief period was to send John de Earley to his own elder brother John Marshal, to make known to him that, after many years, his younger sibling had returned to England.

FitzPeter returned to the Queen's presence in Winchester after four days and William was summoned before Eleanor. 'You shall go at once to London, FitzPeter will accompany you. Arrangements have been made for you to lodge with Richard FitzReiner and you will find the Lady of Striguil in the care of Ranulf de

Glanville, lodged in The White Tower.'

William took his leave of the Queen and, with FitzPeter and his mesnie, rode east to London, towards the Conqueror's fortress where the Justiciar Ranulf de Glanville at first refused to allow the ward of the Old King to be released into William's care, having had second thoughts after receiving the commands of both Queen Eleanor and Duke Richard, borne by FitzPeter.

'Why not?' William asked bluntly, as a protesting FitzPeter fulminated at his elbow.

'My Lord I have examined my conscience and until Count Richard is here, in England, anointed…'

'What of the Lady Eleanor's writ and instruction?' FitzPeter put in, 'you gave me every assurance…'

'The Lady Eleanor has been mewed up these sixteen years. What authority may be placed upon such a writ in such a time, my Lord?' De Glanville asked, an air of desperation in his voice.

'I am appointed a Justiciar,' William said shortly, towering over De Glanville, who remained seated at his table, 'we are equals, you and I, but I would have my way in the matter. Bring the lady to me.'

With an obvious show of reluctance De Glanville rose and passed word that the young woman should be brought into William's presence, then he and FitzPeter withdrew. Helping himself to a goblet of De Glanville's wine William stared from the narrow window in De Glanville's chamber, staring down onto the grey waters of the Thames and the marshy surroundings of the low eminence upon which the Conqueror had had his castle built, commanding the lowest crossing point of the wide tidal stream.

Warm summer sunlight danced in a thousand points of light upon the great river and for a moment he forgot for what he waited, so lost was he in watching the various vessels working the stream. Recalling his own voyages, he thought of Robert De Salignac and their last days at sea on their return from the Holy Land and again envied his friend his forthcoming great adventure with the Lionheart. He longed himself to go back, all the more so now that the Holy Places were in the hands of the unbelievers. What was it they were calling the Turks now? The Saracens? As for the tempestuous Channel, he had crossed it but four times and found it a very different experience from that of the Mediterranean which, whilst able to boil itself into a gale, whipped by sudden winds of extreme ferocity, lacked the inherent malice of the strongly tidal Channel with its short and vicious waves, its mists and rain, and lack of marks. And this River of Thames also possessed the strange magic of tidal waters that FitzPeter had told him belonged in some way to the phases of the moon. So lost was he in contemplation of the incomprehensibility of it all that he did not hear the door open and was only roused from his reverie by the discreet cough of a young woman kept waiting for too long. He spun round, recalled to the present with an apology upon his lips.

'Forgive me, Madam,' he said as his eyes adjusted from the bright light of the river to the gloom of the chamber, into which he advanced.

'My Lord.' The slim figure dipped slightly in courteous curtsey and he was aware of an older woman, her hand-maid, no doubt, who waited in the deeper shadows by the door.

'Isabelle?' he said tentatively, holding out his hand and looking at her properly for the first time. Her close-fitting gown was of a pale grey, edged across her breast in gold and silver thread. An elaborate knotted belt was passed about her slender waist and, tied in front, fell below her knees. Her head was loosely coifed in white and a heavy tress of braided hair fell below her waist. It was of a red-gold colour that reminded him of the Young King Henry.

She was staring at him anxiously. She could not have been past seventeen years of age, he thought, with a shock, and he was past forty! Her hand was cool in his and trembled a little. Well it might he thought, unable to find words to break the silence growing between them, until he bethought himself of his manners and offered her Ranulf de Glanville's chair and poured her a goblet of De Glanville's wine.

'Here, my Lady, pray warm yourself against any chill you may feel in my presence. I assure you it is not intended towards you.'

She murmured her thanks and took the wine. He could see her shaking now and caught the faint chink of her teeth against the silver. She was of more than a mere pleasing appearance, he thought, having that creamy complexion that often goes with auburn hair. Her mouth was red-lipped, encarmined, no doubt, but made for kissing, and her eyes? He could not properly see the colour of them, but they were large, and bright under long lashes which she had darkened with soot or charcoal or some other concoction.

She lowered the goblet and William observed the fall of her breasts. He must hold his peace no longer.

'We are to be married, Madam,' he said in a low and –
he hoped – kindly voice. 'It is…was the desire of our
late King Henry and has been confirmed by the Lord
Richard of England, Normandy and Anjou…' He
faltered as she stared at him. This was all unbelievably
pompous and her eyes were grey… no green…or were
they a strange shade of hazel-brown? He coughed
awkwardly. To be past forty and feeling like a callow
youth in front of this girl was a humiliation he had
neither expected nor desired. His carnal tumblings with
the whores of Guillaume de Tancarville's household had
not required such delicate pre-amblings, while his
dealings with the ladies of the Royal Courts of both the
Old and Young Henry's had been more like exercises
with weapons in the tiltyards, feints and blows amusing
to both parties but leading to no serious conclusions.
Only when he thought of his encounters with Queen
Marguerite, consort to Henry the Young King, did his
heart catch and the fog upon his mind lift.

He smiled, and picked up his thread, repeating
himself. 'We are to be married, you and I, and I hope
that I do not displease you, my Lady, for you do not
displease me…' he trailed off, his rhetoric exhausted as
she stared up at him until a cough from her hand-maid or
waiting woman prompted her to respond.

'No, my Lord, you do not displease me.'

It broke the ice, for he found himself laughing. 'Come
Isabelle, pray tell me the truth. I am an ill looking oaf.'

She caught his mood, pleased at his grinning, and he
found himself under proper scrutiny. 'You have all your
teeth, my Lord,' she said in a relieved tone.

'Do I then pass muster, my Lady? Like a horse, to be

judged by my teeth?'

She was laughing now. 'I confess it to have been a worry, my Lord,' she confessed.

'But what about my other features, Isabelle?'

'You have your hair, my Lord,' she remarked, gaining confidence and revealing her anxieties at being told whom she was to marry.

'Then I satisfy you even more. Come, tell me, can you read and write?'

'Of course, my Lord,' she faltered, intuitively sensing the question was loaded. 'Why, can you not yourself read and..?'

He shook his head. 'Nay, to my shame. My education was cut short and I was sent a hostage in war to the encampment of King Stephen.'

'King Stephen?' he could see she was now shocked. 'During the Anarchy?'

He nodded. 'I was a child,' he added hurriedly, going on to tell her something of his boyhood, of his years as a camp-follower, an intended guarantor of his father's good behaviour towards Stephen in a country riven by civil strife and of how his father had so callously and conspicuously abandoned him. 'But God has been good to me Isabelle,'' he concluded, crossing himself, 'and perhaps never so much as now when I meet you. Do you think that you could be my wife?'

'Do I have a choice?' she asked sharply, revealing a quick intelligence that belied her youth and brought a disapproving intake of breath from the older woman who otherwise remained a mute witness to this pretty scene of blundering courtship. William contemplated Isabelle for a long moment. With her came land and power; to take the hand of a Royal ward was a mark of great favour and the young woman had no choice at all, but he could not leave the question open, for she had asked it directly. Their eyes met.

'If you so wish it, Isabelle, you have a choice.'

'But if I reject you, I should like be married to another and my rejection would be seen as yours, would it not?'

William nodded. 'Aye, it would.'

'And it would harm you, my Lord, in the eyes of the King and the Court.' She said it as a statement; here was no *naïf*, William thought, but a shrewd young woman, well versed in courtly matters. 'Aye, my Lady, and I should have to take the cross and travel to Outremere rather than live with the humiliation.'

'You know that my father was Richard FitzGilbert de Clare, known to many as Richard Strongbow, Earl of Striguil, that my mother was Aoife, daughter of Dermot MacMurrough, the last Irish King of Leinster in Ireland, lands which were conquered by my father whilst you, by your own admission…'

'Am almost a no-body, my Lady, a knight banneret, a body knight to the two Henrys, Young and Old, and now to Lord Richard…' William was almost humbled under the young woman's level appraisal. Had he walked like a fool into a trap? Was he about to insult Richard and let slip his one chance of achieving his ambition? Suddenly crusade to the Holy Land seemed less and less attractive, even though the thought was almost a blasphemy in itself.

She seemed amused at the expression on his face. Could she read his mind? God's bones, she had red hair! Was she descended from the Old People, like Angharad ap Gwyn? He felt a sudden urge to cross himself again but if her next remark disarmed him still further it obviated this sudden need for piety.

'But you possess a great reputation for prowess, my Lord, and you broke a lance and unhorsed Count Richard, whom I must thank for the opportunity to escape this grim place after four years of being mewed-up within its fastness.'

'My Lady, you do me too much honour.'

'Thought you that I should not apprehend him for whom I am intended?'

'Not now I know you better,' William said with a laugh, and she caught the sparkling in his eyes.

She returned the smile. 'If I bring you land, William,' she said intimately, 'then you bring me freedom and the only condition I beg of you as my husband is that you allow me that.'

William considered her proposition and then nodded. 'Upon my honour, asking only that therewith comes a fidelity to your oaths of loyalty which you will take at our marriage.'

'Surely, my Lord,' she said with a return to stiff formality, displaying a spirit that William suddenly found not merely admirable but utterly desirable, 'surely that compact must be mutual, being made before God and sundry witnesses.'

He smiled and took her hand again. It was warm and he bent and kissed it before picking up De Glanville's goblet and raising it to her. 'My Lady, I pledge to thee my troth, in all honour.'

'And I to thee, William Marshal,' and so they drank, and William thought he had never heard his name spoken so beautifully.

***

In the presence of Robert de Salignac and others they were married in early August and thanks to the hospitality of Richard FitzReiner and afterwards, Enguerrand D'Aubernon, who lent William and Isabelle his house at Stoke Daubernon, they enjoyed a few weeks of near privacy, awaiting the arrival of Richard. In that time FitzPeter had prepared the writs and patents making William Lord of Striguil, the valley of the Wye - castellan of Chepstow castle on the Wye and of adjacent lands between the Wye and the Usk in Nether Gwent, the southernmost province of the Welsh marches. With Isabelle's hand came a number of properties in Normandy, besides those he had already visited at Longueville and the manor of St Vaast-d-Equiqueville near Dieppe, the castles of Orbec and Meullers. Other lands once held by Richard Strongbow and taken into Henry's hands upon his daughter's ward-ship, remained in either the new King's hands or those of Count John, who retained his titles in Ireland despite his brother's accession to the English throne.

Although William might consider the possibility of recovering some of Strongbow's Irish conquests, he could do little more regarding Leinster. Nor could he gain access to the lands that attached to the Lordship of Striguil in Hertfordshire and Essex, for they were in the hands of Isabelle's mother, the Lady Aoif, widow of Strongbow, as long as she might live. For the nonce he could do little but express his satisfaction at the extent of his lands both south and north of the Channel. As for those to the north, in addition to Cartmel, he now possessed the keys to two great castles, Chepstow and Usk, both of which came with the patronage of abbeys; he had too some lesser fortresses in the borderlands, and a swathe of rich and level land lying to the north of the Severn Estuary which rose to the forest of Wentwood and ran up the valley of the Wye. Along with his estates in Normandy came also the English manor of Caversham on the Thames.

'His Grace the King,' explained FitzPeter, 'is minded to allow you the purchase of the Shrievalty of Gloucester, its castle, and the Forest of Dean.'

William nodded gravely. 'It shall be done in due time,' he said, thinking of the state of his coffers which were far from bottomless and much depleted of late.

'As to your title, my Lord, your wife has in her own right that of Countess but until the King places a belt about you, you cannot in any sense regard yourself as her equal as Earl, only her master as in her lands, no matter what men may call you for flattery.'

William grinned ruefully. 'I must express myself content, Geoffrey,' he said to FitzPeter. And thinking of Isabelle, added: 'and shall call myself William Marshal until the King's Grace be further known.'

'I beg you not to over-reach yourself, my Lord William,' FitzPeter said solemnly. 'There will be those for whom your present elevation will seem intolerable, the more so since the King goes into Outremer and leaves you among those few entrusted with his Kingdom.'

William nodded. And to compound the issue, his lack of formal rank would not endear him either, so that as either parvenu Earl or upstart commoner he would attract enemies. 'But there is something else that I would have you prepare your writs for, Geoffrey. My father favoured the Augustinian Priory of Bradenstoke where he now lies buried, and I would have some canons translated from thence to a new house, to be supported by my lands at Cartmel. You shall ensure within the foundation charter that they are charged with masses for the souls of Henry Curtmantle and my Lord Henry his son, the Young King, from whom I first derived patronage.'

'That is a pious act, my Lord,' said FitzPeter approvingly, jotting down his master's desires that he might draw up the requisite documents. 'And masses for your father's soul, my Lord?'

William considered the question for a long time so that FitzPeter thought him so abstracted as to add: 'My Lord? Your father?'

'Think you it a sin to condescend, Geoffrey,' William asked quietly. 'My father had no liking for me, nor I for him.'

'Did Curtmantle?'

'He was not my father?'

'Our Lord and Saviour preached forgiveness.'

Finally, William, recalling that dreadfully burned and scarred face, nodded. 'Aye, very well, my father too.'

Just as FitzPeter rose to leave William, John de Earley arrived with news of the King's landing. 'You should go at once, my Lord,' FitzPeter advised, 'and join His Grace without delay, he will expect nothing less.'

William gave orders for De Earley to prepare for his departure and went at once to Isabelle. He found her in the little solar, a charming chamber in the borrowed house, deep in conversation with her hand-maid, Susannah.

'My Lady it is necessary that I briefly take my leave of you to meet the King. We shall meet again in London whither His Grace will go directly to be crowned at Westminster. John de Earley shall escort you thither...' It was only then that he realised that he had interrupted them in some matter of importance. Isabelle's eyes looked uncommonly bright, as if she had been weeping. 'Is something amiss? Forgive me if I should have blundered into some private matter.'

Isabelle smiled and stood. 'My Lord...' She ran her hands over her belly. 'William...I am with child.'

CHAPTER SEVEN: RICHARD, BY THE GRACE
OF GOD 1189 - 1190

Not for the first time William stood in the great abbey church of Westminster and was transported by the colour, majesty and music of his surroundings. Only once in his life before had he felt so secure and so content: the hour he had stood humbly within the Holy Sepulchre in Jerusalem. But this was different because, whereas his experience in the Holy Land had been purely numinous, this was a commingling of the spiritual and the temporal. As he felt his spirits soar with the cadences of the choir, his eyes bedazzled by the splendour of the Archbishops coped and mitred in gold, and the vast number of nobles and their ladies in their coloured robes, he was, nevertheless, mindful of the warning of Geoffrey FitzPeter that he should not overreach himself.

But that bright September morning it was difficult not to feel some sense of personal vindication at all this. Besides his private and quite unexpected joy in his wife and her unborn infant, he had been all-but a nobody for so long that to have been selected to carry the King's sceptre before him into the Abbey was an honour beyond purchase. The sceptre betokened the power to rule and in being chosen to bear it before its recipient as rightful King was a prominent mark of Richard's favour and William's surrogacy in this regard; it marked him as among the few chosen as Justiciars. And as he waited in silence among the great men of the Kingdom for the Holy Moment of Richard's Anointing by the Archbishops of Canterbury and York, William caught the eye of his elder brother John, a man from whom he had been long estranged but who now bore the new King's golden spurs in his capacity as the King's official Marshal in England.

The brothers had met for the first time in many years when greeting and joining the King at Winchester as he moved towards London after landing from his installation as Duke of Normandy at Rouen. The encounter had been cool; too many years lay between them and they had not parted as friends. Their father's death had left property to John and his and William's younger brothers, but William had been excluded from his father's will. Nor had John made any provision of his own for his sibling.

Moreover John, though now present at Richard's coronation, had held no proper office under Henry Curtmantle and had all but rusticated in Wiltshire, except for a foray into France in the train of the enigmatic and difficult Count John who had made him his seneschal.

As their eyes met, the brothers exchanged no mark of joy, merely recognition and then the moment was past as the ceremony proceeded and, amid the heightened pomp of Richard's splendid Court, the investiture and crowning of the monarch culminated. Stripped to an under-shirt and breech-clout, his barrel of a breast bared, Richard was anointed with the sacramental chrism upon his head and chest by Archbishop Baldwin of Canterbury. Then, having robed the new monarch in cloth-of-gold, endowed him with sceptre and orb and finally crowned him, the two Archbishops drew back and, in a symbolic touching of Richard's elbows, lifted him from his throne and presented him as God's anointed to the assembled Lords of England.

Richard rose, resplendent in his robes, his ceremonial sword and bejewelled belt about his waist, his orb and sceptre in his hands and his crown upon his head. With his father's powerful physique and his mother's height he assumed the dignity of Kingship and he seemed to William – as to most others witnessing this Holy Moment of transformation – to be enlarged by it.

The abbey rang to the cries of 'Vivat! Vivat!' and then began the long process of the nobles each doing fealty to the new King. In his turn William went down upon his knees to kiss the King's ring and pledge himself, body and soul, to Richard, by the Grace of God, King of England.

***

In the closing four months of the year John and William were inexorably drawn together by the King's will as he sought to construct a party within England whose power rested entirely upon himself. John was appointed Richard's Chief Escheator in England, responsible for recovering for the King land grants to those men who died intestate and for which he was confirmed in perpetuity his own lordship of the Hundreds of Bedwyn in Wiltshire and Bosham in Sussex.

Another member of the family was drawn into this faction, a younger brother, Henry FitzMarshal who, despite initial opposition from the Archbishop-elect of

York, was made Dean of York Minster, the King's will prevailing. Only by this means could Richard leave for the Holy Land in some expectation of his Kingdom remaining quiet during his absence. This was all the more important for there were serious signs of not just intrigue at Court, or rebellion amongst the barons in the shires, but deeper fractures in the social fabric of the realm. Even as they bore gifts to the new King on the day of his coronation, a large party of Jewish merchants were set upon by a large mob, stripped, and whipped through the streets. Nor was this incident isolated. In the months that followed, as Richard's officials implemented his decree to raise money for the Third Crusade, to be exacted by the so-called 'Saracen Tax,' by some perverse popular logic Jewish communities throughout the land were subject to similar humiliations. There would be wholesale slaughter in York and Bury St Edmund's and, in the following spring John Marshal would lose his office as Sheriff of Yorkshire following the murders in March 1190.

But this sudden elevation of the Marshal family, widely regarded by the nobility as parvenus and by the intellectual power-brokers of the Church as men of doubtful worth and self-seeking ambition, began to attract enemies. Henry's appointment as Dean of York had attracted the deep animosity of Geoffrey, Archbishop of York, while a greater enemy had been made of William de Longchamp, Bishop of Ely and the King's Chancellor, a man much experienced in government and the making of the Law under Henry Curtmantle. It would be De Longchamp who led the Government of England Richard was in the process of establishing to rule England during his absence on crusade.

The brothers were thus drawn inexorably together as Richard ordered his new Kingdom. While William was the more cautious and circumspect of the two older siblings, John was more triumphalist. When he was made Chief Escheator William growled at him that 'it was a most appropriate office for a man who had cut his teeth upon dispossession.'

'It was not my decision to cut you out of our father's estate,' responded John.

'No,' riposted William, a hard and bitter edge to his voice, 'but you took scant notice of my fortune. It is not unknown for an heir to make provision for his brother.'

'But you brought your exclusion upon yourself. It was not my duty to disobey my father's intention…'

'Or no doubt our mother's,' William cut in. 'You are not so certain that I bear Satan's mark now that you enjoy office under my patronage.'

'*Your* patronage?' retorted John angrily, 'by the Rood, you set yourself too high! You needed no money from me, since Tancarville set you on the road to riches in the tournament, an indulgence forbidden here in England, and now you are all but an Earl in name with lands that exceed mine!'

'Oh,' scoffed William, 'blame that on being Satan's imp,' he added with heavy sarcasm. 'It was not your money that I wanted, brother John, but my mother's affection which I learned to live without. Do you take some advice from one who has seen something of life, do not crow when you are raised up. The smiles of Kings can prove fickle and when they die the world changes, the wolves who never cease to circle are eternally hungry. I warn you of this now, for your conduct, whatever it shall be, shall not bring me down in any ruin you achieve by your own folly.'

'By God, William, must I remind you who is the elder...'

'You do not have to do that. I shall allow you the privilege of precedence but never forget that wherever you tread you do so in my footsteps and take my good name with you.'

Discomfitted, John sneered. 'By the Christ, but you speak like a mealy-mouthed and canting priest.

'Aye,' nodded William, taking up a goblet of wine, 'I learned the art in debate with King Stephen when I was what..? D'you remember? A hostage at five, six years of age? But what would you know of that, content at Marlborough or Hampstead Marshal, curled-up in the hearth among our father's hounds? Eh?'

Bereft of a reply and breathing hard John stared at William, his only reaction being a shake of the head.

'Well,' said William, passing a goblet of wine to his older brother. 'The matter is past now. Our father tends the Devil's grindstone in Hell and doubtless our sainted mother, God rest her soul, finds some employment in the many mansions of Heaven.'

To William's gratification, John's mouth fell open at the extent of the impropriety and he crossed himself, half in fear of William and half in respect for his late parents.

'May God forgive you,' he breathed at last. 'Perhaps our mother was right regarding your marking,' he added, referring to the red naevus that disfigured William's back and resembled - at least according to the Lady

Sybil, their mother – the shape of Satan.

'Perhaps she was,' William responded lightly, 'though Henry Curtmantle decreed it more closely resembled a lion rampant, an interpretation I favoured myself. The Lady Isabelle is of like opinion and whether she brings forth a boy or a girl I should not send either as hostage until they were of such an age as to understand why.'

He made no mention of the canons of Cartmel and their instructions to say mass for the soul of their father. That was a matter between William and God, and no affair of his elder brother.

***

The two siblings travelled in King Richard's retinue when he left England for Vezelay in the early summer of 1190. To John's discomfiture William rode at the head of his mesnie, with William Waleran, Geoffrey FitzRobert, John de Earley and Robert de Salignac at his side and some thirty knights in his train. Without bombast William thereby put John firmly in his subordinate place, realising William's condescension in giving him precedence in the witnessing of several of the King's charters as a mere matter of form.

'You should be watchful of your brother, William,' De Salignac said to him one evening during the march through Normandy towards Vezelay and their rendezvous with King Philippe Augustus of France. 'Do not make an enemy of him. Remember the mischief wrought by Adam D'Yquebeuf.'

William nodded. He recalled the consequences following the false accusations of that wretched man. 'You are a true friend, Robert.'

'It may be the last service that I can render you,

William. I do not see our fortunes prospering in Outremer.'

'Why so gloomy?' William asked in some astonishment. 'You have Richard at your head and Philippe's knights at your back.'

'I have an uneasy feeling...' De Salignac said awkwardly.

'Have you consulted a necromancer? I hear there are many such in the Cathar country.'

De Salignac played the matter lightly, laughing off William's ignorance. 'I do not come from the Cathar country, William, but yes, I have consulted one whose advice I valued, though chiefly on my own account.'

'Your estates, you mean?'

'Well, my future, certainly, and yes, my lands such as they are, and they are inferior to yours now.'

'And...?'

'He saw a shadow over me.' De Salignac crossed himself and William did likewise.

'I shall pray for you, Robert,' he said simply, 'be assured of that.'

***

During the march towards Vezelay William received a summons from Richard who ordered him to go 'with your brother John, who has seen service in Count John's retinue,' and convey certain papers to the King's brother. 'This shall serve as a form of introduction,' Richard had concluded. The diversion took a few days, for John lay at Rouen and while William had been in the Count's presence before, they had never previously spoken.

Ushered into John's ante-chamber where several clerks attended him, they were kept waiting for an hour

113

or two until joined by the Count, who gave precedence to his seneschal, making John Marshal welcome, before acknowledging William's presence. William watched the exchange with interest. He had heard much about the youngest Angevin Prince, little of which redounded to John's credit, and it had always surprised him that of all his sons John had been the apple of his father's eye, endlessly forgiven for his infidelities, except for the last which had killed Henry Curtmantle. To be sure the young man enjoyed good looks, reminding William somewhat of his eldest brother, Henry, the so-called Young King who had predeceased their father and had been regarded by the credulous as possessing the looks of an angel. Count John lacked this, but he had his father's stocky frame, and the red-gold hair of his house. However, there was something about John that William had not seen in either of his parents, or Richard, though he may have taken after his middle brother, Geoffrey of Brittany who was reputed to have been the cleverest of the three. There was a craftiness about him, William thought, a fox-like cunning that ran deeper than the evidence of changing sides and oath-breaking suggested. Richard had done enough of that, when it suited his perverse purposes and harried his father. Nor had Richard any reputation for chivalry, unless it be among equals; Richard would burn a city to its foundations should it stand in his way, and woe-betide such of its citizens as might escape, for Richard would indulge himself in rape and worse, before letting his soldiery loose on a terrified townsfolk. But if John did not seem to possess that uninhibited violence that could be cloaked under the excuse of military necessity, his was a face that softened about the mouth, hinting at sensuality, a grosser appetite and a capacity for intrigue.

When at last he did address William it was to hold out his hand for the documents entrusted to him by Richard. Handing these to one of his clerks he looked from older to younger brother and revealed he knew a great deal more about them than either would have liked.

'So, William FitzMarshal,' he said, finally addressing William, 'you were once like I once was, lacking land, were you not? Neither father nor brother made provision for you, eh'

William could almost hear his brother wince at the jibe. Whether or not Count John meant a joke to ease the company, or whether his levity was a form of dissembling, William did not trouble himself to conjecture. He knew where his duty lay and times had moved on.

'Happily, my Lord, I owe you fealty for my lands in Leinster for which I have yet to do you homage.'

'You may do so now,' said John lightly, 'come.'

And William knelt and placed his hands together between those of Count John of Anjou, long nick-named 'Lack-land,' but now Lord of Ireland.

'There, William Fitzmarshal, you are a great man for the time being,' John remarked ominously when William had sworn the oath and he had called for wine to mark the moment. 'Perhaps our fortunes will rise together, eh? You go to England as my brother's Justiciar, I understand?'

'As a co-Justiciar, my Lord.'

John chuckled. 'Ah yes, as *co*-Justiciar.' He paused, then looked William squarely in the eye and added:

'mayhap we shall meet there.'

Although mindful of Richard's injunction that John should remain in the Angevin heartlands, exercising only titular influence in England, William refused to be drawn.

'Or in Leinster, my Lord. Much lies in God's hands.'

'Indeed,' John remarked, taking a draught of his wine. 'Or so the priests tell us.'

***

If Richard's coronation in Westminster Abbey had been a splendid occasion, a meeting of the temporal and the spiritual, the rendezvous at Vezelay was a glittering affair of purely martial magnificence. A forest of pennons and standards, coloured pavilions and tents, a riot of heraldic devices, men and horses in profusion: knights, mounted sergeants, men-at-arms, foot-soldiers, bowmen, armourers, smiths, farriers and sutlers, besides whores and camp-followers of every trick and persuasion. The air was thick with noise: shouted commands, the chink of harness and mail, the whinnies and neighing of horses, the barking of hounds, the cries of vendors, the hammer blows of the artisans, the whirr of grind-stones. It was full too of smoke which rose from bivouac fires, the camp-kitchens of the nobility, smithies; and of steamy smells, from cooking food to horse-dung, and the sharper odours of dog-shit and human excrement.

William pitched his own pavilion close to King Richard's and was among the Lionheart's retinue as Richard and Philippe, their body-attendants clerks and barons, mingled in the great encampment wherein the two Kings gathered their war-hosts. This was intended to

116

accompany them to the Holy Land. It was high summer and the feasting took place out of doors, the participants conducting themselves in high good humour at the prospect of the coming campaign. At a great Mass on mid-summer's eve the entire company took the sacrament from a Papal Legate supported by a bevy of bishops, orders being passed for the entire army to begin the march south on the morrow.

Shortly before dawn William was roused from his camp-bed by one of Richard's knights. 'My Lord, the King desires you attend him without delay.'

William had been expecting some such summons for several days and was soon in the King's pavilion where Richard was preparing to ride, dressed in a light hauberk and surtout, just as he had been in their encounter under the walls of Le Mans. William made his obeisance as Richard shook off his attendant pages, like a great shaggy dog shakes off water after crossing a river.

'My Lord Marshal,' the King began, indicating a number of rolled documents on a camp-table at which a dark-robed clerk with tired eyes sat at his ink-well. 'Here are your commissions and those for some others among those that I have left to govern England under William de Longchamp. It is my will that Geoffrey FitzPeter be granted lands attaching to the Earldom of Essex and he shall join you, Hugh Bardolf and William Briwerre as co-Justiciar's to support and curb my Chancellor. *Your* especial charge is to mind the actions of Count John, my brother, who is charged with the governance of my lands of Anjou, Aquitaine, Maine, Touraine and all those on this southern side of the sea. You have interests in Normandy now,' the King added pointedly, 'and matters must be left to your diplomatic skills…'

The King went on at some length, reiterating what he had spoken of before, but now he placed the various charters and writs, together with FitzPeter's patent of his ranking as an Earl, into William's hands. It was on William's lips to request some similar signal of his own elevation, but he held his tongue, mindful of the warnings of FitzPeter himself. He suffered an envious twisting of his gut at the prospect of his own confidential clerk being elevated having warned him to be modest; he even wondered if FitzPeter had acted with some duplicity in the matter, but cast the thought aside as being unworthy of both of them. He himself possessed the Lordship of Striguil and other lands, he stood high in the King's favour and held immense power in Richard's name, a fact confirmed by Richard presenting him with a ring as a token both of William's delegated authority and the King's trust.

William went down on one knee in recognition of the honour conferred upon him and when he rose Richard looked directly at him. 'Serve me well, Marshal. Do not give me cause to regret raising you.'

Sensing himself dismissed, William bowed, saying, 'God go with you my Lord King, and lend strength to your arms that you might smite the unbeliever and free the Holy Places.'

For the rest of that long summer's day William and his mesnie remained static as, all about them, the great army of Angevin England and Capetian France broke camp and took the road south, leaving a litter of discarded and broken items, besides midden heaps, ash-pits, fire-wood and lost souls – the abandoned harlots, jugglers and hucksters for whom the great rendezvous had been a commercial opportunity. Besides these opportunists there was a handful of knights, like William and his mesnie, whose attendance on their liege-lords had been obligatory but whose duties required them to remain at home.

About mid-morning Robert de Salignac had come to take his departure from his old friend. Having expressed his envy at De Salignac's return to the Holy Land, William wished him well and presented him with his own sword. 'Strike me some blows in my name, Robert,' he said solemnly, 'that I might not be entirely absent from this great enterprise.' He gestured round him where, amid the rising and falling of a psalm, the clatter of an army on the move rent the soft air of the June forenoon.

'With pleasure, William.' De Salignac drew his own sword and handed it to William in exchange.

'Go with God,' he concluded as Robert leaned from his horse and, without a further word, clasped William's right forearm in amity. Then he straightened up in his saddle, wheeled his horse and – with his squire bearing his standard riding behind him – joined the great throng as it drew out along the road and faded from view in a cloud of dust.

Watching De Salignac disappear amid such a host William was touched with a terrible and poignant sadness. His heart ached to be among those left behind, denied an opportunity to show prowess in the recovery of the Holy Places from this Saladin and his warriors. But then he bethought himself of the great work entrusted to him by Richard, work the better fitted for an older man, a man with a new wife who would soon produce an heir of his body, an heir – perhaps a boy – who bore the blood of Kings in his veins. And he thought too of Isabelle herself, and of how Angharad ap Gwyn would have approved, for close acquaintance had convinced him that Isabelle was herself one of the Old People for whom William had always nursed a private affection. He could almost hear his old nurse approving the title marriage to Isabelle had brought with her: Lord of Ystrad Gwy; Lord of the Valley of the Wye, which transliterated into Striguil in the Anglo-Norman tongue.

The day drew on and the dust settled. As the great host disappeared into the forests to the south, William had great reason to be satisfied. Just as he had taken the Young Henry's cloak to the Holy Land in symbolic pilgrimage, Robert de Salignac would convey his own sword thither and do great work with it. Instinctively he touched the pommel of Robert's weapon that nestled in its scabbard at his own hip.

That night William remarked to his brother that they ate their meat as though upon a field of battle such as he had seen in the Holy Land, such had the two armies stripped the neighbouring country for game and firewood.

'This is nothing,' John responded, his tone grim. 'Your Lionheart hath stripped England with his Saracen Tax. Methinks the chalice His Grace has conferred upon you as Justiciar is poisoned, brother.'

CHAPTER EIGHT: JUSTICIAR OF ENGLAND
1190 - 1194

'Pray be seated,' said William de Longchamp as he settled at the head of the table in the Council Chamber of the White Tower, motioning the four co-Justiciars to their seats. On De Longchamp's right sat Geoffrey FitzPeter, and beside him was Hugh Bardolf. Opposite FitzPeter sat William Briwerre, next to William Marshal. A clerk occupied a side table to record the deliberations of the conference, his quill poised while the five men addressed the business of the morning.

All looked to De Longchamp, Bishop of Ely, Chancellor of England and Guardian of the Tower. William Marshal did so with an especial interest. For a man who had been to the Holy Land there was an uncanny resemblance in De Longchamp's features to those of the rock apes seen there. And besides this unfortunate cast of feature the Lord Bishop of Ely limped and had an unsavoury reputation for an unholy interest in young boys. For all that, he was a man of parts, cunning and unscrupulous, with a reputation for law-making in the service of Henry Curtmantle, and trusted by the now absent King Richard.

'So,' Longchamp remarked contentiously, looking round the table and fixing his gaze on William, 'it seems we have Marshals with fingers in every pie in England.'

The clerk's pen remained poised, the other co-Justiciar's drew in their breath and, after shooting glances at William, lowered their eyes and regarded the parchments in front of them. They all knew that William was illiterate, that he could barely scrawl his name to a charter and that De Longchamp regarded him as ill-equipped for his new role. But William's reputation for prowess in the field and a certain sagacity in Council posed a dangerous challenge to the Chancellor's authority.

William had been anticipating some such assault and stirred in his seat. 'I had hoped to make of my Lord Chancellor a friend,' he said in level tones, addressing his fellow co-Justiciars, 'but it seems that he is set upon a path of enmity. Why else would he personally attack my castle at Gloucester whilst I was absent in Wales, huh?' William stared about him, staring directly at De Longchamp and adding, 'perhaps my Lord Chancellor, you would say precisely to which pies you allude.'

A smile flickered across the face of Geoffrey FitzPeter and William heard Briwerre expel his breath.

'Mark this in your record, Master Clerk,' William said, turning to the scribe who looked anxiously at De Longchamp.

'That will not be necessary,' De Longchamp said sharply. 'I am sorry my humour missed its mark,' he went on, his tone of voice now oily with dissimulation. 'I intended to congratulate the Lord of Striguil on his success, along with that of his brothers.'

William smile wryly. 'I think your humour hit the mark right well,' riposted William, 'and in another place I should have knocked you down for it,' he concluded with a chuckle. 'But that is no explanation for why my Lord Chancellor laid siege to Gloucester whilst I relieved the castle at Aber Tawe after it had lain under siege for ten weeks.'

'There were reasons,' De Longchamp stirred uneasily in his seat. 'Now, shall we, proceed…'

'Reasons of state, no doubt,' persisted William.

'Just so, now…'

'Which would, of course, be beyond my understanding.' William pointedly flicked at a parchment on the table, as if contemptuous of those who pushed a goose-quill.

'It is unwise to put words into the mouth of another man,' De Longchamp responded.

'It is unwise to wrest from *me* what the King has given me in fief, though you may be inclined to act thus to others.'

De Longchamp flushed. William's threat was not so veiled as to be unclear. 'We must to our business messieurs,' he hurried on, anxious to change the subject.

'He is as deeply bound by perceptions of honour to the House of Anjou as are you, William,' FitzPeter said to him afterwards, but he sees you, thanks to the connection of your brother John, to be Count John's man. Longchamp rightly entertains suspicions of Count John's intentions, for all that Richard made him swear to keep his feet off English soil. For the nonce you are suspected of a greater loyalty to John than Richard.'

'By the Rood, Geoffrey, it was the King who appointed me a Justiciar, and warned me against both De Longchamp and Count John.'

'Exactly, Will, and De Longchamp probably knows your first charge, if not your second.' William shook his head. 'But you dealt with him on his own terms with gusto, Will,' FitzPeter chuckled, 'and he wasn't expecting that from an old knight best known for battering his foes into submission with a mace.'

'I rarely use a mace,' William replied solemnly, until he realised FitzPeter was guying him. 'God's bones, I am too old for this game,' he said as both broke out into open laughter.

***

As the weeks passed, the Council of State settled down to its affairs. De Longchamp's provocation of William, part deliberate and part in contempt, left the two men in a condition of mutual suspicion. They often voted against each other, but FitzPeter's skill and the good sense of Briwerre and Bardolf, generally managed their business well-enough. The Customs Dues of the ports were properly levied, the differences between two contending trade-guilds in the City of London satisfactorily and amicably settled and De Longchamp's only direct move against the interest of the Marshal brothers, the removal of the Shrievalty of York from John Marshal on account of the ill treatment of the Jews in that city, was voted down. The event did, however, increase De Longchamp's power by bringing into his camp the Archbishop of York, who was equally hostile to Marshal influence.

Reports arrived from Normandy of the King's slow progress towards the Holy Land. He was known to have lingered in Sicily, where a marriage contract was arranged with the Lady Berengaria of Navarre, intelligence that brought with it the probability of a rupture between Richard and Philippe Augustus over the repudiation of the long-standing betrothal agreement that

124

Richard would marry Alice of France. This intelligence came directly from Walter Des Coutances, Archbishop of Rouen, who was among the informants of Queen Eleanor who redirected his couriers to William Marshal. By thus opening a channel of communication with Des Coutances, William had the benefit of confidential counsel with a man of wisdom, a faithful servant of the House of Anjou to whose nephew William had, upon King Richard's desire, surrendered his lordship of Kendal.

At first this correspondence, carried by John de Earley, had consisted of letters concerning the increasing difficulties Des Longchamp was causing within the body politic of England. His disregard of the co-Justiciars was bad enough, but his arrogant encroachments upon the rights and privileges of the Barony was dragging the Council of State into a mire of the Chancellor's own making, and none of the co-Justiciars was prepared allow matters to run on thus or, as Briwerre remarked, Richard would hear of it.

Des Coutances advised the co-Justiciars to isolate and dispose of De Longchamp and then, out of the blue, sent a warning of his own. Rumours had reached him that Count John was making secret preparations to break his word and cross the Channel into England.

***

William was at Winchester when FitzPeter sent word of this to him from London. Here he and Isabelle had been enjoying a few rare weeks of domesticity with their first-born, a son named William after his father. Here too they spent some time in the company of Queen Eleanor and it was to the Queen-Mother that William went directly that the intelligence of John's intentions reached him.

'Your Grace, I would have your counsel,' he said, coming straight to the point after having made his obeisance. 'I am pledged to the King, though my lands in Ireland I hold in fief from Count John. Howsoever, it is to the House of Anjou that I am chiefly pledged and Count John swore to remain in Normandy and I fear for your own lands, for Philippe is, so it is said, returning from his crusade for fury of King Richard's intended marriage to this Lady of Navarre.'

'An alliance with King Sancho of Navarre might be to some advantage,' the Queen mused, 'but should John make mischief in England you are right to be apprehensive, FitzMarshal,' the Queen nodded, her eyes as shrewd as ever. She sighed. 'We are no longer young, you and I, and yet it seems the world still lays its troubles at our feet.'

'Indeed Your Grace…'

'You hesitate?'

William bit his lip. 'Aye, Madam, for while I fear for Aquitaine, the late King, your husband, laid upon me a specific charge.'

'And what was that?' Eleanor asked coolly, her long estrangement from Henry Curtmantle falling over them like some dark shadow.

'That England must be my first concern, for there the Crown lies…'

'While Aquitaine is little more than an ungovernable Duchy,' Eleanor said, smiling ruefully. 'There, I have finished your thought for you, to save you the embarrassment.'

'Madam, I mean no disrespect, but a man cannot be in two places at once and I have but lately come from the Welsh marches where there has been trouble ever since Rhys ap Gruffydd raised his standard on hearing of my Lord Henry's death.'

'And that has nothing to do with your lands in Nether Gwent?' Eleanor asked, one eyebrow raised under her coif.

'Aye, Your Grace, it has everything to do with Striguil, but Nether Gwent I hold in fief for the Crown of England.'

'I should not tease you, FitzMarshal, it was ever a fault of mine and you are right to consult me.' The Queen rose and walked to a window which looked out over a small rose-garden. William, standing behind her heard her whisper to herself the one word: 'Aquitaine.' Then she fell silent and remained staring out over the vista. A sharp shower was falling, but sunshine was not far behind the clouds which were swept across the sky and threw their swift moving shadows across the garden and the stone walls that enclosed it.

'Marshal,' she said without turning her head, 'come hither.' William moved across the chamber and stood next to her. 'Do you recall the affair at Lusignan, when you saved me from ambush and seizure?'

'Aye, My Lady, and Your Grace ransomed me after my own capture.'

'The years have grown long since then.' Eleanor paused, still regarding the rose-bushes where the sunshine now twinkled on raindrops. 'But the Lusignans have proved only their eternal faithlessness, now as on that day, for the Holy Land has fallen to the infidel,' she mused, her voice quiet, confidential. 'Meanwhile Richard tarries in Sicily or Cyprus, God knows what Philippe intends and now John has come into England, from which no good will issue.'

'Nay Madam.'

'God forbid that what my Lord Henry and I built-up should be torn down, but for the sake of holding Aquitaine I should not give-up England.' She suddenly turned to face William. 'I thank you for your courtesy in coming to me, FitzMarshal. Loathe as I am to do so, and much as I have disliked my long exile in this damp and unenchanted island, England must be our chief hope. I cannot tell you how to handle Count John, he defies all predictions, but do you cleave to your liege lord, who is Richard. Should Richard return from his crusade, he has yet years enough to undo whatever damage John's conduct will effect in Normandy, Anjou and Aquitaine. What will ensue in England I likewise cannot guess, I am too removed from the heart of things here, but your place now is in London.' She smiled at him and held out her right hand. William dropped to one knee and kissed it.

'He is like to come here, Your Grace,' William said, concerned.

'Count John?'

'Aye.'

'And you would have me tell you what I shall say to him?'

William shrugged. 'That is not a matter for me to say, Your Grace.'

'God go with you, FitzMarshal.'

***

'What are we to do?' Geoffrey FitzPeter asked William. 'The fool has now fallen-out with the Archbishop of York and half the barons in England and should we have John claiming the right to rule the Kingdom as his brother's Regent in de Longchamp's place...' FitzPeter let the speculation hang.

'Longchamp must go,' William said decisively. 'He is not indispensable and we must have a free and unencumbered hand...'

'But we cannot act alone, what of Bardolf and Briwerre?'

'Summon them,' William said. 'I surmise John will make first for Winchester and will be here in London a day or so later.'

'But that plays into the hands of all those who say that you at least are John's man.'

William nodded. 'Aye. I am bound to him for my Irish estates,' he said ironically, 'and so too is Hugh Bardolf.' Then, suddenly intense, he went on: 'but Geoffrey, Longchamp is cunning whereas John is fickle; John we can manage, John we can cajole, flatter, John we can throw over when Richard returns.'

'And Bardolf?'

William shrugged. 'We can out-vote him. Come, let us send word to Richard by confidential messenger. 'Tis best to be open about this. Summon Longchamp and the others and let us oust him from the Council.'

FitzPeter nodded. 'Very well. Des Coutances is of this opinion,' he said uncertainly. 'I have a man suited to the task of reaching Richard if you can find him escort.'

'I have men from my mesnie who will relish it...

Come what yet troubles you?'

'By what means do we unseat the Chancellor?'

'Leave that to me.'

The Council sat in the White Tower next morning on the pretext of considering what must be done to confront the problem of Count John's undesirable appearance in England. Unaware of what awaited him, De Longchamp made a fatal mistake in his opening remarks.

'I suppose, FitzMarshal, you welcome this intrusion?' he said sarcastically as the five men sat down and wine was served.

'On the presumption that I owe Count John allegiance?'

'You have been heard to say so.'

'Indeed, but that is not, in fact the case. The truth is, my Lord Chancellor, the matter touches yourself more closely than it touches me.'

'How so?' asked De Longchamp, suddenly wary.

'We require that you surrender the Great Seal into our care...'

'What?' roared De Longchamp, interrupting and jumping to his feet. 'That you may hand it to Count John? Have a care, FitzMarshal, you are not the only man to command men-at-arms, I can muster a force...'

'By God's Love not at all,' William interrupted, looking round at his fellow co-Justicars who, with the exception of Hugh Bardolf, watched the unfolding drama with detached interest. 'Have we discussed any such action, my Lords?' He asked each in turn and all denied any such conspiracy. 'There, my Lord Chancellor,' William went on reasonably. 'The fact is, we do not consider you to be suitable for your offices, neither that of Lord Chancellor, nor that of Bishop of Ely, though that lies outside our jurisdiction.'

De Longchamp was white and trembling with rage. 'Why…why, in God's name… You have n…no right…' he eventually spluttered.

'That you have roused half the Barons of England against you I would count a distinction, my Lord, but my Lord Archbishop of York, a man with whom you have until recently been in amity, has much to say against you these days. I understand that you gave orders for his arrest and upon grounds unrevealed to this Council. In this light, common justice, with which you yourself might agree, denies you possession of the Great Seal of England.'

'On wh…what grounds?' De Longchamp stuttered, beside himself, though William could see the shadow of prescience fall across De Longchamp's ape-like features before he had even uttered the words.

'Why buggery, my Lord Bishop.'

***

'How did you know?' asked FitzPeter later.

'I did not *know* anything, but I found no grounds for De Longchamp's order to arrest Geoffrey of York, and presumed a guilt-ridden conscience. Besides, there have been rumours of the deaths of two choir-boys at York,' replied William.

'I had heard that,' added Briwerre in eager if unfounded corroboration.

Bardolf shook his head, plainly disbelieving the assertion. 'You acted boldly, FitzMarshal, think you to do the same with Count John? By all accounts an accusation of buggery would not trouble him and you are his liegeman in respect of your Irish lands.'

William shrugged. 'As are you too, Master Bardolf, but Count John is Richard's for Ireland itself while we are all Richard's co-Justiciars for England and I propose that we invite Walter des Coutances, Archbishop of Rouen, to come hither to join our Council. What say you all?'

But before the Archbishop of Rouen could take De Longchamp's place it was Count John who sat at the head of the Council of State.

'I am come to sit as my brother's Regent,' he said smoothly, 'to guard his throne lest anyone in England should see in the discomfiture of De Longchamp, my brother's chosen Chancellor, some means by which to rise in revolt.' John stared round the table, his eyes coming to rest on William. William met the Count's gaze without a flicker, expecting some such sally and staring John down. 'It was a cruel and disloyal thing to act so against the fellow,' John remarked conversationally, sifting through the parchments laid upon the table in front of him. 'I hear he has escaped into France disguised as a woman hawking wares of some sort and there excommunicated all four of you.' The Count chuckled. 'Word will reach Richard who is even now on campaign in the Holy Land, God grant his arms success,' John went on piously crossing himself, 'and we shall have to await my brother's pleasure in this respect.' John smiled and regarded each one of the co-Justiciars, as if relishing Richard's vengeance at the dismissal of his appointee. William was reminded of a cat playing with a mauled mouse. No-one said a word, waiting for John to reveal his hand.

'But no doubt you have other things on your minds, eh?' the Count went on smoothly. 'Such as why I have come over to England when I might have been expected to sit upon my arse in Mortain, which my generous brother added to my demesne. Well, you have heard that my Lord the King wed the Lady Berengaria of Navarre in Cyprus last February, thereby securing an alliance with King Sancho which will secure his southern lands from Philippe.' John smiled and looked about him. 'Such a coup renders my presence in France superfluous, my Lords.' John shrugged, picked up a parchment and pretended to read it. Without looking up he said, 'You, FitzPeter, and you, my Lord of Striguil, were not the only prude-hommes granted land in England. King Richard granted me also estates in Devonshire and Cornwall, besides his castles of Marlborough and Ludgershall. Nor, for that matter,' he went of affecting a lighter tone of voice, 'are you the only man, FitzMarshal to benefit from marrying an Isabelle, for know you all that I am betrothed to Isabelle of Gloucester and with her come not only Gloucester and Bristol Castles, but marcher lands west of the River Usk and through Glamorgan.' John positively leered at William. 'We shall be neighbours FitzMarshal, besides your owing me allegiance for your lands in Leinster.'

'You have no grounds to remind me of my allegiances, my Lord Count,' William responded coolly.

'Good,' John sat back and called for wine. When he had been served he looked round the table and asked, 'why all the long faces? Have I disturbed your cosy nest, messieurs?'

'My Lord, notwithstanding my Lord King's alliance

with Navarre which may well protect his southern lands, I had supposed you were bound by an oath to remain in Normandy to defend your House's ancestral lands against possible incursion by Philippe who is said to have been mightily displeased with the King's marriage,' William said.

'Pah!' John waved aside the mention of any oath. 'Where did you hear such nonsense? Philippe is in the Holy Land…'

'I think not, my Lord Count,' put in FitzPeter. 'We have some intelligence that he is returning to France.'

'Well, no matter,' John responded dismissively. 'King Philippe will respect the Papal interdict and leave Richard's lands alone, so long as he is on crusade. He is merely piqued that Richard has rejected the Lady Alice, but why would he not? He has prevaricated long enough and, besides, she is no virgin…'

Geoffrey FitzPeter raised an eyebrow. All knew of the supposed seduction of his son's betrothed by Henry Curtmantle, but it was clear that Count John knew well enough that Philippe was on his way home from Outremer.

'I am glad you have faith in King Philippe's respect for the Pope's interdict, my Lord,' remarked William with heavy sarcasm. Although his co-Justiciars appreciated William's scorn, John affected to ignore the reproach to his light attitude to such strictures.

'Come, now to the business of the day…' John said, resuming his aimless riffling through the parchments awaiting the Council's perusal.

***

'By the Christ, 'tis cold,' complained William

Briwerre drawing his fur robe about him as they awaited the arrival of Count John. With the exception of Hugh Bardolf, Briwerre might have spoken for the mood of the co-Justiciars, for ever since the arrival of John they had found themselves in a constant argument with him as he poked his nose into any means of gaining power and money. The young Prince seemed to regard the ruling of England as a game and the co-Justiciars as pawns to be used to fund his excessive pleasures. William was hard put to see in him any virtues or reasons why Henry Curtmantle had once-upon-a-time given his youngest son preference over Richard. At least they had Walter des Coutances as Chancellor now, but that was small consolation for the news coming out of the Holy Land where the campaign did not seem to be going well.

After the expected reports of early victories depressing rumours had reached the Courts of the west, rumours of fallings out among the chief commanders, of jealousies and internecine warfare leading to defeats. Richard, having heroically retaken Acre from Saladin, had resorted to his usual barbarism of massacring his prisoners. At this point he had been abandoned by Philippe as had been long whispered and, free to act alone, Richard had ordered a final advance on Jerusalem. But the triumphant news of the defeat of Saladin at Arsuf was followed first by silence and then disquieting uncertainties.

That summer of 1192 William had learned that his old patron Guillaume de Tancarville had died in Outremer and the news reminded him, if he needed it, of his own mortality. He was nearing fifty years of age and feared for the future. Although he had been impressed by

Richard's demeanour on his assumption of kingship, William did not consider his absence in the Holy Land boded well for his empire. The alliance with Navarre seemed to William insubstantial and set against the enmity aroused with Philippe, worthless. Besides, in John the feckless and wilful conduct of Henry Curtmantle's brood showed no signs of abating. A growing sense of impending trouble had descended upon William and at the fall of the leaf he had taken his retinue into Nether Gwent where he had ordered the building of a new gatehouse and stone wall at his castle of Chepstow standing on its eminence overlooking the River Wye. He intended it as a safe haven for Isabelle, little William and their second child when his wife was brought to bed, and it was December before he was back in London.

By then it was known that Richard had been forced to turn back within sight of the walls of the Holy City, his army ravaged by disease, worn by fatigue, its lines of supply over-stretched and incapable of mounting the siege operations that the recapture of Jerusalem required.

While they awaited the arrival of Count John, Des Coutances and the co-Justiciars were debating the latest intelligence, now months old, that Richard had secured a settlement with Saladin. The news had arrived with the first of the crusaders to return, among them Hubert FitzWalter, Bishop of Salisbury, who had covered himself with glory in the fighting and now revealed that King Richard and a small retinue intended returning overland. The Council had put Fitzwalter forward as candidate for the vacant See of Canterbury, whither he was duly translated.

As for other news, it was tossed about the Council table like a ball as they awaited Count John.

'It seems Cyprus is to be given over to Guy de Lusignan,' observed Des Coutances, 'and the Holy Places given up.'

'How is that possible?' asked an appalled FitzPeter, to be met by shrugs of incomprehension.

'So, Richard is on his way home overland,' ruminated William. ''Twill take him many months.'

'Perhaps he is making alliances against Philippe,' Des Coutances said hopefully.

'Let us hope no great mischief is done before his arrival,' remarked William gloomily.

'But then the sparks will fly,' added Briwerre with an attempt at cheerfulness.

'Aye, by the Christ,' put in Bardolf, biting his nails.

'We have nothing to fear,' William said, looking round him, but his words fell on deaf ears, for each fell to his own thoughts. That his old enemy Guy de Lusignan had retained something akin to a throne irritated him, but his chief thoughts were for Robert de Salignac and how he had fared in this grand débâcle.

An hour later John arrived and, dismissing the matters laid before him by FitzPeter, ordered funds from the Customs Dues of the River of Thames diverted to his coffers 'for the better improvements of Nottingham Castle'. The request was cunningly couched for none of the co-Justiciars could in all justice deny the necessity for the disbursement, though all knew equally that John was making of Nottingham a stronghold in the heart of England for himself.

'My Lord,' argued FitzPeter, 'This is not the proper

use of such monies…'

'Nottingham is weak, FitzPeter,' John broke in, 'and much in need of improvement. The Lord of Striguil has put in hand some augmentations at Chepstow, and very wise he is to do so. Nottingham is in like case.' John sat back and took up his goblet of wine. 'Do you direct the sums Coutances.'

'My Lord,' protested the Archbishop, 'the Lord of Striguil is paying for the improvements at Chepstow from the revenues of his own lands.'

'So he should,' snapped John. 'That is precisely why he is enfieffed!'

'But so art thou, my Lord,' riposted Walter des Coutances.

'Damn you, Archbishop, for your effrontery!' John banged the table. 'I am Regent and Nottingham is to be improved in the King's name, not mine!' The Count rose to his feet and began striding up and down the chamber. 'God rot the lot of you. De Longchamp was right to excommunicate you.'

'My Lord…' Bardolf half rose in protest at being lumped with his fellow Justiciars.

'The excommunication was invalid, my Lord,' soothed Des Coutances, ignoring Bardolf's feeble and self-interested intervention. 'And well you know it. You have four thousand per year from your estates, a half of that would buy you the whole shire of Nottingham, let alone its castle…'

'You shall *not* thwart me!' John turned and slammed his hand on the table under Des Coutances' nose.

The old Archbishop looked down at the Count's hand then up at his face, and an ominous silence hung in the air. No-one moved as the two men confronted each other. FitzPeter shot a glance at William but even he seemed paralysed by this naked confrontation. Then Des Coutances said slowly, as if to a child, 'my Lord, no-one at this table is going to sanction funds for Nottingham from the Customs Levies of the River of Thames – no-one.'

Hugh Bardolf moved uneasily in his seat, as though minded to contest the Archbishop's assertion and prove himself Count John's man, but the moment passed.

Count John seemed to visibly deflate, then turned on his heel and bellowed for wine. 'You would not deny me that, I presume, Archbishop?' he snarled over his shoulder.

But it was not a page with wine who entered the chamber; instead the door was pushed open by an unknown knight whose state showed that he had travelled long and hard. He was accompanied by a sergeant at arms of the Tower guard who protested the fellow's importunity and apologised for the intrusion.

'He insisted, my Lords, and carries a commission…'

The knight bore the look of a desperate man and, holding out his hand as if to reassure the Council that this lone fellow was not about to murder them, William rose to his feet. 'I know you,' he said, calling for wine, 'you are of De Salignac's mesnie. Here, take my seat.'

Near total collapse the exhausted knight sank into William's vacated seat as the Council stared in apprehension at this strange disturbance.

'There is no good news here,' said Des Coutances anxiously awaiting the revivifying effects of the cup of wine, while John motioned for a goblet of his own.

Eventually the man stirred, shook his head and looked about him.

'My Lords,' he said uncertainly, 'I am in search of William Marshal, Lord of Striguil…'

'Who sent you?' Count John asked abruptly.

'I bear news of my Lord the King.' A frisson of trepidation ran through the Council, all fearing the death of their distant monarch. Only Count John's eye gleamed at the prospect.

'What of him?' he snapped.

'He is taken prisoner by Duke Leopold of Austrian, my Lords, and a great ransom is to be demanded.'

'By the Christ!' blasphemed Briwerre. Des Coutances crossed himself as a low murmur ran round the table. It was broken by John who chuckled.

'Taken prisoner, eh? Well, well; how Richard will enjoy his incarceration.'

The archbishop was the first to pull himself together. 'Dost know the amount asked for?'

The knight shook his head. 'No, my Lord Archbishop, only that the Duke avenges himself for some slight he had at the King's hand during the crusade.'

'Oh,' John almost shouted, sitting up and slapping his thigh with something akin to undisguised glee. 'My brother was ever intemperate!'

'This will do you no good,' snapped Des Coutances as the messenger stirred uneasily.

'If it pleases your Lordships…'

'Come fellow,' said William offering an arm as the knight rose to his feet. 'You shall have a bed.'

William led the knight out of the Council chamber in search of a couch and, as the man lay down an anxious

William bent over him and asked, 'what of Robert de Salignac?'

The knight's eyes were closed and for a moment William thought him already asleep. Then he stirred and said: 'Dead, my Lord, of a fever and a bloody flux...'

**

'Gone? What? Into France?'

'Aye Your Grace, for the time being, to do Philippe homage for his lands held in fief from the French crown,' William explained, though there was little need for explanation to this shrewd old woman who had seen some seventy years come and go. It was more for his own comprehension that William laid out Count John's perfidy. Such entanglements as occupied the Princes of the House of Anjou had always taxed William.

'And the ransom?' asked Queen Eleanor.

'Every possible means of raising the sum demanded is in hand, my Lady. Hubert FitzWalter of Canterbury, and Richard FitzNeal are the custodians appointed to secure the sums in St Paul's cathedral. Scutage and redemption at twenty shillings on a knight's fee are being levied, there is a general tax on all chattels and revenues at one quarter thereof; the whole wool-crop of the Cistercian and Gilbertine abbeys has been sequestered, parish silver is to be surrendered...'

'Enough,' the Queen held up her hand. 'Will this prove sufficient?'

William shook his head. 'I do not think so, my Lady, for the sum is unprecedented...'

'But it *must* be raised, FitzMarshal, for if we fail, Philippe will *buy* Richard and all will be lost.'

'But there is more, Your Grace, I hear it said that to

Duke Leopold's demand of twenty-five thousand silver
marks, the Emperor requires a further sum, a total of one
hundred and fifty thousand marks.'

'Philippe will never raise that much,' Eleanor mused.

'And his attempt to raise the French barons for a
campaign into Normandy was rejected for fear of
excommunication.'

'Thank God for that, but he took Gisors,' Eleanor
pointed out, 'and has since over-run the Vexin.'

'But Robert of Leicester, holds Rouen yet, my Lady.
The best that can be said is that we hear His Grace is not
held in close durance. Duke Leopold has released him
into the custody of the Emperor; he has sent for his
hawks and several of his intimates have visited him. We
have had report from William Briwerre, whom we sent
to Worm to conduct negotiations that His Grace the
King and the Emperor Heinrich are in amity.'

'Perhaps something may be thereby rescued from this
débâcle,' Eleanor observed.

'I fear mischief yet, Your Grace,' William said
solemnly.

'John,' responded the Queen shrewdly.

'Aye, Madam. I fear so.'

Although he had no knowledge of it, besides the co-
Justiciar Briwerre, another of Richard's intimates
visiting Richard at Worms, where he had held something
of a Court, had been William Longchamp.

***

'I had not thought I should live to see such a day,'
William growled to John de Earley as he rode the lines
of the encampment. Although no longer William's
squire De Earley had assumed the role of William's

standard bearer when he had become Lord of Striguil, for the red lion rampant now no longer featured on the pennon of a knight banneret, but graced a gonfalon, halved green and pale gold.

'Think these men a rabble or an army, my Lord?' De Earley asked of William who, in full mail, rode a magnificent new destrier named Coeur de Lion in honour of the absent King Richard. Besides the batailles of mounted knights, the sergeants in their gambesons, the arbalestriers armed with their cross-bows and haubergon-clad foot-soldiers were numbers of common rustics armed with scythes and extemporised spears.

'They will do well enough,' William replied grimly.

The review to the east of London was the result of a great feudal levy, held in the wake of a huge mobilisation such as England had not seen since the Anarchy. It was but one part of a grand strategy to defeat the threatened invasion of King Philippe in support of Count John who had slipped back into England and ridden hard for Windsor where he had holed himself up in the castle there, claiming the English throne for himself. In the face of both rebellion within and invasion without, oaths of allegiance to Richard had been extracted wholesale. The London merchants and the Cinque Ports had provided ships to watch the Flemish ports where the enemy were assembled, ready to embark and within the kingdom, the aged Archbishop of Rouen, Walter des Coutances, had laid siege to John at Windsor. John's garrison at Nottingham was likewise under siege while, further north, the even older Prince-Bishop of Durham, Hugh de Puiset, had dug-in before the Count's stronghold at Tickhill. Marlborough, Lancaster and St

Michael's Mount were also invested or watched, pending besieging.

To substantiate his claim to the throne Count John had sent out heralds and messengers claiming that King Richard was dead. No-one on the Council of State believed the rumoured was true, not least because there were several inconsistent versions of it, but it gained ground elsewhere persuading those who owned fealty to Count John that it was Hubert FitzWalter and the co-Justiciars who had seized power.

More credible to the Councillors in the White Tower was the story that followed John out of France, for it rang with the truth of the Count's duplicitous character; moreover, it was soon confirmed. Despite his betrothal to Isabelle of Gloucester, it was learned, that while fawning at Philippe's Court, out of policy John had married the Lady Alice, only to renounce her the following day.

'But he said himself she was no longer a virgin,' an incredulous Bardolf had said.

'What a purblind fool the man is,' Des Coutances had remarked to everybody and no-one as the Council had broken-up and its members – with the exception of Bardolf - had departed London to implement the provisions they had decided upon. 'He would throw all away by his intemperance.'

'But this places him in King Philippe's camp,' persisted Bardolf in his dismay.

'Aye, Alice's bed is too close to Philippe's, Master Hugh, you must watch your liege Lord for fear he shall drag you to hell.'

'Or the devil in Richard catches you by your tail,'

William had added pointedly.

'Well, messieurs,' Des Coutances had put in, 'pity the Lady Alice. She has been ill-used.'

'So has England,' William had growled as the orders were issued to rouse the country against Count John and those whom he had summoned to his cause. As a last resort the Council had despatched a herald with a heavy escort of knights from William's mesnie to summon Count John from Windsor to appear before them in London but he had returned a defiant answer, hence the general demand for affirmations of oaths of allegiance to Richard.

They had excused Hugh Bardolf, dismissed him from their board and, with great firmness three of the four co-Justiciars announced the sequestration of all Count John's English lands in the name of King Richard and took up arms against the Count.

Throwing off his cope, Des Coutances had belted on his sword and summoned his own knights as William had passed word for the great levy and drew up the plan of campaign, summoning those Barons known to be loyal to Richard and ignoring all those who, like Curtmantle's uncertain and pusillanimous Norman vassals sitting on their fence at Alençon, awaited the outcome of events.

Largely ignorant of Richard's diplomacy on the continent in which he sought and made alliances against Philippe, William's actions in taking up arms against Count John represented a technical revolt against his liege-lord in Leinster but the imperative of securing England for Richard's return over-bore all. Bardolf pleaded a more delicate conscience and, likewise owing allegiance to John, demurred and received his quittance. But if William and his fellow Justiciars were ignorant of the abasement of John who, prior to his return to England had secured an alliance with King Philippe, they were not insensible to its implications. If he was frustrated in damaging Richard, Philippe could destroy his presumed heir, 'with a fatal and fraternal bear-hug,' was how Des Coutances expressed it. In this way Philippe, having seized the Norman Vexin, now filched further Norman territory and, to the south, Touraine, thrusting ever westwards towards the Angevin heartland of Anjou.

But while John de Earley marvelled at the sight of the assembled war-host as William and his retinue rode down the lines, William was counting the cost. His many months of acting as co-Justiciar, added to his new role as Lord of Striguil and the stewardship of the lands he had by way of Isabelle de Clare, taxed him both mentally and financially. His personal clerks, men recommended by FitzPeter, even FitzPeter himself, assisted him in this complex and unfamiliar task, making up for his lack of literacy and numeracy. However, as well as the additions and improvements to his own castles, he had borne the brunt of ordering the immediate strengthening of no less than thirty-three castles as a result of Count John's opportunistic rebellion. The financial cost had been supervised by Archbishop FitzWalter, the co-commissioner for raising Richard's ransom and a man Des Coutances now drew into the Council of State itself. William was wary of FitzWalter for he was in close touch with the ousted Longchamp who had been negotiating with the Emperor in Richard's behalf and insidiously rehabilitating himself by proving indispensible to the absent King. As for Count John, the author of their present predicament, William could see only the slippery treachery and blind opportunism that so characterised the sons of Henry Curtmantle.

'The bastard has earned whatever befalls,' he had growled to FitzPeter as that worthy reluctantly donned mail to join William in the review of the great levy. No soldier but supported by others, FitzPeter was to assume nominal command of the force once William had completed his present duty.

William sighed, recalling himself to the present. It was beginning to rain and the war-host was as readied as it could be. He looked at the darkening sky; the rain was borne on a wind and the wind was from the west. Philippe's ships and his Flemish mercenaries were unlikely to trouble them for some time yet, if at all. He turned in his saddle and nodded to the knights of his mesnie to disperse. 'I thank you messieurs for your duty. I am confident,' he said, raising his voice that his comment might be heard by others and thereby passed throughout the camp, 'when he hears of our *grande bataille*, as he surely must, King Philippe will not come when it is Normandy and Anjou that he most wants.'

A murmur of assent ran through those closest to him, then John de Earley jinked his destrier forward and, standing in his stirrups, raised William's gonfalon. 'For King Richard and the Marshal!' he bawled.

'King Richard! The Marshal!'

They took up the cry and it spread through the ranks, reverberating back to the knot of horsemen forming

William's mesnie who echoed it, some flourishing drawn swords.

'King Richard! The Marshal!'

Wheeling his charger De Earley returned to William's side, his broad face split from ear to ear by a grin.

William's expression was sardonic. 'I thank you for the courtesy, John, but by God I know not how long we must maintain this war-host, nor what its cost will be in victuals.'

'Thank God it is a feudal levy of true-born Englishmen, my Lord, and no mercenary horde,' De Earley responded cheerfully.

***

'My Lord is not pleased?'

William turned from the contemplation of his second son, whose wrinkled face had drawn from his the unhappiest of memories, and stared at Isabelle. She lay on the pillow, her beautiful auburn tresses spread about her face.

'Forgive me, Isabelle, I am well pleased, well pleased. If I seemed distracted I was thinking…'

He had arrived at Chepstow Castle earlier that day, after a hard ride from Gloucester as he made his tour of the west.

'I know this rebellion has much preoccupied you…'

''Twas not that of which I thought,' William said with a sad smile, looking at his wife. 'I was thinking of my own boyhood, being the second born and unwanted.'

Isabelle frowned. 'Unwanted, William, how so?' She patted the skins covering the bed and he sat and took her hand.

'I have never told you.'

'We spend so little time together…'

William chuckled in an attempt to lighten his mood. He did not wish to burden Isabelle with memories of his childhood and, rarely giving the matter any thought, had been surprised by the strength of the emotional tug on seeing his second born son for the first time. 'We spend enough time together to beget sons,' he jested.

'Tell me,' she persisted.

'What, of my mother, or of Angharad ap Gwyn who was better than a mother to me?'

'Of them both, of them all…'

And for an hour he sat on the bed and related the circumstances of his boyhood as the afternoon drew on and the sun westered, casting Isabelle's chamber in the keep of Chepstow castle into deep shadow. When he had finished he seemed to return from a far distance, looking about him as though he had never seen the place before.

'What is it William?' Isabelle asked, seeing the shadow cross his face.

''Tis nothing, only that…'

'Only that?' she prompted.

'Only that my mother, Sybil, sister to Patrick, Earl of Salisbury, gave birth to me in a chamber far inferior to this… Are you happy Isabelle?'

'Why, my Lord, why should I not be?'

'Because my mother was not happy and it was as much that she married my father as she bore me…'

'The "Imp of Satan," ' Isabelle jested.

'Aye,' replied William solemnly, 'the "Imp of Satan." '

'No, I do not regret my marriage to you, my Lord,' Isabelle said after a moment's reflection. 'Your mother may have been Sybil of Salisbury, but she was not Isabelle de Clare.'

'Perhaps it is because you *are* Isabelle de Clare that I ask.'

'Such questions, William.' She dismissed his concern and asked, 'What shall we call the boy. Methinks Richard; Richard, for the King. What think you of that husband?'

He smiled at her. 'Richard, eh?' He considered the matter a moment, then nodded. 'Yes, Richard is fine.'

They were interrupted by a knock at the chamber door and Isabelle's hand-maid Susannah announced the arrival of a courier. William rose from the bed and slowly withdrew his hand from his wife's. 'I am sorry we get so little time together,' he said, smiling sadly down at her. She returned his smile and watched as, pausing to take a peek at the wrinkled boy in his cradle, he made to leave the chamber when Isabelle called after him.

'William!' He half-turned at the door. 'He carries no birth-mark.'

'Thanks be to God,' said William nodding, leaving the door for the waiting Susannah to re-enter her mistress's room.

William found the messenger in the hall below. He was not what he had expected, a courier from London, recalling William from the inspection of the improvement works of the castles in the west upon which he had been engaged by the Council. While the threat from Philippe had abated on the news that Richard had been released from captivity, that from an ever more desperate John had yet to be dealt with.

The man had a plain, rustic look about him, oddly familiar, yet somehow alien. William was wary. It was not beyond Count John to send such a man bent on murder of one of his enemies, for Count John had his back against the wall

'My Lord Marshal,' the man said, making his obeisance.

'Aye. What conference would you have with me?' William kept his distance, annoyed with himself for not even carrying a dagger. He thought of calling for De Earley, but the messenger, a sergeant-at-arms by his habiliments, quickly relieved him of his anxiety and replaced it with something akin to regret.

'My Lord, I bring you news of your brother's death.'

'My brother? John?'

'Aye, my Lord.'

'I am sorry to hear of it. May God have mercy upon his soul.' William crossed himself, asking, 'where did he die?'

'At Marlborough, my Lord, with the Lady Aline. It was she who directed me hither.'

William nodded. 'I see.'

Marlborough Castle was one of John's, and his brother had been close to Count John at one time, but there was no point in dwelling on that. Calling for his steward William had the man taken to the kitchen, fed and given a bed for the night. He withdrew himself to his small private chamber and knelt in prayer, but could summon little feelings of grief for brother John. John had always been his parents' darling and in the spoiling of him had formed a man for which, even in adult life, William could find little love for. Odd that, not an hour since, he had been ruminating on his childhood. He wondered about John's wife, the Lady Aline de Port. There had been no children and so, he realised slowly, after being cut-out of their father's will and John having denied William anything, he had, in the end, inherited what remained of old John's estates and title of the King's Marshal. Not that the lack of it, like the lack of an Earldom upon his marriage to Isabelle de Clare, had either affected him or the mode by which he was addressed or known. The great levy in Essex had shown that, with John de Earley riding out like a moonstruck page-boy to raise cheers for Richard and the Marshal. But now, unless Richard deprived him of it, he was without doubt the Marshal of England and, instead of mourning his brother, he rose from his feet in lighter mood than when contemplating his second son's birth.

For a moment he reproached himself, dropped to one knee and said a hurried Paternoster. Crossing himself again he rose to his feet. Then he sighed. 'Tomorrow,' he murmured to himself, his shoulders sagging with a sudden weariness, 'tomorrow I must needs ride to Marlborough when I would rather watch my Lady Isabelle and the boy a-suckling.'

But William never rode to Marlborough, nor saw his elder brother buried, for hard on the heels of the messenger from the Lady Aline came three knights and a dozen sergeants-at-arms from London who clattered up to the half-built new gatehouse of Chepstow Castle and demanded entry in the name of King Richard. Brought before the Lord of Striguil they announced that, three days earlier, on the 3rd March 1194, King Richard had landed at Sandwich in Kent.

'You are commanded to attend the King's presence in London, my Lord,' he handed William a small parchment, sealed with red and bearing – for by now William was familiar with the name – the sign manual of Archbishop Hubert FitzWalter.

'The King is come home,' he told Isabelle when he visited her that evening, 'and tomorrow I must leave for London.'

'What of your brother's widow?' his wife enquired.

'I must send John de Earley thither. He will do what must be done.'

Isabelle extended her hand and he knelt at the bedside and kissed it. 'You are worthy of Strongbow's daughter, my William,' she said, smiling tiredly. 'The Earldom must follow when God wills it.'

CHAPTER NINE: THE KING'S MARSHAL 1194

William entered the plain room of the house in which King Richard had made his headquarters. It lay close below the castle rock above which the ramparts of Nottingham Castle reared. Hubert FitzWalter, Archbishop of Canterbury, coifed and coated in chain mail, stood next to the Earl of Huntingdon in the half-lit chamber and William nodded to both men after making his obeisance to Richard who turned from the window as William made his entry.

'Hola, Marshal! D'you have news of the petraries and trebuchets?'

'Aye, Your Grace, they are half a day's march away on the Leicester road.'

'Come hither,' Richard peremptorily jerked his head. 'What do you say to an immediate attack?'

Without ceremony the King summoned William to join him at the open casement, scarcely giving William time to draw breath from his ascent of the steep staircase. Such breathless action seemed the hallmark of the last few days for Richard had hardly arrived in London ere he was on the move, acknowledging only the welcome of the citizens, before giving orders for the forces mustered against Philippe turned north and west, to bring to an abrupt conclusion the rebellion of his brother, Count John of Mortain and Anjou. Although disbelieved in many quarters, the news of Richard's return had swept through England like fire through brushwood, so-much-so, it was said, that the castellan of St Michael's Mount in Cornwall, Henry de Pumerai, had died of an apoplexy on the spot.

William had been in no doubt of the truth of Richard's arrival in England. Sending John de Earley to Marlborough and his brother's widow, he had ridden north and east, to join the King at Huntingdon, along with other barons of the realm, including the Earls of Chester and Ferrers. Thereafter the main Loyalist force under the King marched on Nottingham where the garrison, still loyal to Count John, held out in the belief that Richard was dead.

William had ruined two horses in his headlong dash across country with only a handful of his household knights in train. Happily, his favourite destrier was reserved for battle and, unridden, was in good wind for whatever might befall. On the march north, De Earley had re-joined his master.

'What news of the Lady Aline, John?' William had asked him.

'She is well enough, my Lord, and sends you greeting,' De Earley had replied. 'You will have no trouble from her respecting her husband's office.'

Now William joined Richard at the casement and studied the outer barbican of the castle. It was a largely wooden structure and, given the fortress's otherwise commanding position on its great rock above its river, was the castle's weakest feature, a point obviously not lost on Richard. From time-to-time the head of a defender appeared as the garrison prepared for an attack and it was clear that with every hour that passed the advantage slipped from the attackers.

'This must be swiftly concluded, Marshal,' the King growled in William's ear. 'I am unwilling to invest the place and embark on a protracted siege. You have Ferrers and Chester with you?'

'Aye, Your Grace, they are quartering their horses and will be with you directly.' Richard grunted. And as footsteps sounded on the wooden staircase, marking the arrival of the two Earls, William asked, 'Any news from Tickhill, Your Grace?'

'Aye, Marshal, The Bishop of Durham, God bless him, has taken the place and marches to our reinforcement.'

'Have we a ram sufficient to batter those gates?'

'Aye, Two, both iron-shod, and Greek-fire should it prove necessary...' Richard paused, considering. 'My master-engineer Urric is on the road from London, but I am reluctant to await his arrival. We might force that barbican today...'

Something caught William's eye and he cried out a warning. Both men instinctively drew back as a cross-bow bolt struck the timber window-sill with a thud and stuck there, vibrating.

Richard stared at William, then laughed. 'Well?'

'Attack, Your Grace.' William snapped.

Richard turned from the window, addressing the assembled nobles and the Prelate. 'Very well, messieurs, muster your men. We move at once!'

As they left the room and clattered down the gloomy staircase in single file William felt a hand like a vice upon his shoulder. He half-turned in the half-light as Richard, two steps above him lent forward. 'I mislike what is happening here, Marshal,' Richard said, his tone suddenly sinister. 'Have you one to bear your standard?'

Uncomprehending anything more than he seemed to have incurred Richard's displeasure, William met the King's gaze and eased his shoulder so that the King loosened his grip. 'Aye, my Lord,' he replied evenly, 'John de Earley.'

'Very well, then tell John de Earley that he has the honour of bearing my standard and you, Marshal, have the greater honour of leading the assault.'

For a moment the two men, hidden from all others, stared at each other. This was the first moment they had had alone since the King's return and William had no idea of how he had offended Richard. But this was no time for such considerations, and William nodded. 'As you command, my Liege,' he said, descending the stairs and hurrying out into the street where troops were milling and jostling under the cover of the adjacent houses. Shouting for John de Earley and finding him with William's assembled mesnie, William passed Richard's instruction and was met by incomprehension and then a dawning light.

De Earley frowned. 'Doth he mean us killed, my Lord?'

'Perhaps, but I think his greater purpose is to force that gate. We attack, and on foot. Get rid of this horse.'

Although the gate itself was out of sight, there was no mistaking the beetling ramparts of the castle. 'By the Christ,' breathed De Earley.

'Go find the King's standard, John and remember: "For Richard and the Marshal". '

'And what of your own device?'

'Tell Geoffrey FitzRobert to bear it.' De Earley nodded, then William added, 'and tell him to bear it close by the King.'

De Earley grinned. 'For Richard and the Marshal then.'

'Aye,' William said slapping the haunches of De Earley's horse. 'And mayhap for England too,' he muttered as he sought out his own squires, arming himself with sword and shield.

For twenty minutes the streets of Nottingham seethed with preparation as the barons and knights banneret sorted their mesnies and supporting troops, a riot of noise and suppressed fear and excitement. A few of the citizens stared from their windows, though most hid, for fear of the ravages of Richard's war-host, though several taverns and a few whores did a brief but roaring trade as the leading knights laid about them with the flats of their swords, bringing order to the unruly mob.

John de Earley returned to William's side on foot, the great red banner of England with its golden leopards, now three in number, floating about his steel casque.

William nodded and crossed himself. 'God go with you, John.'

'And with you my Lord.'

Then Richard was among them on horseback, lightly coifed as he had been wont to be in the Holy Land, silencing them and giving the order to move. Standing in his stirrups he roared: 'Bring up the rams!' There was a swirl in the crowded street as a party of foot-soldiers, covered by arbalestriers, drew out to the end of the street where it turned through a right angle leading up to the castle.

'Advance my standard!' bellowed the King.

William hefted his long shield covering his body with

his left arm and took his post alongside the head of the battering ram, sword in hand. John de Earley marched close behind him, bearing the King's standard with two squires covering him with shields.

'En avant! Forward!' William shouted. 'For Richard and England!'

The shambolic muddle of knights, men-at-arms and foot-soldiers, moved forward, and in rounding the corner transformed itself into a purposeful column that stamped up the gradient towards the wooden barbican. Men fell instructively into step to avoid tripping over each other's feet as they kept a close and mutually protective order and the speed of the column changed into a loping run. Above them flew a dark cloud of bolts and arrows, forcing the garrison to keep their heads down, but then one, two, three cross-bow bolts penetrated William's shield. Their successive impacts forced him to stumble and the heads poked menacingly through the steel, but he recovered his pace as the wretched men carrying the ram, exposed as they were to the hail of fire from the top of the gateway, began to fall.

But it took a moment or two to load and fire a cross-bow, and the numbers the gate-tower and adjacent ramparts could accommodate were limited, particularly as those firing to enfilade the attack, must needs lean outwards, against the sky, where the arbalestriers of the King, now firing from good cover among the houses, picked them off.

Within a few panting moments the assault column fell under the shadow of the gate-house and with a steady thud-thud, the ram was put to work. Stones were now rained down, but those carrying shields, with aching arms, could give a measure of protection to the foot-soldiers coming directly under this hail of missiles as they battered at the gate.

Then up came the second ram, along with archers and arbalestriers, and the swarm under the arch of the gate-house began to gain ground as the timbers of the gate itself began to give way. The wooden barbican accommodated no portcullis and there was little William and De Earley could do beyond giving what support their shields might offer to those working the rams and urging them to greater efforts, until, with a sudden crack, the locking beam fractured and the shattered gates swung wide.

William forced his way forward, slashing left and right, Robert de Salignac's sword light in his powerful hand. Behind him De Earley bawled at the men who had dropped the rams at the moment of their success to lug out their short swords and bollock knives and follow where William and his mesnie, now shoving past in close order under the protection of their shields, thrust the defenders back through sheer weight of numbers.

It was bloody work and William took an ear-splitting blow to his head before hacking down the man who administered it, cleaving the knight's mail coat so that it split like a pig's hide. There was neither quarter nor ransom given nor expected and as Richard led in reinforcements to keep up the momentum of the assault, the King and his followers had to clamber over a heap of the dead and the dying.

After two hours of strenuous fighting the gate-house was carried and the Loyalist forces had occupied the outer bailey, all but a few of the garrison retreating within the middle bailey as the sun set. The prisoners were herded back under guard into the town and locked up for the night.

Richard withdrew from the barbican for the night. The entrance to the outer-bailey was soon swarming with dogs and rats which rooted among the corpses, attracted by the stink of gore. Taking stock after nightfall the King stared at the loom of the central keep of the castle, his Barons gathered about him. William, aching from cuts, bruises and strained muscles, nursed a feeling of ill-will towards Richard, furious, in the anti-climactic aftermath of battle and the physical exertion that it had demanded of him, that the King had so privately ill-treated him.

Taking the King's standard from John de Earley shortly after the fighting had died out, William had personally handed it back to Richard with the curt observation that: 'By placing this in the hands of Sir John de Earley, Your Grace risked its loss as much as I risked the loss of a valued knight.'

But Richard had merely motioned to the Earl of Huntingdon to relieve William of the great flag and remarked, casually, 'I did not think either in much danger, Marshal.'

The compliment was veiled, and at odds with the King's earlier behaviour, further irritating William so that he attended the King that evening with something like resentment burning within him. Eventually the King turned and spoke to his Barons and the Prelate. 'Messieurs we must eat,' and, retiring into an adjacent and empty dwelling house, called for meat and wine. Here, in the parlour of an unknown and absent merchant, the flower of English chivalry shuffled for somewhere to hunker down with a bowl of warm mutton stew brought up from the King's camp-kitchen.

After finishing their meal and setting guard, they all settled down for the night, being woken an hour before dawn when the knight commanding the middle-guard entered the crowded chamber and announced that the garrison had salled and set fire to the barbican, whereupon Richard leapt to his feet. Summoning William and FitzWalter to follow him, the King strode out to reconnoitre.

'This is much to our advantage unless I am much mistaken,' Richard observed. Turning to William he ordered timber brought up from the town in order for a large gallows to be erected in the outer-bailey as soon as possible and as soon as the sun threw a baleful light over the outer ramparts and into the outer bailey, Richard sent a herald forward to summon the Constables, Ralph Murdac and William de Weneval to surrender.

They returned a defiant response. They were not fooled, the herald reported, by the advancing of the King's standard, for it had been the device of William Marshal, one of the co-Justiciar's, - that had been conspicuous. Had the King been with them they should have observed the fact.

During the forenoon, as the siege engines arrived from Leicester, Richard and William began a close investment of the castle, the King sent Archbishop FitzWalter forward under the protection of a pair of heralds and again summoned the garrison to surrender. The Prelate, caparisoned for war and riding a huge bay charger, informed the Constables that Count John's cause was lost, Tickhill had fallen and that His Grace the King was indeed present.

'Surrender to the King's mercy!' the Prelate shouted up at the walls surrounding the middle-bailey. 'Your cause is not only unjust, it is lost! You have been deceived, for thanks be to Almighty God, King Richard is restored to the throne of his father!'

'Give us proof!' came a hail from the gate of the middle-bailey and, under safe-conduct, the Archbishop brought back to the King's presence two knights, Fouchier de Grendon and Henry Russel. The two men shuffled awkwardly as Richard stood in the merchant's parlour, surrounded by his chief commanders.

The King seemed amused for he remarked, 'I know neither of you and neither or you know me.

'Are you not William FitzMarshal? De Grendon asked.

Richard turned. 'Would you dare wear the leopards of England, my Lord Marshal?' he asked as William stepped forward.

'No, your Grace.'

The two knights now stared at William, then, turning back, bent their knee to the King.'

'Go, tell the Constables what you have seen. You have half an hour to capitulate.'

But Murdac and De Wenneval remained unconvinced and night fell without any resolution of the affair.

Now Richard called for the timbers assembled by William to be made into a gallows by carpenters newly arrived the day before with the siege-engines from Leicester. That night the Loyalists occupied the brunt wreckage of the barbican as the gallows were erected in the outer-bailey so that the garrison might wake-up to see what the King had hung from it.

Shortly after daybreak the King had two of the prisoners taken at the first day's assault brought out of their confinement and strung up, to die of slow strangulation. One, a plain-hauberked sergeant-at-arms, took three minutes, struggling against the inevitable, writhing horribly, his legs streaming with piss and shit, to the delight of the watching Loyalists. The other took rather longer, affording perhaps greater amusement to Richard and his men. He was a Norman-French knight, Alain de Gisallon, a man of stocky build, enormously powerful shoulders and thick neck, who sought to cheat death for as long as possible by hunching his shoulders and drawing his head down to keep his wind-pipe open. Those on both sides watched in open-mouthed admiration as, in a remarkable display of self-control, De Gisallon seemed to succeed for some long minutes, until at last he could no longer support the weight of his body from his neck. Twitching at first, his legs soon began to kick uncontrollably, and the air started to wheeze and then whistle in his slowly contracting throat.

As the affair reached its climax a rising roar of appreciation greeted the spectacle until, in a great spasm, De Gisallon gave-up, his bowels opened and in a terrible arching of his back he snapped his own spine at the neck. Hanging, his head on one side, his body swayed slightly from his last exertions on earth.

'There dies a brave man,' Richard was heard to remark as he turned aside and called for victuals to break his own fast.

William watched this spectacle, his face grim. Richard's ruthlessness had accomplished far worse, but this was the first time William had seen it for himself. 'Doubtless more will hang before sunset,' he remarked savagely to De Earley as the two men followed the King in search of viands.

But none did. It seemed the expression of callous savagery proved Richard's identity and the Constables sent word asking for terms. Having so barbarically executed the two prisoners, Richard then offered generous conditions, accepting the Constables' excuse that they had been misled by Count John's misinformation and the unwitting effect of Richard's *ruse de guerre* employing William and his mesnie in his vanguard.

Ralph Murdac and William de Wenneval had little option but to accede and Richard entered the castle in triumph, followed by his principal Barons, Archbishop FitzWalter and Queen Eleanor who had arrived from Winchester. Here he convened a great Council, the first business of which was to deal with Count John's garrison. Most of the knights serving under Murdac and De Wenneval were no more penalised than if they had been taken in a tournament.

The evening's feasting was marred by a squabble between Archbishop Hubert FitzWalter of Canterbury and Geoffrey, Archbishop of York, the latter arguing that FitzWalter had no right raising his Cross within the great See of York where he, Geoffrey, was Primate. After allowing the two high churchmen to make fools of themselves, Richard put an end to their dispute and made them make the sign of Peace, declaring that: 'I would have it that such dissensions are ended in this, my Kingdom of England.

The following day the King reconvened the Council which first discussed the question of Count John. Noting the Council had stripped him of his English lands, of which the King approved, Richard demanded John should present himself before his brother within forty days. The convocation then turned its attention to the means of raising the unpaid portion of the King's ransom. The Duke of Austria had been bought off by the Holy Roman Emperor, Heinrich VI, who had taken Richard over as his own prisoner, though allowing him considerable freedoms and had generously remitted seventeen thousand marks to prevent Richard from making peace with King Philippe of France. Nevertheless, there remained outstanding a substantial sum and the King in Council settled upon a series of fines from the supporters of Count John, plus a tax on those possessing funds of ten shillings and upwards.

While these measures troubled several sitting in the great hall of the castle, what disturbed the Council most was the revelation that in order to return to England Richard had rendered homage for his Kingdom to Heinrich, and thereby made of himself and his entire barony, vassals of the Empire. For several of the assembled nobles and churchmen this expedient seemed a step too far, though none challenged the King. This fell circumstance was revealed by William Briwerre on the King's behalf, Briwerre having with Longchamp, been forward in negotiating the conditions for the King's release.

Richard sat stroking his beard throughout Briwerre's revelation of this shift in the King's powers. His eyes rove over the assembled notables, seeking to read each man as they listened to the co-Justiciar's words.

William was non-plussed by the disclosure and wondered if the King had lost his wits. His long association with the intemperate characters of four Angevin Princes led him to consider the possibility. The King's conduct on the staircase of the house from which they had reconnoitred the castle but three days earlier still lacked any explanation, but, like the others sitting at board, he held his tongue as Briwerre concluded. It was Archbishop FitzWalter who broke the awkward silence.

'May it please Your Grace,' he said, 'that I might prevail upon you to entertain a solemn crown-wearing by way of giving thanks to Almighty God for your safe return from the Holy Land and to reassert your resumption of your throne and the dissolution of the Council of State.

'It would please me greatly,' Richard said. 'I intend to pass directly into France but, my Lords, we shall spend some time at Winchester gathering our force. There shall you, my Lord Archbishop, perform your high office,' the King rose to his feet and all present jumped to their feet as Richard swept out of the great hall. For a few moments the members of the Council turned from one to another discussing the morning's discussions and revelations as they prepared to leave the hall themselves. William met Geoffrey FitzPeter's raised eyebrow and then found William Briwerre beside him.

'FitzMarshal,' Briwerre said quietly, 'I am to inform you that the King desires your presence in his private chamber.'

William found Richard sitting and scratching a large hound; he made his obeisance and Richard sat back and, again stroking his beard, stared at William.

'Why did you do it, Marshal?' he asked at last.

'Do what my Liege?' William asked frowning.

'Dismiss Longchamp.'

William blew out his cheeks and gathered his wits. 'My Lord King, you have oft told me to use a mailed fist if a velvet glove doth not prevail. Your Grace will recall entrusting me with some powers to watch the Chancellor and, should he exceed his powers and disrupt the tranquillity of your Kingdom in Your Grace's absence, act accordingly. It so happened that the Chancellor was stirring-up trouble among the Barons, one against the other and there was no policy in it beyond what he himself gained in power thereby. I was not alone in the decision to remove him, though I am prepared to withstand the accusation of having done so.'

'Have you anything more to say?' the King asked sardonically, concealing a half smile under his hand as he played with his beard.

'No, Your Grace.'

The King nodded slowly then changed the subject. 'Once we discussed war, FitzMarshal, d'you recall?'

'Aye, it was before Neufchâtel-en-Bray…'

'And much has happened since.'

'Indeed, Your Grace.'

'As soon as this business in Winchester is concluded, I intend crossing to Normandy. You shall come with me. Your brother is dead, God rest his soul, which confers upon you the office of Marshal, a title you have long held in his name, for I never knew much of him, nor he of me. We shall have conference about our campaign in Winchester, but for the time being you should know that you have made an enemy of William Longchamp and I repose trust in him, as I do you.'

'I understand, Your Grace.'

The King grunted. 'You may go.' Richard called for wine and bent to fondle the hound curled about his feet.

'Your Grace…'

'What is it?' Richard asked, without looking up.

'I would seek a step to match my Lady's fiefs and estates, some mark that better enables my people to hold the March of Nether Gwent.'

Richard continued to tumble the wolf-hound's ears but turned his head and looked up at William. 'Striguil, eh? You press me for an Earldom, eh?'

Richard sat up and put his finger-tips together, touching his lips and regarding William over his two hands. Then he shook his head. 'It shall not be, Marshal. I observed your dislike of my accommodation with the Emperor. Besides, your accusation of Longchamp as a bugger offended his dignity as Chancellor, an appointment I never removed, nor have removed from him, though I do not think you acted unwisely in replacing him with the Archbishop of Rouen.'

'Your Grace, the remark touched him like a hot poker. He ran from the Kingdom in woman's clothes, with a disguise to match, including wares to vend.'

If William intended to play upon Richard's partial approval in co-opting Des Coutances, it misfired. Instead of softening, Richard's face grew hard.

'No matter,' he responded curtly, waving William away.

William bowed and withdrew, recalling rumours of Richard's sexual proclivities. In dismissing Longchamp as a sodomite, had he unwittingly touched a raw nerve in Richard? If so, it had cost him an Earldom.

***

William rode south with King Richard's train. To all outward appearances his demeanour was unruffled, but inwardly he was seething at Richard's curt dismissal, of the King's lack of gratitude towards himself and the news that Longchamp was awaiting the King's arrival at Winchester, fully and pointedly reappointed to his old office. Even the presence of FitzPeter, whose warning to William that he should not over-reach himself, had no effect as a dark mood took hold of William, for FitzPeter *had* been rewarded with the estates of the Earldom of Essex long since, though the title of Earl as yet eluded him. Nevertheless, it was the ownership of *land* that mattered, for land equated to income and with income a man could buy and sell, wield influence, make advantageous marriages and secure a future for his family. With every mile they travelled to the southward William's feeling of having been hard done-by increased. Besides the political decisions William had made, or contributed to, in the King's absence, Richard owed the swift capture of Nottingham Castle less to his own Lion-hearted valour than to William's raw courage. As King, Richard's participation in any assault was voluntary; as a vassal William did his duty as assigned to him, and he was under no illusions that Richard deliberately sent him forward in the post of greatest danger with a calculated deliberation.

On 17th April 1194, in Winchester Cathedral, among his Barons, with the Archbishop of Canterbury and his Prelates in their golden copes all assembled and the

Queen Mother, Eleanor of Aquitaine looking-on, King Richard underwent a solemn 'Crown-wearing' during which William bore the Sword of State. Seen by many as a second coronation, the ceremony was an affirmation of his kingship after his long absence, but it contained significant undertones.

After the Archbishop's blessing, as in his first and proper crowning, Richard required his chief Barons to swear fealty and establish the legitimacy of their own powers within the Kingdom. However, on this occasion, this otherwise routine feature of the feudal system meant a submission of the Barony to Richard's own expedient submission to the Holy Roman Emperor. Although all knew that with much of the King's ransom still unpaid and the pressing necessity for Richard to forge alliances to cover his forthcoming war with Philippe Augustus to recover Normandy and elsewhere, it sealed England as a fiefdom of Heinrich VI.

One-by-one the great men of the Kingdom shuffled up, knelt before the King and, as if in prayer, placed their hands between the King's. A long and tedious process, largely of mumbling oath-taking as a herald read out the feudatories for which each man pledged his troth, William broke the dreary observance and electrified the congregation.

Having sworn allegiance for his English and Welsh land, William said nothing as the herald read out the estates in Ireland that had come to him through Isabelle's father's conquests. Thinking William had not heard, the herald read them out again, and it was the repetition that gained the suddenly attention of a largely bored congregation.

'You do not swear, FitzMarshal,' remarked the affronted King, still clasping William's hands, though now pressing them together, hard.

William looked up at Richard. 'No, Your Grace,' he said, his voice icy with a cool conviction and in a tone that could be clearly heard by many standing about the throne. 'As all the world knows, it is unnecessary. Count John is Lord of Ireland and to him I shall do homage as soon as he does homage to Your Grace.'

Then William pointedly slid his hands out from between the King's as the words and gesture were met by a gasp of astonishment. William Longchamp shouted out, 'beware, my Lord King, Marshal plants vines!'

Richard looked at William, ten years his senior and saw the implacable expression upon his face. 'What mean you by this?' he asked in a low voice, but before William could answer, FitzPeter, greatly daring but avoiding any address directly to the King, countered Longchamp's mischievous assertion.

'My Lord Chancellor, the Marshal is strictly correct and doubtless wishes the Count of Mortain brought to the King's feet with all speed. Your direction to the herald is faulty and reprehensible.'

A palpable ripple ran through the assembly as the King bent and hissed in his ear. 'God's blood, Marshal, I admire your courage.' William rose, bowing to the King and withdrew, stared at by all present who had heard the exchange.

'God damn you, William, but you press your friends hard, FitzPeter said to him afterwards. 'Have I not told you…'

'Aye Geoffrey, many times but by God if I serve with

172

honour by honour I shall be served. Unless I am much mistaken, Richard knows that.'

'You will be banished...'

'What? To Ireland?' William riposted with a laugh. 'Let us see, my friend. The Lionheart will need a new military establishment for the coming war with Philippe, something more durable than the fyrd which cannot be conveyed to Normandy where, in any case, the general levy there will prove inadequate, only being in the field for forty days. I will wager you fifty marks he will require some better means of raising a host and someone to effect it.'

'You?'

William shrugged. 'Both you and me, perhaps.'

'Those English Barons who have lost land in Normandy and have given-up hope of recovery are less likely to hazard their dwindling fortunes on Richard's gamble against the growing power of Philippe,' said FitzPeter.

'Damn them then,' William retorted. 'If we can make some swift inroads and gain booty to add to scutage and tallage, then sufficient money may be raised to fund a war-host from knights banneret, sergeants-at-arms, routiers and Welsh mercenaries such as will serve as long as Richard feeds them blood and treasure to gorge upon. For God's sake, Geoffrey, you know the methods by which he makes war. He will have little trouble finding footloose men of low birth either back from the Holy Land or like those fools drawn out of Sherwood forest after he took Nottingham.'

William's gamble proved his judgement correct. He heard little further from the King regarding the affair of his cleaving to Count John beyond a rumour that Queen Eleanor had approved his action and the almost symbolic deprivation of the shrievalty of Gloucester. No vengeance was taken elsewhere and his younger brother Henry remained secure in his Palace as Bishop of Exeter, the See to which he had been appointed the previous year. As for William, within hours he was caught up in the business of preparing the King's war host which, in its first wave, left Portsmouth on 12 May and crossed the Channel in upwards of one hundred ships, leaving the government of England in the hands of a sole Justiciar, Hubert FitzWalter, Archbishop of Canterbury.

As the men, horses, stores and such supplies as they had brought with them, were landed at Barfleur, Richard ordered a march on Lisieux where, so word had it, Count John awaited his coming. And in Richard's train rode William Marshal, with John de Earley at his side bearing the rampant red lion on its ground of pale gold and green behind which rode William's mesnie.

CHAPTER TEN: WAR WITH PHILIPPE
AUGUSTUS 1194 – 1199

Thus did Richard, nick-named Coeur de Lion, pass over the seas into Normandy. He arrived in all his murderous splendour intending to retake what his brother had lost, to a rapturous reception given him by the citizens of Barfleur. He, and others in the host including William Longchamp, would never set foot on English soil again, but for the first months of his campaigning, Richard maintained his reputation as a fearsome warrior.

At Lisieux, in the presence of the Queen Mother, Count John grovelled in contrition before his brother, an act made all the more specious in its character by the actions of the Count in deserting King Philippe. In fear of Richard he had but a few days earlier repudiated his oath to Philippe by quietly abandoning his post in command of the French garrison at Evreux. Richard made a gracious speech accepting John's penitence after Queen Eleanor had spoken in her younger son's favour. Richard told his brother he had been misled like a child but Eleanor's politic intercession made it easier for William to boost the reconciliation between the two royal siblings by paying a conspicuously public homage to John for his Leinster lands.

'Well, well, Marshal, you have truly compounded with the Devil's brood now,' Richard had casually and sardonically remarked to him the following day as the

King mounted his horse.

'I am bound by loyalty, My Liege,' William replied solemnly, looking up at the King as Richard took the reins from the attendant page.

Richard laughed. 'Come William,' he growled, patting the palfrey's neck and leaning down so that only William could hear what he said. 'We are neither of us fit to waste our lives at Court,' Richard chuckled. 'We are warriors and there is work to be done.'

'To Vernueil then, Your Grace?'

'Where else?' Richard spurred his mount forward and William motioned for his own palfrey to be brought up. As he swung into the saddle and shoved his feet into his stirrups, he looked about him. As always John de Earley was at hand, his own horse almost choking on its bit as foam flecked from its lips in the creature's eagerness to be off.

'My Lord is in favour again,' remarked De Earley with his engagingly broad grin.

'By God, John, you grow too big for your boots,' William remarked without rancour, supressing his own smile. 'Aye,' he added, 'Richard is himself again, God help his enemies and the common people of this fair land.'

***

And, as the King had said, to work they went. With the repentant Count John in company Richard's war-host stormed south deeper into Normandy, the King concerting a plan for the relief of Verneuil and the taking of Evreux with his brother and William.

'Marshal,' the King said in conference with William one night as they broke their march in a small village from which the peasants had fled, 'it is my purpose to divide my force. The Count of Mortain will advance on Evreux and prove his repentance by taking the city of which he was lately Philippe's castellan. As for Verneuil, I place you in command of half my remaining force.'

William bowed his head obediently. There would be many among the King's Barons who would regard the King's favour as misplaced, but age and experience, added to his reputation for prowess, secured William Marshal's claim to this preferment. He listened as the King went on: 'I shall employ the chevauchée and lead a division of my heaviest chivalry to cover as many bowmen as we can mount and supply with a few days' victuals directly through the enemy lines. They will reinforce the garrison and shake the enemy's spirit. Once I have seen them into Verneuil I will rejoin you, and you, in the meanwhile, shall take the remainder of our host east and cut off Philippe's legs, after which he can only fall.'

William nodded. 'You will need to give me two days' start if I am to successfully cut King Philippe's supply lines, my Liege.'

'That will be too long to conceal your movements from the fox; shall we say one?'

'As Your Grace wishes.'

'Good. Then let it be so, but we shall need additional horses...'

'Aye, but you may leave that to me. If we act quickly we can use our own pack-animals for half our needs, the rest I shall take from the countryside. We can mount two bowmen on any decent beast.'

'Aye, that is good,' the King said smiling with a disarming and almost boyish enthusiasm. 'By the Christ, Marshal, 'tis good sport to hound this French bastard, is it not?'

'So long as he does not escape us, my Liege,' William responded seriously, 'though it is always the chase the pleases most,' he added, catching something of Richard's mood.

As planned, one morning in the third week in May, the van of the Angevins suddenly appeared out of the woods near Verneuil, Taking the besieging forces completely by surprise Richard sent his mounted column directly up to the city gates where the besieged, recognising the devices and colours of the approaching force and the confusion it was causing among the French, threw open the barricaded gates.

In the meanwhile William, with the greater part of the war-host marched east and severed the Paris road, then turned west and approached the embattled city. However, as he had feared, word of the turning movement had reached Philippe who had thrown-up the siege and was in full and disorganised retreat to the south-east as fast as horse and legs could carry him and his men.

Nevertheless, if Richard had failed to nail his enemy, he was in high good spirits when he met William and the bulk of the Angevin army as it neared Verneuil and encountered the scattered remnants of the Capetians.

'Well, the fox has escaped, but we shall catch him next time,' Richard said cheerfully but William was disappointed. A quick and conclusive victory was surely essential, but Richard seemed to glory in a perpetual struggle and William realised that conflict was meat-and-drink to him, a conclusion confirmed in the following days.

After a triumphal entry into Verneuil when Richard ordered William to ride alongside him to the ringing cheers of the citizens, and Richard having dismounted and symbolically kissed as many of the garrison as were close-by, the King gave his orders for a further advance. The swift Angevin victory had persuaded many of the hesitant Barons to throw in their lot with Richard and the King's war-host grew in size. Unfortunately, before they left Verneuil, news reached them that although Count John's chevauchée had been equally successful in retaking Evreux, its accomplishment was already notorious.

'He seeks to beat me at my own game, damn him,' Richard remarked to his assembled Barons. His face darkened as he read the despatch borne to Verneuil by one of John's knights who was clearly an informant for the King. 'And in so doing brings my cause into disrepute.' He flung the message aside.

'How so, my Liege?' someone asked.

'It seems, my Lords,' Richard said in clipped and furious tones, 'that my brother approached Evreux with every appearance of amity and that the garrison, unacquainted with his reconciliation in our cause at Lisieux, and thinking that he arrived with reinforcements welcomed him and restored him to his place at the head of their board as they sat down to their meat. As they enjoyed their wine and discourse, my brother had his own knights rise and decapitate the very men he himself had commanded in Philippe's name no more than a month since,' Richard concluded with an air of disgust.

The pronouncement was met with a silence. No-one there was unaware that Richard had employed such methods himself, though only when he deemed the utter destruction of the enemy was – in his eyes, politic, and rarely by such a deceit. He had exercised restraint at Nottingham, and it had paid off, but John's conduct at Evreux was judged infamous not only by the treachery he employed in heartlessly killing men with whom he had broken bread a fortnight earlier, but that he then had had their severed heads paraded on poles and lances and paraded them through the streets.

'This will damage our cause,' growled Richard. 'From the heart of such a man no good can come.'

To assuage his anger and with an energy reminiscent of his father, Henry Curtmantle, Richard recalled John to his standard and again divided his forces. One column drove east to retake the castle at Montmirail which guarded the border of Angevin Maine, while Richard hurled his main body further south, towards Le Mans. The city swiftly capitulated without resistance, augmenting the King's war-chest with twenty thousand marks as a proof of their repudiation of loyalty to Philippe. William, who rode with Richard, led the host into Tours as it passed into Touraine and, in a swift and brilliant chevauchée retook the castle of Loches in an assault that lasted a mere three hours.

Such a swift return of Touraine to the Angevins drew down the might of French chivalry and Richard, secure in his mind that King Sancho of Navarre had crossed the Pyrenees and therefore covered Avquitaine, next turned north to meet Philippe on the borders of Angevin Maine and the Capetian Orléannais.

'We have Philippe by his bollocks now,' Richard remarked genially one evening in early July, indicating the French heralds that stood awkwardly beside their horses as Richard greeted William coming in from his rounds of the entrenched encampment at Vendôme. Drawing William into his pavilion the King ordered wine and explained.

'Philippe is quartered at Fréteval and sends his heralds to issue challenges on behalf of his chief knights. What say you and I take them up, eh? When we have routed them, Philippe will be bound to submit for I would deliver him over to death or take him alive.'

'And if you failed, my Lord King?' William cautioned.

Richard sighed. 'You are right, though 'twould have been fine sport, eh? We shall assault them in a general mêlée tomorrow but I shall send back that I will meet him in combat at the head of his host.' William nodded his agreement. 'Send them back with such a message then, Marshal.'

The following morning the Angevin camp was astir early, broke its fast and was marching towards Fréteval before the sun had burnt the dew off the grass. Word of its coming had preceded it but the French forces, rather than drawing up their array, was in full and disorderly retreat. The Angevin war-host, consisting of two bodies, the main force under Richard, and the reserve under William, deployed for the attack.

As they did so Richard himself rode back to William, drawing up his magnificent destrier, sword in hand. 'Do you hold you men in check, Marshal. I shall press the pursuit, but for fear that the fox Philippe had prepared a grand ambush or that my own division get out of hand in the chase, I would have you follow in support!' He tugged his charger's head round, then threw back over his shoulder, 'Be sure to restrain your men!' Then he was gone.

Richard urged his mounted troops - knights, sergeants-at-arms and routiers – to the charge, covered by archers and backed-up by foot-soldiers with their murderous knives. William slowed his own advance until, just before dusk, word came back that Richard had caught-up with what was left of Philippe's shaky rear-guard.

As Richard's division pressed the remnants of the Capetian host to a rout, William's men followed, advancing over the wreckage of men and horses slaughtered by the fury of Richard's onslaught. The reek of blood was everywhere, causing the horses to champ on their bits, while the cries of the dying and wounded was piteous enough to invite their off-hand butchery by the passing men of William's reserve as it moved along the line of march.

From time-to-time a little group wearing Angevin colours pinned-down or held a French nobleman, captured for ransom. Others stripped dead destriers or looted and despatched dying knights.

'By God, they fall away like pigeons before the hawk,' John de Earley remarked incredulously as William's reserve rode over the scene of wholesale slaughter. Richard turned back at midnight, it having become apparent that Philippe had deserted his army and escaped, a circumstance that had almost immediately caused a collapse in morale among his followers. When, about midnight, Richard rode back to Fréteval having lost the French King in the pursuit, he was furious at having been deceived.

'A bastard of a Brabantine mercenary set me on the wrong road and the fox escaped by another,' he roared, greeting William at a tavern in the town around which the victors billeted themselves for the night.

Bawling for wine and meat, Richard received the reports from his senior Barons. Despite the escape of the King's chief quarry, the loot and booty were immense; apart from the flower of French chivalry and their chargers, the Angevins had taken treasure, tents, silken banners, palfreys, roncins, arms and supplies, all of which could either be turned into money or subsumed into the Angevin army. Even Philippe's seal and his private papers had fallen into Richard's hands, revealing those who, with Count John, had betrayed him.

Loud were the boasts and claims of prowess made by the Barons and knights who had served in Richard's force, most of whom guyed those in William's whose part in the battle had been merely supportive.

At one point this became intolerable, for one knight asked 'where were you?' and provoked a general roar upbraiding William's men with cowardice. In the highly charged and intoxicated atmosphere, swords were drawn, whereupon Richard stood and bellowed for silence.

'I shall not have this day's work further spoiled!' he thundered. 'The escape of the bastard Capetian is enough. The Marshal and his gentlemen did as they had been bid and obeyed my orders. They are beyond reproach. Suppose that Philippe's retreat had been but a ruse and he had turned about and fallen upon our flank, or rear. What would many of you have done when down on your knees stripping the harness off a dead chevalier, eh? Whoever has a good rear-guard need fear no enemy. Come Marshal, take wine with me for I esteem thy skill in holding these blackguards in check that we might better haze the Capetian pigs!'

***

But though victorious at Fréteval, the Angevin forces were not left to enjoy the fruits of their triumph, nor was Richard allowed to bag the fox.

Having seen Richard turn away to the northward after the retaking of Loches, the Barons of Aquitaine had sought to further their own interests, calculating that Richard and Philippe would ruin or exhaust themselves in their private, dynastic war while King Sancho would venture no further north than the line of the River Adour. But what amounted to a rebellion in Aquitaine was more than Richard could stomach; of all the lands to which Richard laid claim, Aquitaine was his, he felt, by birth-right of his mother. Once again his army reversed its line of march, striking deep into the Duchy, his forces deployed hither and yon, in sieges and chevauchées in which his senior knights, William among them, wrought havoc. But such warfare, whilst it had its impact upon the attacked and in its successes refilled the war-chest of the attackers, could ultimately only have one result, the inevitable if slow depletion of the victor's resources and man-power. Besides a gradual leeching of treasure, disease, wounds, desertion and death, the sight of two Christian Kings ravaging the fair lands of Christendom excited the ecclesiastical authorities to combine and a truce was arranged by the churchmen on both sides.

Although unratified by King Richard and not destined to last, he acquiesced, the breathing space allowing him to replenish his coffers. Sending to England for men and money the Angevins sat down and awaited the next move.

'Read me this,' William asked De Earley one day in September, handing his friend a letter from the Lady Isabelle. William's illiteracy troubled him, but the faithful De Earley had proved the soul of discretion and read of the doings of William's growing sons, to which William listened with pleasure. The letter ended, however, on a less happy note, for Isabelle kept her husband informed of not merely the finances of his estates, and the reports of his seneschals, castellans and stewards, but of the state of things in England.

' "Know you, therefore, husband",' De Earley read in his halting manner which nevertheless impressed his master, ' "that the City of London hath been plagued by a fellow of rude manners who hath set himself up as the King of the Poor. One William FitzOsbert hath lately been among those complaining of the taxes being levied in support of Our Lord King, Richard, and his desire to make war against King Philippe. He was raised up by the citizens who called him Longbeard and a rebellion was feared until he was betrayed and mewed himself in a church tower. This being set on fire he was driven out, taken and stabbed in the bowels. Not being killed thereby, he was dragged at a horse's tail to the Tower where Walter FitzHubert tried and condemned him. Taken to West Smithfield he was hanged, whereupon the citizens who had revered him but allowed him to be taken, claimed him for a martyr. Coming so hard upon the taxes required for the King's ransom, such additional moneys as are required for this war against Philippe are causing deep resentment throughout the Kingdom...'

'My Lady is bold,' remarked De Earley, concluding the letter some few moments later.

'Destroy it,' William ordered brusquely, nodding at the letter. He shook his head. The circumstances of Longbeard's being burnt-out of a church reminded him of his own father's escape when, seeking sanctuary in an abbey, his pursuers had sought to evict him by setting fire to the place. Afterwards, finding him charred, left him for dead. His father had come-to and walked several miles to safety, but his face had thereafter been a scarred mess, possessing only one eye. The hideous mask was a mark of John Marshal's loyalty to the Empress Matilda, who had escaped while her body-guard had immolated himself in her name.

William shuddered. There was in Longbeard's death that other coincidence, a sudden and appealing martyrdom that, like the end of Henry, the Young King, enjoyed a brief and rapturous enthusiasm, reputedly working miracles among the credulous. William intensely disliked these 'connections' for they resurrected others, more personal. As the truce with Philippe broke down and William was sucked into a long and desultory war with periods of strenuous activity interspersed with short-lived respites, he also crossed back into England and spent time in his wife's bed where, one night in October 1194, Isabelle unintentionally and uncharacteristically struck a raw nerve.

Lightly touching the raised and granulated flesh of her

husband's naevus, she ran her finger over it. Neither made any comment, for their love-making had rendered them tired, but William could not sleep for thinking of the mark. His dead brother John had last spoken of it, he recalled. 'Perhaps our mother was right regarding your marking,' he had said, for the shape of the bloody birth-mark had reminded the Lady Sybil of the shape of Satan. Although others, Henry Curtmantle and his nurse Angharad ap Gwyn chief among them, dismissed this as nonsense, saying the mark more closely resembled a rampant red lion – the device William in due course adopted as his own – he could never quite let his mother's fears go.

Now, with Isabelle breathing softly in his arms, her glorious hair magically silvered by the light of a full moon that penetrated the imperfect shutters of her chamber, it seemed to haunt him. Somehow Henry Curtmantle's assertion that it was a lion seemed now a specious deception, for he had, as Richard had reminded him, in full compact with the Devil's brood, and rode at Richard's side, for better or worse.

Nor did it escape William in such a lonely moment of self-assessment as only a sleepless night can provide that he had grown a great dissembler and that while Richard trusted him for his military skills, he yet withheld the Earldom that William knew he had earned many times over. That this was because, despite everything odious about the Count of Mortain and Anjou, William remained punctilious in his loyalty to John for his Irish lands. From time-to-time Richard would guy him about it, making of something deeper an open jest, reminding William that, high though he stood in the King's favour, his conduct at Winchester and several protestations since, had not yet wiped away William's apparent defiance of King Richard.

In this and subsequent visits in the spring of 1196 and the fall of the leaf two years later, William left Isabelle with child. However, although William enjoyed the prospect of his growing family and marvelled at the precocious skills of his older two boys in the tilt-yard, the chief purpose of his forays into England were to refill his coffers and oversee the administration of his estates. These lay largely in the able hands of Isabelle herself, assisted by the officers of William's household, such as Nicholas Avenal and Master Joscelin, and provided him with a generous income.

Elsewhere among the peasantry and mercantile classes the protracted war was bleeding England white. William agreed to take his dead brother's bastard son John into his mesnie and supported Richard's lifting of his father's ban on tourneying in England, since that raised a number of new warriors with incomes to support their bearing of arms in Normandy. This was necessary for Richard, for all his skills, had failed to bag his fox and the wily Philippe still held the Norman Vexin which threatened the Richard's ducal capital of Rouen where he held his Court..

Here he was visited by the Papal Legate Pietro di Capua. Sent by Pope Celestine III to make peace between Richard and Philippe in order that they would combine and lead a forth crusade to recover Jerusalem for Christ, Pietro had preached peace and cited numerous breaches of faith by Richard, not the least that he held in captivity the Bishop of Beauvais, caught, fully armoured in the field, contrary to the accepted practice of the day.

The King had – in the presence of his Barons - roared his defiance at the Legate.

'Where, in the name of Almighty God, was Papal authority when I was in the Holy Land bleeding in the name of Christ blood while the Capetian ravaged my lands in defiance of the Papal interdiction on war against a Christian Prince on crusade, eh?' he stormed. 'Did the Holy Father excommunicate his friend the King of France? No, by the Rood, he did not! Neither did the Holy Father lift a single fat finger to ease my confinement in the hands of Austria or the Emperor! Now I am told that I ill-use a Bishop caught in rebellion!' Richard was incandescent with a rage reminiscent to those who remembered them, of his father's tempestuous furies.

'By the Christ Legate, I swear I shall bite the bollocks off your fat body should you accuse me of bad faith. Go tell your Holy Master to...' but the King got no further and seemed to choke upon his own words as he was assisted to his private chambers to recover.

As a terrified Pietro hurried away, William was called by an equally frightened body-servant to Richard to attend the King.

'My Lord, I fear for his life. He has discharged me and will see no-one. If he should have an apoplexy...' the man left the sentence unfinished and William entered the darkened apartment to find the King on his knees, clenched fists before his face, his whole body shaking with rage.

'Get out,' Richard gasped, his breathing uneasy and barely able to speak, such was his anger.

'My Liege...' William said tentatively, advancing cautiously, for Richard was dangerous in such a mood. 'The man has fled,' he said, 'fearing the loss of his balls...'

The crudity mollified Richard. His shoulders rose and fell with less frequency and William realised the root of his great and fearless courage in battle was rooted in his temper. Slowly Richard turned his head and recognised William.

'Would that I had castrated him but in the withholding of my hand...' William sensed Richard was marvelling at his own restraint as his words tailed off.

'He was the Papal Legate, my Liege,'twould have done no good.'

'It would have taught the bastard a lesson for he is adept at trickery.'

'Aye, my Liege, but you left him with a face as yellow as a kite's claw.'

'Did I?' Richard caught his breath and held up an arm for William to help him to his feet. 'My God, Marshal, but I am surrounded by perfidy.'

'Not quite surrounded, my Liege,' William said, adding, 'make peace with Philippe and buy time. It can only do your own cause good. The Pope's plea will unseat Philippe more than Your Grace.'

The King stared at William for a moment then clapped him on the shoulder. 'You are right, Marshal, you are right.' Richard called for wine and as William made his obeisance, jested, 'if you continue to be right I shall have to place a belt about you.'

'As Your Grace pleases,' William replied.

***

But there was little peace to be had. Richard sent the Bishop of Beauvais's coat of mail, stained by blood, to Rome and went, once more, to war. In the months that followed Richard, with William at his side and his military engineers led by Uffric managing his petraries, trebuchets and mangonels, attempted to bring the war to a conclusion. The Norman Vexin still lay in Philippe's hands and Richard, in concert with William and his senior Barons and Uffric, began a complex and hideously expensive strategic programme designed to secure for all time the Vexin. A wet-dock was dug out of the water meadows of the Seine at Les Anderlys and to protect it, high on a near-by rock work began on the building of a massive fortress christened Chateau Galliard, the 'Castle of Impudence'. But although a master of siege warfare Richard did not neglect the chevauchée, sending out fast hit-and-run raiding parties aimed at rendering opposition to him null and void.

As the works at Les Anderlys and Chateau Galliard continued, in May 1197, the King's forces made a raid deep into the Beauvaisis. Leaving the routier chief, Mercadier, to attack the city of Beauvais due east of Rouen, William, with Count John, assaulted the castle of Milli-sur-Thérain some six miles to the north-west. As the attackers escaladed the walls, the scaling ladders were hurled back, the defenders using flails, forks as well as knives and bows. Flung back, the ladders breaking under the strain, hurled men into the ditches below where they writhed in an agony of broken limbs. The assault had conspicuously failed and its repulse was accompanied by shouts and cries of glee and insult. Having been thrust back from the ramparts, one ladder remained near vertical, its base jammed in some rocks, shaking as it shed all its load but one, a Flemish knight who clung to its upper rungs, his body transfixed by a fork.

No more than a few feet from them and almost on a level, the Fleming now served as a target for a group of bowmen who shot at him repeatedly, though he clung on through some perverse reflex.

'Come FitzMarshal,' John said, watching with William from the far side of the ditch, 'we can do no more.'

'God's blood!' roared William, 'I do not take a castle as you do,' he leapt forward and leaving John open mouthed at the effrontery, calling for more scaling ladders and his household knights, William shouted, 'follow me who will!' and impetuously led the first ladder party forward. As the foot-soldiers placed the ladder in the bottom of the ditch, William leapt on it and as it reached the vertical he climbed as fast as his mail allowed. Towards the top his weight carried the ladder through its final arc with such rapidity that the upper end crashed against the ramparts with a shudder and William leapt down amid the enemy. Most were still distractedly taking pot-shots at their sitting duck who by now hung like St Sebastian, pierced by arrows, 'like a hedgehog,' as John de Earley afterwards observed. As they realised a large knight had suddenly appeared in their midst they turned on William who, kicking the nearest man aside, lugged out his sword.

With wide-sweeps of his weapon, William swiftly cut down the unarmoured and astonished bowmen. He was too quick and too close for them to use their bows and only a few had the opportunity to draw their knives so that, within a minute, William had cleared the vicinity of the head of the ladder and was receiving the support of his followers. De Earley and John Marshal were soon beside him as the castellan and a party of armed knights came running towards them and a furious mêlée took place. As William and his followers continued to keep the defenders at bay and a portion of the ramparts clear, other scaling ladders appeared and more and more of the Angevins were coming over the top of the stonework.

Now out of breath, William was confronted by an approaching knight running towards him. William hefted his sword and took a mighty swing at the knight's head; he felt his sword blade bite as it cut through helm and the mail coif beneath. The man fell with a clatter and William looked about him. His men had almost cleared the ramparts and were already forcing their way down the steps leading up to them. Winded by the fury of his exertions, William sat down upon the body of the fallen knight who still lived and caught his belabouring breath. It was there that John de Earley found him ten minutes later.

'The place is ours, my Lord,' he said simply, bending to wipe the gore from the blade of his sword on the fallen Castellan's surtout before sheathing it. With a tired gesture William held up his own weapon and a grinning De Earley did the same for his master.

'I am grown too old for such adventures, John,' he remarked.

'It should have been Count John who led such a bold assault, my Lord Marshal.'

William chuckled, 'I do not think he has it in him,' he replied.

'No,' responded De Earley, laughing. 'We had better open the gate that he may ride in like a conqueror.'

'Aye,' said William, getting to his feet with a groan. 'Who is this fellow?' he asked, looking down at his still breathing opponent.

'He wears the device of Guillaume de Monceaux, my Lord, the Constable of this place,' De Earley informed him.

'Well, you shall have the ransoming of him John.'

When he heard of it, King Richard upbraided William for reviving the faltering assault on Milli-sur-Thérain. 'A knight of such eminence and my field commander should not expose himself, my Lord Marshal. It deprives the younger men of an opportunity to gain prowess.'

'The younger man who was your commander in the field,' William said pointedly, 'was for giving up, my Liege, as for my being a man of eminence, you speak of one who was an Earl, not a mere Banneret.'

Richard looked at him sharply, then smote his thigh and broke into a laugh. 'We'll see, Marshal, we'll see…'

But Richard had other priorities, both for himself and William. Having secured the south by a marriage of his younger sister Joanne to the Count of Toulouse, Richard sought an alliance with Count Baldwin IX of Flanders, and sent William as part of the delegation to seek this. William had known the new Count's father and had received fiefs at St Omer until they had been lost to Philippe, so he had an interest in suborning Baldwin from his traditional alliance with the French King. Accompanied by John Marshal, among others, and laden with gifts and the promise of money, William and his fellow negotiators succeeded in prising Baldwin from the French King's side.

***

The campaigning of that year of 1197 sputtered out as the contending forces retired into winter quarters. Richard had almost completely recovered the lands lost by John, but from Rouen he eyed the portion of the Norman Vexin that remained in Philippe's hands and urged on the works at Chateau Galliard and Les Anderlys. If the Vexin gnawed at the King's bowels, the year ended with one distinct feather in Richard's cap when he was released from his oath of allegiance to the Holy Roman Emperor by Heinrich as he lay upon his death-bed.

'England is mine again,' he confided to William, betraying the underlying anxiety he had borne, and of which he knew William had disapproved.

'I am right glad to know that, my Liege.'

Both William and the King rode frequently along the banks of the Seine and the building of the new castle rose above its rock, pushing the construction through the winter months so that, by the opening of the campaigning season of the new year the place should be finished, though the cost at twelve thousand pounds was staggering. As the King inspected the building, William encouraged the small force of mounted knights and sergeants-at-arms who covered the rising ramparts from any raid by Philippe's forces.

'So, my Lord Marshal,' Richard said, addressing the problem of the coming campaign as they returned to Rouen after one such review, 'you know our problem well enough.'

'Aye, my Liege, Gisors.'

Richard nodded. 'Gisors. A mighty enough fortress, which would not trouble me other than that it is too easily relieved if we lay siege to it, so, we move all our might into the armed camp at Les Anderlys which will be admirably covered by Chateau Galliard and from there move small columns into the Norman Vexin gradually isolating all Philippe's posts therein.'

'A war of encroachment,' William responded.

'Aye, and if we prove successful then every minor fortress in the Vexin will be isolated and eventually capitulate, and if Philippe sends out a mighty chevauchée…'

'We simply retire into the fastness at Les Anderlys and Galliard, then sally and strike at his over-extended lines and cut him off.'

Richard laughed. 'We are of one mind.'

'Why should we not be?' William asked, smiling.

In the campaign which followed Richard's war-host ravaged the land, terrified the peasantry and finally met Philippe in open battle near Gisors. Fought near a crossing of the River Epte the fighting was furious, Richard rode unattended into the mass of French chivalry and engaged, unseated and captured three knights. William was not present at the battle of Gisors, Richard having left him and his household at Chateau Galliard to cover his rear, but Philippe's army was completely routed and flung back over the Epte, the bridge over which collapsed under the weight of fleeing and panic-stricken men. Afterwards Richard, having recovered the Vexin, boasted that he had made Philippe 'drink the waters of the Epte,' but complete though his victory over the French King was, the King was not left to enjoy his triumph.

The death of Pope Celestine III was followed by the installation of Innocent III who took up his predecessor's plea for a new crusade. Archbishop Hubert FitzWalter crossed to Rouen, leaving the government of England in the hands of a sole Jusiticiar, William's old friend Geoffrey FitzPeter.

FitzWalter negotiated yet another truce, ostensibly for five years, between Richard and Philippe but the confirmation of Richard as Lord of all his father's lands was swiftly disrupted by news of a rebellion in the Limousin where Viscount Aimery of Limoges, having concluded a secret treaty with the ever devious Philippe, repudiated Richard as his overlord. The young nobleman had been stirred-up by Bertran de Born, 'a vile treasonous troubadour who cloaks his intrigues in honey words and would kill his mother for her jewels,' Richard complained.

'I know him of old, My Liege. A treacherous bastard to be sure, and one whom I should have best sent to his death long since.

'God's strewth, Marshal,' Richard snarled as he outlined his plan to deal with Aimery, 'it seems I must put Aimery in his grave ere I can sit down to meat and drink, let alone set the Holy Places free of the infidel. I must and shall leave you here, in Normandy, for I do not trust that fox in Paris, while I, by the Holy Rood, despatch this insolent upstart and devastate the bastard and his land with sword and fire.' Richard rose and William stood aside as he moved to leave his chamber. Then Richard turned and indicated the desk, full of parchments. 'There are ducal pleas to be heard, here in

Rouen and at Vaudreuil; do you watch my rear and see to them. The clerks will assist you.'

The following morning William watched Richard ride south before turning to the duties of justice and administration that the King had left him with. He was disappointed not to accompany Richard as his trusted companion-in-arms, but sensed that Richard felt the discomfiting of Aimery of Limoges was no great matter while compelling William – whom Richard knew was illiterate – to some sort of administrative and judicial test, preparing him for the honour of an Earldom.

***

After years of warfare William found the Ducal court at Vaudreuil dull. He had a fair grasp of the Common Law as established by Henry Curtmantle and Richard's clerks did his reading for him, but the sheer volume of cases, many held over during the vacillations of open warfare endured by rich and poor alike, made his task a heavy one.

Heavy cloud-banks drew a curtain of premature darkness over the city one afternoon in late March 1199 as William sat in judgement in the great hall. Outside a rising wind presaged rain and the doors had been fast shut so that, although not late, candles had been lit and torches set in the sconces. The atmosphere had grown soporific, heated by the clerks setting out their cases and three hours had been spent on a land-dispute before William had the easier duty of condemning three men to death for stealing livestock. The preliminary arguments for the next case were in progress when the door to the great hall flew open and a gust of wind swept across the clerks' tables, lifting documents and scattering them, to the scrambling consternation and indignation of the black-clad law-officers.

One had been whispering a brief of the plea into William's ear when he looked up at the disturbance. Two knights, in both coifs and coats of mail, strode into the hall and advanced directly towards William on his elevated chair.

'My Lord Marshal...'

The two men dropped on one knee and handed William a rolled and sealed document which he immediately passed to his confidential clerk and bid the two men to rise.

'What means this intrusion?' William asked.

'The King, my Lord, is grievously wounded,' one of the knights said, getting to his feet.
 William was shocked. Ordering the court cleared and all cases and pleas suspended, William withdrew with the knights and his clerk, who bore the written message. When the four of them were alone, William asked: 'How and where did this happen?'

'At Chaluz, my Lord. The castle was within a day of falling to our arms and His Grace went out to reconnoitre prior to making a final assault when a cross-bowman spotted him...'

'Was he armoured?' William broke in.

'No, my Lord, not beyond his light coat of mail and with but one companion...'

'God's blood,' snarled William, grinding his teeth with fury at Richard's stupidity.

'It was dusk, my Lord,' the knight explained, seeing William's suppressed fury.

'Go on,' William growled.

The arbalestrier aimed his quarrel well and it drove deep into the King's left shoulder. Though the head has been extracted, the wound is thought be poisoned and like to mortify…'

'Christ Jesu,' whispered William rising to his feet and going to the casement where he crossed himself, the thoughts tumbling about in his head. A heavy silence hung in the room then William asked of the clerk, 'what does the letter say?'

The clerk cleared his throat. 'That it is the King's will that you return to Rouen and secure the city and his treasury there, My Lord.'

'Aye, aye…' said William nodding, thinking fast. Then turning to the two knights he asked, 'the Queen Eleanor is at Fontevrault, has word been sent to her?'

'Aye, my Lord. She is called to the King's side.'

William nodded again. 'Very well. You shall have meat and wine and a bed this night, then, upon the morrow, I would have you return to Chaluz and from there keep me informed.' He turned to his clerk. 'We ride for Rouen at once, round-up your fellows and send John de Earley to me.'

With his mesnie and household William was at Rouen the following night and here he told only Archbishop FitzWalter of the King's plight. For days they waited, preserving to all outward appearances an air of normality, though their private discussions were all about the succession and the uncertainties and likely disaster that would befall the Angevins should Richard's wound prove fatal. Day followed day then, one evening in mid-April, as William prepared to retire for the night, the news that he had most feared arrived by the hand of the same brace of knights whom he had seen at Vaudrueil.

'The Lionheart is dead, my Lord.'

Crossing himself, William drew on his discarded leggings, put on his shoes and wrapped his cloak about him. Ten minutes later he was at the door of the Archbishop's lodgings demanding to see FitzWalter. William's face told the Archbishop all he needed to know and William handed the parchment brought by the knights to FitzWalter for him to read.

FitzWalter sat and scanned it in silence then set it down and called for wine, looking up at William. 'Do you sit, my Lord Marshal. You do not know what is herein?' William shook his head. 'He named Count John his successor,' FitzWalter said, shaking his head.

All the worst features of the two men's arguments of the previous days now confronted them.

'You were right in your supposition, William,' FitzWalter said sorrowfully. 'So shall you cleave to Richard's instruction or do what seems better for the Kingdom?'

'How say you, Geoffrey?' William countered.

'As I have repeatedly reasoned, the argument for Arthur as son of Count John's older brother is strong…'

'Maybe for Normandy, Aquitaine and the rest, but even so he is but a boy and will succumb to Philippe. As for England he will prove useless and an untrammelled, un-enfiefed England is to whence we must look. There lies your See, Walter, and all your influence and power.'

'But you William could stand Guardian or Regent for the boy Arthur,' FitzWalter suggested.

William scoffed. 'I am past fifty summers, Geoffrey.

Besides, I would be seen by those whose claim on such a position is far greater than mine by blood, office and title as an upstart, even perhaps a pretender to the Crown, a usurper... No, it must be John, John with my support as long as I may render it.'

FitzWalter sighed and for a few moments seemed plunged in deep thought. William waited patiently, aware that FitzWalter's decision was crucial, that the influence he commanded and could bring to bear upon the opinion of the Barons of England, who had no love for John, would be critical. Eventually the Archbishop looked up and nodded. 'Very well, William, but I must warn you that you will never come to regret anything you ever did as much as what you are doing now'.

'I have no alternative,' William replied grimly. 'Loyalty binds me.'

'To John then,' the Archbishop said, raising his wine-cup. 'And may he be wisely governed and govern wisely.'

'Amen to that at least.'

PART THREE: JOHN LACKLAND 1199 - 1205

CHAPTER ELEVEN: THE KING'S CLOAK 1199 - 1202

'My Lord Archbishop…Marshal…'

John slumped in his chair, his left hand clasped about the stem of a silver goblet. FitzWalter made his obeisance, followed by William, who – displeased with John's demeanour – was further repulsed by the nails of the man's right hand: they were bitten to the quick. The formalities disposed of, John came to the point:

'You have secured England, eh?'

'We have obtained a sufficient promise of fealty as warrants you crossing the Channel, Your Grace,' FitzHubert said smoothly, 'but Your Grace is not popular…'

'Pah!' John waved the Archbishop's concern aside. 'I have an army and the treasury here, at Rouen,' he added with a satisfied expression, as though increasing the pay of his late brother's mercenary routiers and seizing Richard's war-chests at Chinon was the answer to everything.

'And,' said FitzWalter, summoning assistance with a glance at William, 'we understand that, although no opposition was raised to that, Your Grace, the Barons of Touraine, Anjou and Maine are already in league with those of Brittany in supporting Geoffrey's boy, Arthur.'

'By the Christ!' snapped John, suddenly sitting upright, 'do you brook my claim to the Crown, Archbishop?' By God's bones I shall…'

'Do not make the mistake that your father made, my Lord,' said William, speaking for the first time. John was nineteen years his junior and unprepossessing with it. Moreover, during the exchange between him and FitzWalter, William had suffered a profound sense of weariness. In referring to Henry Curtmantle's ill-judged remark that had caused the death of Archbishop Becket, he had subconsciously avoided the form of address John might have felt himself entitled to expect; nor had William's tone been conciliatory.

'Who ever said my father made a mistake,' sneered John, half-smiling at his own wit but deceiving no-one: he stood in awe of the Marshal for his prowess as much as the Archbishop for his intelligence.

John sat back in his chair and began chewing the nails of his right hand. 'But you *have* secured England?' he asked again, betraying his anxiety no less than the value he placed upon the services and influence of the two men before him.

'Aye, Your Grace. At Nottingham we proclaimed you rightful King as named successor of Richard, as son of Henry, the Second of that name, and grandson of the Empress Matilda and Count Geoffrey of Anjou. A promise of fealty was forthcoming from most of the Barons...'

'Most?'

'Most,' said William. 'Those that were not attending to the defences of their castles.'

'Hell's teeth!' John swore.

'But I think that you may safely pass over the sea into England, Your Grace,' added FitzWalter in the honeyed tones of the real diplomat. 'You already wear the Ducal coronet of Normandy,' he pointed out, John having wasted no time in appearing in Rouen cathedral where he had assumed the Dukedom. 'As for the rest,' FitzWalter went on, referring to the rebellion said to have broken out to the south and west, 'you must, I fear leave all to chance until after your coronation at Westminster.'

John nodded. The brief weeks FitzWalter and William had spent in England soliciting sufficient support for John had been exhausting and neither wanted to be delayed by the resumption of a war over the Angevin provinces.

'Howsoever, there is one thing, Your Grace, that must be dealt with first,' FitzWalter said, and William wondered what required any further priority than to get this idle, pleasure-seeking and heartless youth off his arse and invested with the trappings of kingship. Whatever it was, it went beyond the points he and FitzWalter had agreed upon.

'You have great need of the Marshal's services, the Archbishop went on. 'He has made conspicuous his loyalty to you as his liege lord for his Irish lands in the face of Richard's claim to unreserved homage. It is necessary that you recompense him...'

Both John and William were staring at the Archbishop, the former quizzically, the latter with astonishment. It was John who blinked first.

'What would you have me do, Archbishop?'

'An Earldom for those lands he has by way of his wife, Isabelle de Clare, daughter of Strongbow, and further lands direct from your own hand.'

'Have *you* instigated this?' John asked William, his

tone sharply vicious. 'is that your price for your *loyalty*?'

'No, Your Grace,' William responded, genuinely surprised and quickly turning over in his mind how such an honour as was now in John's gift might compromise him if things ran ill.

'The Marshal must have authority before you cross the sea, Your Grace,' FitzWalter explained reasonably, 'otherwise he will be challenged by all those opposed to you.'

John curled his lip and responded, looking from one to the other. 'Do you not think they will see this as my buying favours? If my kingship is in doubt, will that not invalidate such entitlement that the Marshal achieves from my hand, eh?'

'Not at all. The late King, your brother, was minded to elevate the Marshal in regard of his wife's lands. I can swear to that, Your Grace, and like Richard's choice of you as his heir, it is deserving of respect and may be presented thus.'

John suddenly chuckled. 'You churchmen are devious. Richard never made any such declaration in my hearing.'

'What of, Your Grace, your right to succeed him, or of the Marshal to be belted an Earl?'

John looked shocked. 'You mean…?'

'I mean, Your Grace,' FitzWalter ran on soothingly, 'that if you require the one to be confirmed on oath, then the other must follow.'

John again looked from FitzWalter to William and back again and both men saw the same calculating train of thought. Without such powerful allies bound to his cause, John knew very well, all support might fall away at the first sign of trouble.

'But I have Wolfscar and his mercenaries,' John responded after pondering matters for a moment, referring to the leader of his routiers others called Lupescar.

'True, Your Grace,' smiled Fitzwalter, 'just as long as you have money, but I submit that Your Grace needs to look beyond the immediate…'

John blew out his cheeks in submission. FitzWalter was right, of course, and he knew it. There was no point in protesting further. Besides, to alienate the Marshal would be a stupid thing to do and John knew he needed allies and friends, the more powerful and the more bound to him the better. He nodded.

'Very well, my Lords, it shall be so…'

'And lest you forget in the haste of departure, you shall attest to it now, before we depart from this place. I have a patent…'

'You would command me, Archbishop?' John said, leaning forward, an unpleasant look upon his face.

'Aye, Your Grace, I command thee as I would command thee to confess your sins.'

'But this is a temporal matter…'

'Which Holy Church most devoutly desires, my Lord King,' FitzWalter said tellingly. John sighed and called for goose-feather and ink, whereupon the Archbishop made his obeisance and withdrew. William followed him outside the chamber where FitzWalter made off at high speed with William following. Once out of the immediate ears of any sycophantic and self-serving courtier, the Archbishop slowed and William fell into step.

'By God, Hubert, but you have bound me hand and foot to him now.'

FitzWalter stopped abruptly and turned to William. 'It is the only way, William. Once you had made to me your declaration of support for John, I could see no other way. All the weeks we were in England proclaiming John as rightful successor I was troubled by a lack of authority, not for my own part, but for yours. The English dogs will tear you apart when that foolish turd reveals his true nature and Philippe begins playing his games, yet I see no other solution for England's peace now that John has been proclaimed... Besides, few will object to your assumption of the title in regard of your wife's lands; you are already Lord of Striguil. Let John rule well for a year and grant you more lands in the Welsh March and you will leave something for your sons.'

'I do not know whether to thank or curse you...'

'Do not concern yourself with me,' remarked FitzWalter over his shoulder as he resumed the brisk walk to his lodgings. 'To be sure, you will curse yourself often enough. Now do you get John de Earley over the sea and rouse Geoffrey FitzPeter. I shall have a despatch for him within the hour, then you and I shall dine together, for I do not think His Grace is likely to invite us to sup with him this night.'

***

Out of cunning, malice and a further binding of William to his person, before he and his retinue left Dieppe for Shoreham, John informed William that he would invest him with the Earldom, but with-hold the actual grant of the Pembrokeshire lands which Richard

Strongbow had lost to Henry Curtmantle in the settlement ending the Anarchy. True, there was a promise to restore these estates to the fiefdom in due course, but in terms of revenues enabling William to support his new status, little had changed.

Nevertheless, William had reason to be pleased and wished Robert de Salignac had lived to know of his rise, for he was, at long last, incrementally increasing his power. During his foray into England with Archbishop FitzWalter and the grand colloquy they had held at Nottingham Castle to obtain promises of fealty to John should he cross the Channel, although many of the Barons had declined to attend, those that did formed a powerful caucus. They had included Ranulf, Earl of Chester, Richard, Earl of Clare and David, brother to William I of Scotland.

Although William had moved in such circles before, he had never done so as an equal, only as a military leader whose skills were acknowledged to be essential. Now, however, he was able to more closely integrate, binding others to him as John bound William to himself. It was one thing to take up his elder brother's bastard, John Marshal, and add him to his own mesnie, but quite another to augment his authority by association with other powerful men and, best of all, if such men had had a chequered rise through prowess rather than land and birth. William Longsword was the new King's half-brother, a bastard of Henry Curtmantle, who, by betrothal to the little Lady Ela, the six-year old daughter of William Marshal's dead cousin, the Earl of Salisbury, assumed the title of Ela's father. A companion-in-arms of the Lionheart and William, the new Earl of Salisbury had an enviable military reputation of his own. Linked by birth to the King and by marriage to William, Longsword was a natural and unequivocal member of the loyalist party, and drew closer to William for all these reasons.

If he was apprehensive about the fulfilment of John's promise of land, once crowned, John could not go back on his undertaking to invest William as Earl of Pembroke. On 27th May 1199, in Edward the Confessor's great abbey church of St Peter at Westminster, the assembled Barony of England heard Archbishop FitzWalter declare John, Duke of Normandy, the legitimate King of England. John's right rested on lineage and - FitzWalter asserted with great cunning and referring to an ancient form of elective kingship – had been chosen by the chief noblemen of the land at the great Council held at Nottingham. In short, FitzWalter stressed, His Grace possessed all the regal qualities enjoyed by his late, great brother, at which declaration there was a good deal of foot shuffling and exchanges of glances, though the ceremony passed without obvious dissent.

The chief Barons having done homage to the new monarch, William Marshal and Geoffrey FitzPeter were called forth, girded with belts and swords and declared the Earls of Pembroke and Essex respectively. Thereafter they too did homage. That evening at the great banquet William Marshal and Geoffrey FitzPeter attended the King, serving him his meat as befitted their new status.

The Lady Isabelle and her two eldest boys attended both the coronation and the banquet and in bed that night

Isabelle mused upon the ironies inherent in the day.

'I can see no resemblance to the Lionheart in the new King,' she remarked, laying her head on William's breast. 'The Archbishop has a ready tongue and employs it in his cheek to good effect, do you not think?'

In high good humour William chuckled his agreement. 'Aye, and has been made Chancellor for his pains.'

'And FitzPeter makes a goodish Earl, though he is no knight and will have to pay scutage. Still he has had the usage of the Earldom of Essex for long enough while you, husband, get the title with no land.'

'Not yet. The King promises it…'

'Like Richard promised the Earldom that is yours as readily as Longsword got his by his mere *betrothal* to little Ela.' Isabelle uttered the word scathingly. 'Besides, William, the Pembrokeshire lands were my father's…'

'I know, my sweet Lady, but if we wait we shall get them back for our boys.'

It was Isabelle's turn to chuckle as she snuggled down, her own shoulder in William's great arm-pit. 'Ah, yes,' she said, 'our dear sweet boys. God grant them long life.' She paused, then raised her head to add, 'but you, William, along with Hubert FitzPeter, William Longsword and Geoffrey FitzHubert have become the King's cloak. For God's sake avoid being torn off in the thorns of this life.'

Soon afterwards the Lady Isabelle lay asleep in her husband's arms while he lay awake, staring into the darkness, her words of caution still in his ears.

***

'There Messieurs,' King John asked, looking around the Council board, 'do you not think that I have done well?'

There was an awkward silence. It was the end of May 1200 and John had been on the throne for a year, a year of turbulence and upheaval in the Angevin lands but that month the King had signed a two-year truce, the Treaty of Le Goulet, with Philippe of France in which, according to his own lights at least, John had secured his continental lands.

John blew out his cheeks, called for wine and asked, prompting some reaction, 'well, my Lords, has my diplomacy struck you all dumb?'

No-one wished to broach the subject of the King's diplomacy; it was short-term, stupid and answered nothing. But the last year had given rise among the Barons, particularly those in England, to the exposure of the King's essential weaknesses. Apart from his emerging moral turpitude, which could be tolerated as long as he sought his pleasures among his inferiors, his lack of judgement and unreliability combined with his vindictiveness when thwarted, to render opposition to him useless – or exceedingly dangerous. With John showing a disturbing interest in the wives and marriageable daughters of the nobility, he was rendering land-holders nervous. William, now at last granted the estates of Strongbow in Pembrokeshire and having had the Shrievalty of Gloucester restored to him, knew that John could – and would – strip him of all of it upon a whim if crossed.

'My Lord Chancellor?' John goaded. 'You were part architect of our accommodation with our cousin Philippe...'

'Indeed, my Liege,' FitzPeter observed cautiously,

'but I think the treaty flawed. To render homage to Philippe for your lands over the sea, as your father and brother did, is one thing; easy to repudiate if an infringement is precipitated by the other party. But to pay a sum of twenty thousand marks is an act of submission that any breaking thereof will detract from the lustre of your name.'

'But we have settled the question of Arthur,' John insisted, betraying his continuing anxiety over his right to the English Crown. 'He holds Brittany under me…' he cast about for some analogy, 'just as the Marshal did homage for Leinster to me and not directly to Richard.' John sat back with an air of satisfaction and took up his constantly refilled wine-cup.

'All this is at the expense of Evreux and part of the Vexin,' William pointed out. Having been directly implicated in the debate William now spoke out. 'And at the collapse of our long-standing alliance with Flanders which I…'

'Yes, yes, Marshal,' snapped John testily, 'which you negotiated three…four years ago.' John waved the concern airily aside.

'And, my Liege, the clause of betrothal of your niece, Blanche of Castile, to Philippe's son Louis may prove problematical.'

'Pah!' John retorted. 'My mother approved. Indeed my mother crossed the Pyrenees to bring Blanche into Aquitaine, having settled the Lusignan question by granting Hugh de Luisgnan the County of La Marche…'

John finished his wine and dismissed the Council, leaving the chamber followed by two wolf-hounds. In his wake the Councillors rose, broke up into small groups and discussed the pass to which matters had so speedily come.

'I was about to say that I deplored the loss of the Flemish alliance as I have land at Longueville,' protested William in an unusually peevish explosion, 'and the region will be mine to defend should the Count of Flanders decide to invade.'

'As he most certainly will, once Philippe is ready,' added FitzPeter. 'As for bringing Queen Eleanor's initiative into it,' the Chancellor shrugged, 'what man – let alone a King - seeks his mother's approval?'

'This one does,' growled William in a low voice. 'I also hear rumours that, having had his marriage to Isabella of Gloucester annulled, he intends to seek the hand of Isabelle of Angoulême.'

'But she is no more than a child!' exclaimed FitzPeter, ' of what? Ten or twelve years of age?'

'For the love of God, is this lechery or diplomacy?' asked FitzWalter.

'If it is true it is trouble, for I suspect the diplomacy is all Philippe's' added William. 'The girl has been promised to Hugh de Lusignan and that hornet's nest will not take the matter without reaction.'

'Which is *exactly* what Philippe wants,' snapped FitzWalter.

'Should they marry,' said William with an air of resignation, 'we shall have been entrapped.'

And upon William's opinion the four men remaining in the Council chamber dispersed with an air of something like despair.

***

William looked up at the young man before him in his

lodgings in London. All about him were preparations for departure: packed chests of arms, clothing and money littered the inn-room and from the yard below came the shouts of William's retinue and retainers, the clatter of movement and the quiet snickering of horses, palfreys and roncins, all making ready for the journey west. In the corner of the room, at a small table sat William's confidential clerk, one Thomas; he was busy with pen and ink, possessed of an air of urgency. About the table, dressed in travelling clothes, their cloaks about their shoulders as if for imminent departure, sat the senior knights of William's mesnie: William Waleran, Geoffrey FitzRobert, the young John Marshal and the ever-present John de Earley. All now regarded the latest recruit to their number, Jordan de Sauqueville.

William smiled up at him. The younger man was unfamiliar with England and made no secret of his desire to return to Normandy whither William was sending him with his blessing.

'You will proceed first to Longueville and then Meleurs. Ensure they are brought forward into a state of preparedness for war. I would this were accomplished with some discretion and a lack of show, but whatsoever of the defences need attention, put it in hand. Then you should repair to Arques, a place you know well and a place the significance you know well of too, for it stands guard over the valley of the Béthune and thus marks the frontier of my Norman lands.' William spelt out the responsibility he was laying upon the young Norman knight, emphasising the personal importance of the castle of Arques to his Lord's fortune.

'I understand, my Lord,' De Sauqueville

acknowledged.

'Have you the commission ready?' William asked of his clerk and Thomas rose, bringing the document along with wax and candle. William fished for the small and modest seal he had had made when first a knight banneret and which he clung to out of sentimentality and superstition, fearing that to have a new and ostentatious seal bearing his title as Earl, might provoke fate and the King too much. Thomas dripped the hot wax and William pressed the seal into it, giving the sealed document to De Sauqueville.

'Here is your authority, Sieur Jordan. God go with you,' he said as his knights mumbled agreement and all there crossed themselves. De Sauqueville made his obeisance and left the room.

When he had gone William addressed the remaining knights. 'Well, messieurs, to Striguil. Then Pembroke and Leinster.'

They rose as one and clattered down into the inn-yard as Thomas supervised the last of the chests secured to the pack-horses. The mesnie mounted up, leaving Thomas to settle affairs with the landlord, and led by De Earley they took the road to the west, towards the Welsh March and, beyond the Western Sea, Ireland.

***

'Are you happy, husband?' Isabelle asked as they walked, hand-in-hand through the woods above the Wye in a rare moment of marital peace.

William blew his cheeks out and, after a moment replied. 'It is not a question I feel I can ask myself, Isabelle. My life has too much of the uncertain in it to qualify for happiness, methinks. How is it with you?'

She looked up at him. 'I could have married worse,' she said, her green eyes sparkling.

Looking down at her upturned face, William stopped and said, 'I think that I am happy *now*.' They kissed, then continued their walk. He was thinking of his mother and her own husband, John, and the Marshal's awful, scarred visage. For the first time in his life he wondered if the Lady Sybil had even been happy. Squeezing Isabelle's hand he added, 'yes, I am truly happy now.'

Isabelle laughed. 'And I am pleased we have my father's lands back. There will be something better for the boys than empty lives in fear of the caprice of this dreadful King.'

'Have a care what you say about John, my Lady,' William growled. 'Whatever you think of him, think it privily and remember that though you consider the lands I now hold as having been your father's, he held them from Henry and, just as Henry had taken them back, the son can do the same again.'

'I know. But what about the lands in Ireland? The King would have trouble wresting them from you should you decide to hold them…'

'What? In defiance of him?' William asked with mild astonishment.

'Yes, should it become necessary,' Isabelle retorted quickly.

'I forget sometimes that you are Strongbow's daughter,' he chuckled.

'And that my mother was Aoife, daughter of Dermot MacMurrough, King of Leinster,' she added sharply, stepping slightly aside, so that, hands clasped, their arms swung between them.

'Well, my love, we shall shortly see what effect the name of the daughter of King Dermot has upon the unruly inhabitants of Leinster,' William bantered, 'for I would that you accompany me thither when I go thence.'

'I had no intention of allowing you to go without me,' Isabelle riposted with a smile.

William laughed. 'I knew that,' he said, then lowered his voice and drew her close to his side 'but to a more serious matter, Isabelle. If, as you surmise, life under John becomes intolerable, a retreat into Leinster may become indispensible. Since neither you nor I can stay there for long until at least such a moment occurs, whom do you think we should appoint our seneschal?'

'Geoffrey FitzRobert, William,' Isabelle replied without a moment's hesitation. 'He has been loyal to you and I think he would find my half-sister Basilia warmed his bed to a nicety.'

'God's blood, Isabelle, you plot like the most seasoned courtier!' William said admiringly. 'But it is a good and expedient notion; would the lady oblige?'

Isabelle laughed ironically. 'A lord's male bastards can usually find some useful matter with which to occupy their lives. Their female equivalents,' she explained, 'find such things less easy. Besides, she lies in your gift.'

'Neither fact had ever occurred to me,' William said ruminatively.

'No,' said Isabelle with more than a hint of sarcasm, 'more's the pity such thoughts rarely occupy a man's mind.'

'Isabelle, you chide me!'

'Aye my Lord, I most certainly do.'

'Well then, it shall be so, if Geoffrey will have her.'

'Huh, she is not ill-looking. He would be a fool to turn her away.'

***

'I am at a loss to know whether this land is blessed or cursed,' William remarked as he sat his horse and looked down upon the shallow valley below him. His horse chinked at its bit and snorted its agreement.

Beside him Geoffrey FitzRobert grunted agreement.

'Methinks we are still at sea,' William grumbled on as the drenching rain fell unremittingly, reminding those with him of the fearfully stormy passage they had endured in crossing from Pembroke to Waterford.

The voyage had seemed interminable. Several of the horses had fallen and broken their legs, only to be killed of necessity thereafter. One of their men-at-arms had been washed overboard one dark night and all but the seamen and mariners had been prostrated by sea-sickness. The cold and the damp had affected William's people too, and several had remarked on the contrast with a storm in the Mediterranean, which those who had been to Outremer knew better.

With no experience of warmer seas, the master of the chartered ship in which William had embarked had explained that it was one thing to cross the Channel between Normandy and England where a westerly wind blew upon the beam of one's ship, and thus aided its passage. A voyage from Wales to Ireland was, the fellow said, a very different matter, for the wind, prevailing as it was from the west, was a headwind, necessitating delays and a prolonged journey as they struggled to windward, casting first this way, and then that, hoping for a slight shift to give them an advantage. In fact, the ship-master had declared, with a good deal of satisfaction that William and his knights found hard to comprehend, they had done well to fetch Waterford!

'My Lord,' the man had almost laughed in William's face at one stage in the passage, when William had enquired how long the agony of vomiting upon an empty belly would go on and when they might expect to find some shelter from the land, 'If your Lordship chooses to venture afloat in the season of the spring gales, I fear you cannot escape such weather. However, I vow you will forget this discomfort soon. They say that upon putting to sea, you first fear dying but after a few days you long for it. Pity the poor mariner who must endure it for his life-long.'

'I fear that I am fast approaching that second state of mind, Master,' a pallid William had gulped, shouting the words above the shriek of the wind in the rigging supporting the vessel's solitary mast. Only a shred of sail appeared to be exposed from the heavy yard that crossed it, scare enough, in William's opinion, to wipe his arse upon. He had straightened up from the lee rail; at least they had all learned to spew downwind. 'Can you not ease my concerns as to how long we must yet tolerate this great upheaval?'

The ship-master had shrugged. 'My Lord, out here we are in the hands of God!'

William had drawn his cloak about him and hunkered down in the shelter of the bulwarks, vowing to thank God for all his mercies if they ever reached land again.

And now, a week after landing, this valley suddenly spoke to his soul. He had no idea why this green place beckoned with such a fierce compulsion, but it did and he could no more deny it than he could deny the birth-mark on his shoulder. As he sat hunched upon his palfrey a great curtain of rain swept across the landscape to suddenly ease and then cease. Through the dark and scudding clouds a sudden shaft of sunlight thrust itself, moving across an extended flood-plain, to set a sparkle upon a distant river before gradually fading. Then the rain began to fall again. Touched by superstition as he was, William realised that he must make good his vow and here seemed as good a place as any. If he had founded the religious house at Cartmel to intercede for the soul of his father, there must be yet one more, established here, on this spot, to thank God not only for his deliverance from the perils of the sea, but for his Earldom. And where better than here, where the numinous had suddenly over-whelmed him? Surely, if he endowed a religious house here, Almighty God would grant him security in the tenure of his great possessions? To act upon the impulse of faith was a good and knightly thing to do, he felt sure. And if it were to be a bulwark against the malice of King John, had he not given more years than most to the faithful service of the House of Anjou? He almost sensed old Nicholas de Sarum telling him so, whispering through the hissing of the downpour and the distance of the years.

He was growing used to the voices of ghosts these days; past fifty summers. life could not hold out many more years to him and it was seemly that here he might leave some mark of his true devotion. William had grown a fondness for the Wales of his old nurse, Angharad ap Gwyn, which he had come into as his just inheritance through Isabelle. There was something strangely compelling about these Celtic lands that he could not fathom, but he was touched by a singular *appropriateness* in his coming to Leinster to inspect his lands in Ireland. He was not a man of sufficient intellectual accomplishment to analyse this sentiment, but its power and its *rightness* was overwhelming. To William, who had spent most of his adult life in the Angevin provinces over the sea, where his military skills had been exclusively at the service of the faithless Angevins, the *otherness* of Leinster had a powerful and visceral appeal. He did not trouble himself to rationalise it, but it would be a fitting marker of his sojourn in Ireland to set-up a house of prayer and spiritual observance here, at the extremity of Christendom. If the country was blessed, then a new religious house could only add to its lustre; if cursed, it could only redeem it. Here too he might be buried, or remembered and prayed for after death.

'Here, I think,' he said, turning to Geoffrey FitzRobert.

'My Lord?' FitzRobert asked, uncomprehending.

'Here you will establish a religious house for me.'

FitzRobert said nothing. He nodded obediently, but showed no obvious enthusiasm for the task, far less than he had shown when being sworn-in as William's Seneschal for his lands in Leinster a few days earlier, and that had been little enough. The spring weather of April 1202 would have been pleasant in Striguil, FitzRobert thought; but here, under this lowering sky and pouring rain, it seemed as like being afloat as his master had jested. The prospect of being left in such a wet hell did not enchant Geoffrey FitzRobert. As for his being employed to build a church... He blew the rain off the extremity of his nose with a sudden despair.

'We shall name it Tintern Parva, Geoffrey,' William said firmly. 'I was much taken by the great Mother House above the Wye,' he added, having asked for God's blessing on his forthcoming voyage to Ireland at Tintern Abbey, going there with his Countess, Isabelle and their children, then walking through the hanging woods with his lady.

'Very well, my Lord,' FitzRobert acknowledged.

'You will do me great service here, Geoffrey,' William said quietly, crossing himself. FitzRobert nodded, unconvinced. He had other things on his mind and thought the Marshal should have too, not be diverting himself with Holy intentions; such things were for other men, men who could read and write, and sang songs of futile love to unattainable women who were usually no better than whores. FitzRobert had – at least until now - a healthy respect for the Marshal who disdained such foppish occupations. The Marshal was a man fitted for war and there had been disquieting rumours following them out of Wales for some days now. It was said that a ship had arrived in Cork from Brittany with news that King Philippe had invited Prince Arthur and his mother, the Lady Constance, to Paris where Philippe had knighted the young Prince. No-one aware that Arthur of Brittany owed his first allegiance to King John could be anything but troubled by the story, but it was unconfirmed and did not appear to originate from any source other than the waterfront at Brest.

William smiled at FitzRobert. 'We must go back to Waterford, Geoffrey. My Lady has there someone she intends to make you happy.'

'My Lord?' Two puzzles in one day was a little oppressive, but the drift of the Marshal's argument was not incomprehensible. 'You mean…?'

'Aye, Robert, 'tis time you were married and the Lady Basilia is half-sister to my wife.'

Laughing at FitzRobert, William kicked his horse into a canter, his half-pleased, half-annoyed Seneschal following.

Then, two days after William had decided to establish and endow a religious house at Tintern Parva and told FitzRobert of his future, a message came from the Castellan of Manorbier, in Pembrokeshire, one of William's new vassal Lords and a man who also held lands in Leinster. William lay at Waterford Castle, no great distance from the proposed site of his abbey and it was John De Earley who accompanied the messenger, tactfully on hand to read William the message.

'The King has married Isabelle de Angoulême, my Lord,' De Earley said, mouthing the words. 'My Lord of Essex is seeking your presence in London.'

'It seems marriage is much in the air these days,' remarked William. 'Very well, pass word that we shall remove shortly and do you find us a ship.'

De Earley grinned. 'Have you plans for me, my Lord?' he asked impudently.

'You'll know in good time,' William growled good-naturedly.

CHAPTER TWELVE: EARL OF PEMBROKE
1202

'Truly the man is spawned of the Devil!' Geoffrey FitzPeter, Earl of Essex, was furious. 'He marries Alice of France, then Isabella of Gloucester, throws both over leaving a festering sore with Pope Innocent as regards Alice, then snatches this poor wench, who can scarcely yet be bleeding, from the clutches of Hugh de Lusignan who promptly runs bleating to Philippe about betrayal and treachery – and a good man to do that, by God, for his family stinks in that regard...'

'By the Rood they do,' put in William contemptuously. His long-standing hatred of Hugh's uncle, Geoffrey de Lusignan, extended back many years to the death of his own uncle, Patrick, Earl of Salisbury, father of Longsword's betrothed.

'Well, of course,' FitzPeter went on, 'Philippe seizes upon the pretext to summon our great and glorious King to conference with him. John vacillates and finally refuses, leaving Philippe clear to declare John disobedient, taking away all right John has to any lands south of the Channel Sea. Philippe and Baldwin of Flanders are already on the move.'

William blew out his cheeks. 'This is the second time the bastard has lost everything,' William snarled, 'but now we have no Richard to recover them.'

FitzPeter looked at William. 'I fear you are our Richard now, William.'

William stared at FitzPeter. 'God's blood, Geoffrey, I am too old for campaigning!'

'There is no other, though there are those to support you: 'Longsword, for example, and I shall pay scutage to put men in the field under your standard...'

'And what of the King?'

'A hundred knights and their retinues to follow you into Normandy.'

'Those are his orders?'

'Aye, William. Those are his orders. And he goes thither himself.'

'Well that is something, I suppose. ' William paused, wondering if some well-directed quarrel might strike John as it had his brother and terminate the King's life only to realise that John's death, unlikely as it was in such circumstances, would cause more problems than it would solve. 'So I have no choice...'

'I think not.'

'I hope to Christ Jordan de Sauqueville has Arques in some state of preparedness,' William said ruminatively as his mind switched to the practical problems now confronting him. 'And that Philippe and Baldwin are delayed at Aumale or Eu...'

***

In May 1202 William was in Normandy with his own and the King's one hundred knights, sergeants-at-arms and a war-chest supplied by John. William Longsword, Earl of Salisbury rode at his side as they made for Arques. De Sauqueville had done his best, but there was more that could be achieved to strengthen the great fortress at Arques, and in a flurry of activity during June William dispersed huge sums of money in anticipation of an imminent attack. Everywhere he went now he ordered stone and stone-masons to enhance the more primitive castles of which he had tenure. He had left Isabelle augmenting the fortifications of Striguil and Pembroke, and the newly married FitzRobert was not only responsible for the Raising of an abbey at Tintern Parva, but raising stone castellations in Leinster.

But the border fortresses of Aumale, Eu and Neufchâtel-en-Bray had already fallen at Philippe's feet, surrendered at the French King's first thrust. Then, in July, word came that Gournay had capitulated and that Philippe and Baldwin had turned their war-host and its siege-engines north; their objective - Arques.

John, meanwhile, was at Rouen with a large war-host. A Council had been held there after the King and his military commanders had crossed over into Normandy and it had decided that the Earls of Pembroke and Salisbury should hold the east of the Duchy while the King, supported by William's old companion-in-arms at the escape of Henry Curtmantle from Le Mans, William Des Roches, contained any incursion by the Lusignans from the south or the Bretons from the West.

'The Queen, my Mother, is gone into the castle at Mirebeau,' John had confided to William, in a rare moment of confidentiality. Not for the first time was William perplexed by the conflicted character of the members of the House of Anjou: one moment blowing hot and intimate, the next cold with hatred. 'You must hold the north, Marshal,' the King insisted.

'I will do what I can, my Liege.'

Both William and Longsword knew their situation was weak, if not hopeless. No castle could endure a siege indefinitely and if – or when – Arques fell, then the whole of Normandy lay open to the invader. Nevertheless, as soon as news of the fall of Gournay reached him, William called a Council in the keep of Arques.

'Messieurs, I shall not deceive you. Our position is weak and Philippe's is strong. He is mobile, we are like to be mewed-up here, therefore I propose to divide our forces.' A murmur of shock went through the assembly. One or two made to intervene and challenge William.

'This is a Council, my Lord, you have yet to ask our opinion…'

'No,' countered William. 'And I cannot. I am charged with the King's will. To ask your opinion will invite an endless discussion…'

'But you have already said our forces are weak, a division only worsens our position.'

'I pray you, hear me out,' William pleaded as dissent caught on and voices were raised.

'God damn you! Listen to the Marshal!' roared William Longsword, quelling the incipient rebellion.

'You, William Mortimer,' William went on, referring to one of the King's senior knights, 'you shall hold this place as long as you can while the Earl of Salisbury and I maintain our forces to the westward. Arques will be invested and our presence somewhere other than here will not be known, for we shall give it out that we ride to join the King at Rouen. Once the siege lines are set, we shall launch a series of raids to discomfit the besiegers. Philippe has a history of not standing long at his post. If God favours our arms and the justice of our cause, we may wear him down such that he raises the siege. If he does not, we may have the opportunity of resupplying the garrison from time-to-time and thus prolonging the siege and detaining Philippe's host under the considerable walls of this fortress. With summer comes the sickness men get from drinking river water...' William left the sentence unfinished; they all knew what he meant: the flies and the endless shitting. 'Keep your men to their wells, Mortimer, and do not sally,' he concluded.

Mortimer acknowledged the good sense of William's strategy, by which time the Marshal's confident tone had cleared the doubts of most of the rough fellows who the King had sent to serve under him.

After all except Longsword and De Earley had gone to make their preparations for departure, William turned to Longsword and thanked him for his timely intervention. 'I am obliged to you,' he said with a tired smile. 'God knows we need his aid as much as he knows our cause is far from just,' he added ruefully.

'It is just insofar as Philippe has no right to act as he does,' responded Longsword.

'Aye.' William looked at his fellow Earl. 'Then let us ride out and lose ourselves in the countryside.' Longsword nodded, then De Earley caught William's eye. 'You would have words with us, John?'

'Aye my Lords. There is a man among the routiers who has given me an idea...'

'Go on.'

'Do you recall, my Lord Marshal, after we had taken Nottingham Castle, King Richard rode out into Sherwood forest?'

'Aye. He went hunting, if I recall aright.'

'And there was talk of a band of ne'er-do-wells who robbed travellers and hid deep in the forest glades?'

'Exactly what I intend for us in the coming days, but what has your man to do with our present situation?'

'This routier, in his cups, claims to have been among this band and I heard him boasting of some exploit using a ruse that, upon close enquiry, and a little pressure,' De Earley smiled and touched his dagger hilt, 'he confessed was no lie, though one might have hanged him for it, but which set my mind a-thinking.'

'Tell us, John.'

When De Earley had finished, William looked at Longsword, who nodded his approval and William asked: 'A week, you say?'

'Aye, my Lord. No more.'

'And you would go with this fellow?'

De Earley nodded. 'To ensure he does not betray us.'

'And what is his name?'

'He calls himself Red William,' my Lord, on account of his ginger hair.'

William thought for a moment and then nodded. 'Very well. But you must take care John. God go with you.' And the three men crossed themselves before De Earley withdrew.

'A week,' mused William. 'That should give Philippe's men time to have settled into their siege lines…'

***

It was raining when they set out on that first chevauchée against Philippe's siege lines surrounding Arques, not the torrential downpour of Leinster, but wet enough to depress an army sat down outside the grim walls of a fortress such as confronted the French and Flemish war-host on the banks of the River Bèthune.

Having withdrawn well to the westward, William and Longsword first concealed their force in a small *manoir* whose occupants they held in respectful self-keeping until John de Earley and his accomplice returned. Disguised as a pair of mendicant clerks the two men had pretended to offer letter-writing and other services to the men of Philippe's war-host, mixing among the inevitable hangers-on: camp-followers, whores, quacks and hucksters. In this way they had walked the entire circuit of the siege lines without let or hindrance, withdrawing under cover of night to rejoin William within the allotted sennight.

Having been briefed by De Earley, all but the foot-soldiers had been roused out and prepared for the chevauchée, moving off in three parties making their way south and then east, to cross the road that ran along the left bank of the river, whither the French army had come from Neufchâtel-en-Bray. The smallest of the three divisions, under De Earley, consisted of two wagons requisitioned from the *manoir* and laden with supplies, including forage, cider and grain. A third wagon bore live sheep, and all three wagons were accompanied by a small escort of mounted sergeants-at-arms and some knights devoid of their armour, but dressed like routiers in leather hauberks. The other two parties, one commanded by William, the other by Longsword, comprised their own household knights and greater retinues, including a number of mounted archers, a striking force at the head of which William now sat his horse in the mizzling rain and awaited the first light of dawn.

They had broken the last camp of their circuitous march at about three that morning. Few had slept much that damp night and all were eager to be at their work as the column mounted-up in the darkness and silently made their way towards their objective.

William stilled his destrier as it snickered at the approach of another and Longsword appeared beside him.

'You can just make out the castle,' William said quietly, pointing. Longsword peered through the trees and the drizzle and caught the loom of the great fortress upon which, it was said, William had spent over fifteen hundred pounds in recent improvements.

'We must wait until we can see the ground under our feet,' Longsword observed. 'It will be heavy going after this rain.'

'A matter of nice judgement,' offered William. 'I think we can be no more than a mile from the lines.'

The two men sat in silence for some minutes, then Longsword remarked, 'I think it time,' and William growled assent.

'Get De Earley on the move then,' William said, wheeling his destrier and moving aside as Longsword rode off and motioned De Earley to lead the supply train as if replenishing Philippe's besiegers. After giving De Earley's wagons a head start, without a word, William waved the remainder of the column forward. They cantered along, catching up with and then over-taking the wagons, William's division to the left and Longsword's to the right. As they main two divisions passed De Earley's wagons and their escort, the entire force picked up speed.

There was sufficient daylight now to see, below the ramparts of Arques, the extensive siege-lines and the engines and forces King Philippe and Count Baldwin had massed about the fortress. The pale pyramidal shapes of the pavilions of the chief chevaliers were interspersed with the plainer tents of lesser nobles and knights, while the rising smoke of cooking fires being relit after the night's rain laid a grey pall over the entire encampment as another tedious day began for the besiegers. The vague shapes of men, coughing in the smoke, and moving sleepily about, could now be made out.

But William had scant time to take in these details; his single focus was closing the distance before some shout of alarm or recognition went-up. If the enemy were deceived into thinking he led a column of support they would soon be disabused, so everything now hung upon his and Longsword's chivalry reaching the siege-lines as quickly as possible.

The destrier was in his stride now and it could not be anything other than clear that a force of advancing knights whose mounts shook the wet earth were hostile. Sure enough, a shout of alarm went up when they had yet a quarter of a mile to go. They had left their lances with the foot-soldiers and some of the archers at their base-camp and as the distance closed William drew his sword. As instructed, his division was fanning out, to strike the lines from behind on as wide a front as possible and then to turn north, harrowing the entire encampment, leaving Longsword to execute a similar manoeuvre, parallel to William's, but nearer the river's bank. In this way they hoped to spread confusion and terror along the entire line on the western bank of the Bèthune.

The next moment they were in the thick of it, slashing left and right at tents, horses and men. Some disablement of the siege-engines was under-taken by cutting the ropes on the windlasses, while a few fires were started where burning brands could be lifted off the bivouac fires and flung into the dry trappings of the pavilions. De Earley, meanwhile, sped hell-for-leather for the gate of Arques, holloaing to the startled garrison that they were friends.

'For John and the Marshal!' De Earley raised the war-cry, which was taken up by his men and, although a few arrows and quarrels were fired by the defenders, these soon ceased as, once in the shadow of the walls and outside the gate, De Earley left the wagons, hauled about and raced back the way he had come, to cut his way through the half-rallied wreckage of the besiegers who were still reeling from the rude awakening that had utterly surprised them.

Seeing the abandoned wagons, the besieged flung open the gates and drew the supplies inside before quickly re-securing the defences. It was all over in half an hour of strenuous endeavour; William, De Earley and Longsword departed as swiftly as they had come, and although William laid an ambush under De Earley for any pursuit, it had rejoined the main force by mid-afternoon, reporting that no real attempt at pursuit had been made.

'Some twenty of their chivalry rode to within a half mile of us before they abandoned the chase,' De Earley reported, his wide grin cracking his broad features. 'But they looked wrecked,' De Earley went on, laughing, 'just like us, my Lord, when we landed off that God-forsaken ship at Waterford! Though by no means destroyed, I think the enemy will feel their vulnerability to their rear from now onwards,' he added, relishing the morning's work.

***

'Well, my Lords,' crowed John, lounging at the head of the board as was his wont, a goblet of Bordeaux wine within reach. 'While you have been next to idle, God or the Devil has smiled on me.'

William resisted the urge to remonstrate, though he thought to himself the Devil had more to do with it all than Almighty God; he and Longsword had been far from idle, but the King's achievement was remarkable and it behove him to say so before Longsword, positively bristling at his elbow, said something impolitic.

'Indeed, my Liege, it seems the spirit of the Lionheart lives on,' William murmured diplomatically.

'The Lionheart be damned,' John almost chortled, ''twas an accomplishment worthy of my father, Curtmantle himself.'

'As Your Grace says,' William agreed with a smile.

Sensing sarcasm, John sat up. 'Who else could cover eighty miles in two days and raise a siege, eh? Did you raise the siege of Arques, Marshal? No, you did not, but I relieved Mirebeau, set the Queen my mother free, captured two hundred and fifty two knights and...' and here John sat back again, an expression of malicious satisfaction on his face, 'and I took Arthur of Brittany a prisoner.'

The King had every right to be pleased with himself, though he owed much to the energies of William des Roches and William de Briouze, the actual captor of Arthur. Both men were present at this summoning of the Angevin nobles to Rouen, for it seemed that - thanks to the King's swift chevauchée - the tide of war had turned in John's favour and a grand celebratory banquet was to be held that evening. Such had been the effect of John's unexpected triumph that Philippe and Baldwin had thrown-up the siege of Arques, for fear of John racing north and defeating them in the field, a state-of-mind induced in fact by the hit-and-run raids that William and Longsword had relentlessly maintained against the besiegers' supply lines and foraging parties.

'And Her Grace, the Queen Mother, my Liege; is she well?' William asked.

'Indeed, Marshal, she has retired to Fontevrault Abbey,' John said smoothly.

'Then, my Liege, your position is transformed.'

'Indeed, Marshal, it is,' responded John, only too obviously pleased with the triumph of his arms and the complimentary acknowledgement coming from a warrior of William's prowess.

Later that same night as William rose from the festive board, half sozzled with wine and anxious to find his bed, he bumped into Des Roches returning from the garde de robe.

'I have drunk too many toasts,' William said apologetically, seeing his old companion-in-arms. 'But you did well, my friend,' he added generously.

'Aye William, but God save us, I fear he will throw it

all away for he has ordered all his captives into fortresses here and in England.' Wine had loosened Des Roches tongue but the assertion puzzled William for a moment.

'What d'you mean?'

'That there is no intention to ransom them. He intends them to starve. Many are friends...relatives of mine.'

'You have heard him say so?' William was incredulous.

'Aye, to Hubert de Burgh. And the Count of Brittany is to be held close...too close for my liking, for I am Arthur's man before I am John's... None of this bodes good, only evil...' Des Roches belched and wiped his face with his hand.

William frowned, struggling to comprehend the utter stupidity of such a policy. Knowing he was befuddled with drink he thought Des Roches might be similarly encumbered.

'D'you mean...?' Under the influence of far too much wine William's reasoning powers were as slow as his speech; he frowned as he tried to tease out Des Roches' meaning. Des Roches stared back at him, the two men swaying slightly in the stone passageway, their weather-beaten faces, both lined by years of campaigning thrown into craggy chiaroscuro by the flickering of a near-by torch in its iron sconce. 'But if what you say is true,' William went on, 'he throws all that he has gained away and, in the process loses all honour.'

'An' all support,' added Des Roche, with an air of finality as he took his leave of William and reeled off to his bed-place.

William stood for a moment, supporting himself

against the cold stone wall, watching Des Roches stagger away. The fall of the leaf was already upon them and the campaigning season at an end; much mischief could be done in the wintery months and Philippe's deficiencies on the field of war could be more than made up by the skill and cunning of his diplomacy. William shook his head clear of the fumes of the celebration. John must not be allowed to treat his captives as Des Roches suggested he intended, but the key to everything lay in Arthur of Brittany.

If Arthur was to repudiate Philippe and pay homage to John, all might yet be well.

CHAPTER THIRTEEN: ARTHUR OF BRITTANY 1201 - 1203

'My Liege, I would have colloquy with you.'

William braced himself for the King's retort, for he knew enough of John's character to anticipate it.

'Has my Lord Earl insufficient work in attending to my horses that he must importune me in matters of state, for I presume it is of matters of state that you wish to speak, eh?'

'Aye, my Liege,' William replied, his tone of voice level, controlled.

'Remarkable for a man who can neither read nor write,' John remarked in a snide aside to his clerks, seeking to belittle William.

'It never stood in the way of the service I have rendered your brother or your father,' William responded smoothly. 'Nor does it do much good to alienate men by such means, my Lord King.'

'You speak frankly.' John was looking directly at William now.

'Would you have me speak otherwise?' There was an edge to William's voice now.

John let out a sigh and motioned the clerks to leave them. 'Well?' John asked curtly when they were alone. 'What *colloquy* would you have of me?'

'My Liege, I understand that of the many knights taken at Mirebeau none are to be ransomed, but all held in durance.'

John looked at William, moved uneasily in his chair and reached for his wine. 'That is my intention, and may the bastards all starve for their disloyalty.'

'But that is contrary to all the usage of war...'

'All the usage of war *hitherto*, my Lord of Pembroke,' John said pointedly, taking a draft of the red Bordeaux. 'Richard might have ransomed them or he might have castrated them, or perhaps, if he had been in good humour, merely had them killed outright. If I *remove* them and imprison them, they are beyond either martyrdom or rebellion; being unable to return to their lands; as a consequence, their provinces will remain quiescent and untaxed for the burden of ransom. Why, they should be grateful to me for leaving them in peace for they are all my fiefdoms, Angevin lands whose overlords have proved treacherous. Thereafter their revenues will come to me.'

William had not considered the wisdom of John's action as a deliberate policy. It surprised him, but he clung to his less elevated argument. 'It will not be seen thus by others who can yet raise rebellion against you, my Liege,' William pressed his point, though nursing a growing awareness of the cunning in John's reasoning.

'But I hold their lords as hostages.' John's logic seemed increasingly impervious to reasoned argument and the King had been watching the dawning comprehension in William's expression. He smiled. 'You can find no argument against this policy, I see, my Lord Earl. Perhaps you should attend the horses, after all.'

But William swiftly changed his approach, raising another matter, a matter of dynastic importance. 'And the Duke of Brittany, what of him?'

'He is my guest,' John responded.

'I do not see him at your table, my Liege.'

'Did Des Roches put you up to this importunity?' John had lost the initiative and stirred uneasily, reaching again for his cup of wine.

'No, my Liege, but I know him to be distressed by the treatment your castellans are meeting out to two of his kin, and this upon your orders, he tells me.'

'I think you have said enough. Go, before I am provoked…'

My Liege, while your arguments may have some validity, they will not prevent further rebellion and you miscalculate if you think otherwise.'

'It is not given to Kings to cavil and bend. Get out!'

'My Liege,' William shouted back, 'you have secured all that was lost, and by a brilliant feat of arms! No man could have done better. Not even the Lionheart! I beseech you that you do not fling it away!'

John sat fuming, glaring at William, whose persistence and disobedience at not withdrawing at the King's command, angered him. John rose and paced up and down the chamber, suddenly stopping in front of William and staring up at him.

'Why should ransom work this time around, eh?' He paused and William felt John's breath hot upon his own face. 'Did it work for my cunning father, or did he exhaust himself in endless warfare and die like a dog covered in shit and sores for his trouble? Eh, tell me that, for you above all men know the answer to *that*. Did it work for my lionhearted brother with his ruthless quest for victory anywhere, anyhow? Has my sainted mother, with all the sagacity that her many years are supposed to have conferred upon her, found a method of holding her beloved Aquitaine for longer than a year without the Lusignans or some other upstart house troubling the peace of the people she affects to hold in such esteem?' John broke off to resume his furious pacing, leaving William a moment to reflect on the King's meaning. 'God's blood, William,' John went on, his tone now suddenly confidential, intimate and conciliatory, 'I am neither my brother nor my father but, by the bones of the Christ, I would have peace if I could, as the Lord Jesu is my witness.' John piously crossed himself and William quickly followed suit. 'But every which-way I look I find men's hands turned against me that I must find some other method.' Again he stopped in front of William. 'Can you think of any other means by which I can stop this incessant warfare?'

An idea struck William with an almost physical impact. Both he and John could be the losers by it in the short-term, but perhaps, in the long run, they might make something of it. Staring at William John divined something in William's eyes.

'Well? What is it?'

'I may speak freely, my Liege?'

'Yes, yes,' replied John testily, quite forgetting that a moment before he had ordered William out of his presence. 'Is it not obvious that I invite your counsel.'

William brushed aside the irony.

'Then give up Normandy, my Liege, give up Anjou, Aquitaine and the rest. Rule in England. England untrammelled could make you stronger than expending blood and treasure as half a King north of the Channel

Sea and half Philippe's vassal to the southward of it. Let Arthur do you fealty for Brittany, if you wish, for the Bretons have no love of Philippe of France...'

Listening to William's proposition, John had been staring open-mouthed and now he interrupted, crashing his fist down on the board. 'By Christ, Marshal!' he roared. 'What kind of fool d'you take me for? Or what kind of a fool should *I* take you for, for such counsel?'

William raised his hand, 'My Liege, I beg of you that you will heed this,' he interjected, quietening John's outburst, 'that your father once charged me, in the name of your brother, to ever hold England for the power of the Crown, your Crown now, My Lord King.' William paused, for he had John's attention again. 'Make Arthur your sworn vassal, invest him with Normandy if you will, but remove yourself from Philippe...'

He got no further. As John imbibed the meaning of William's words he flushed with renewed and intemperate rage, raising his voice. 'God damn your soul to Hell, Marshal! Better you had stilled your tongue when first I told you to, for you have truly provoked me now!' John waved William away with a withering: 'Go!' bawling at him to: 'Tend to the horses and mind the affairs of your office lest I give it to another! My clerks are better company than you!' John roared. 'Get out! Get out! For the love of God go lest I...' John broke off and turned his blazing face away. As he withdrew, William heard John mutter to himself, 'whoso is afraid let him flee. I myself will not flee...'

When William left the King he felt the onset of an immense depression. In one sense he saw John's plight, even admired his attempt to devise a method of breaking the endless chain of cause-and-effect. William had long ago given up all hope of comprehending the minds of any of his Angevin masters, but that was when he wielded no influence whatsoever. Now matters had changed; his foray into Ireland, brief though it had been, had taught him that there existed alternative lands to those under the notional suzerainty of the King of France and that John as King of England would in many way be immeasurably more powerful unencumbered by the turbulent dynastic fiefdoms of Aquitaine, Anjou and the rest.

Impressive though John's attempt to break the endless circle of feuding, broken oaths and worthless treaties might be, he could not act alone. He would have to cede both power and reputation to Philippe, even if he was, in the end, the winner in France. As for the long-term advantages that might be procured by quietly starving all his captives, it would not answer in the short-term. William feared that it would, by default, more likely lead to the loss of John's lands south of the Channel in any case. Better to submit with an air of dignified willingness and thereby gain some advantage to the English Crown by way of indemnity, than to lose all by ignominious and inglorious military defeat.

***

And William's fears proved far from groundless. In the event it was the defection of William Des Roches to Philippe that started the rot, much as William had predicted. After Des Roches, baron after baron went over to Philippe, many the sons of those whose fathers John was holding and of whom no news was forthcoming, though there was rumour a-plenty.

John had crossed into England to hold a miserable Christmas Court at Canterbury, leaving William in Rouen and it was here that Des Roches came to William to announce his intentions.

'You will not reconsider?' William had asked.

Des Roches shook his head. 'He is not to be trusted…'

'Is Philippe?' William countered.

'Philippe has more guile and gains power by the month. He has bought Baldwin of Flanders who will not, I think, return to his old alliance with the House of Anjou, for it has cost his family too much. Philippe's star is rising, that of the Devil's brood must be in decline.' Des Roches crossed himself. 'Besides he has the Pope's ear and John has only his heel.' Des Roches paused and looked shrewdly at William. 'You have lands in Normandy, William; cleave to John and you will lose them.'

'Aye, but I have greater lands and greater title in England, the Welsh March and Ireland,' William responded ruminatively.

Des Roches shrugged, picking up and drawing on his gauntlets. 'As you will. I must bid you farewell then,' he said abruptly and was gone into the night.

As the spring of 1203 approached and the warmth of the sun began to lure the green shoots from the ground, further disturbing rumours followed the King's return to Rouen. Although few, except his own restless and independently-minded tenants, had given much thought to him, people began asking the whereabouts of Arthur, Count of Brittany. No-one, it appeared, knew anything. He had been confined in the castle of Falaise, it was said, but if true he was not there now. There was a story circulating in the water-front taverns of Rouen that a fisherman had hauled a body out of the Seine. It was richly dressed, and clearly of a young man, though the corpse was so bloated as to be unrecognisable. Enquiries as to what had happened to it, yielded nothing convincing: it has been buried somewhere, perhaps at the priory of Notre-Dame-des-Pré, but no-one could say for certain. An interrogation of the Prior yielded nothing of substance. Perhaps a young noble-man had fallen into the Seine, the Prior had said, but none could say who he was.

Some had heard that the King had declared his brother the Lionheart would have had the boy blinded and castrated, thus rendering him harmless and no threat to the existing order. Others averred that the King, being in a furious and drunken rage, had personally stoned the young man, or strangled him with his bare hands, or cut his throat with a dagger, or his eating knife as he sat at meat with Arthur beside him.

Yet another finger of accusation pointed at William de Briouze who pushed aside Hubert de Burgh, the Prince's official jailer, to kill Arthur and ingratiate himself with John. Few ever knew the truth, for the truth was too shocking, though a distraught De Burgh sought absolution for his marginal part in it, or so William heard. All William knew for certain was that Arthur had ceased to exist some time before Lady Day that year and that John, De Briouze and De Burgh had all hand some part to play in the matter.

Coming so soon after Des Roches' defection to Philippe and the start of a steady leaching of loyalty away from John towards the French King, the news of Arthur's non-existence – he was never declared dead – proved the fulcrum of fate. All the gains of Mirebeau lay in the dust and by that summer William was at war again.

***

The King's Council held at Rouen in the spring of 1203 was as unhappy as John's Christmas Court at Canterbury. Having secured the Duchy of Normandy by his triumph at Mirebeau, John's conduct in indefinitely and secretly incarcerating the barons who had thereafter fallen into his hands had swiftly borne a terrible fruit, just as William had predicted. Des Roches was swiftly followed by many others in his defection to the French camp, including the Lord of Alençon, whose lands bordered Maine and offered Philippe a southern gateway into Normandy. Both William and Longsword privately agreed that they were embarking upon a lost cause, such was the alienation of John, but both owed everything to John and in turn the King looked to them for support and for the devising of a strategy to combat the new threat to the House of Anjou.

As the King sat, biting his nails to the quick and quaffing from his goblet, William addressed those loyal lords, barons and senior knights banneret assembled in the King's presence.

'My Liege,' he began deferentially before turning to those who must defend the King's rights, 'my Lords and Gentlemen, we face a war on three fronts. In the west the turbulent Bretons must be met with force and it is My Lord the King's will that William Longsword moves with his chivalry and all his armament to meet them. In the meanwhile His Grace and I shall maintain our power here, relying upon Robert FitzWalter to hold Vaudreuil and Roger de Lacy Chateau Galliard, should Philippe advance along the line of the Seine or come by way of the Vexin. If he does, Wolfscar and I will harry him to destruction. If, on the other hand, he should march west to Maine, join Alençon and seek to come at us from the south, perhaps with some notion of linking up with the Bretons, then we will shall move against him there....'

'All depends upon the movements of Philippe,' put in Longsword awkwardly, emphasising, if it needed it, that John's strategy was, of necessity, defensive.

'My Lords,' said the King, rousing himself from his wine-induced torpor and looking about him, 'I rely upon you to assert my just cause...' There was an awkward shuffling among the assembly, as John went on, almost plaintively, his voice slurred by wine. 'And I shall not forget my gratitude to you when we prevail.' John forced a smile and turned to William. 'My Lord of Pembroke will stand exemplar of my powers to elevate a worthy man who plies his sword and directs his chivalry in my name.' John let the words hang in the air for a moment before rising unsteadily, leaving William grinding his teeth in supressed fury at being so used as all present also leapt to their feet. 'God go with you all,' the King said piously, crossing himself as the barons and knights followed suit, then fell back and made way for him as he lurched from the chamber.

'Longspear's force shall move on the morrow,' growled a flushed William, wrapping up the Council's deliberations, 'after a Mass has been said to our success. Go to it, my Lords and Gentlemen.'

He and Longsword shooed the two clerks from their writings and watched the nobles, barons and senior knights banneret as they left the room to be about their individual preparations. When they were alone, William leaned forward, both fists clenched upon the table and blew out his cheeks. 'By the Blood of Christ, I mislike this business more and more with every day that passes, Will.'

'Aye,' agreed Longsword. 'Did you ever see such a crowd of dogs with their tails in the mud? God grant De Lacy and FitzWalter hold their posts…'

'Amen to that,' William agreed, nodding.

'And pity his poor little Queen,' Longsword added in a low voice, 'that she should receive him into her bed in that condition every night, if indeed it is the Queen's bed to which he repairs.'

'Would that she would conceive and bring forth a boy,' William remarked, straightening up, 'and give us some meaning for our labours.'

'Aye.' Longsword lingered as if wanting to say more.

'Now,' remarked William, 'we must not be tardy ourselves…'

'Hold hard a moment, William, there is something that greatly troubles me.'

William guessed what was coming, but asked, 'and what is that?'

Longsword looked William in the eyes and asked, 'Do you know what became of Arthur?'

William shook his head. 'No, and if you doubt it, I would willingly swear to it upon the bones of Christ himself,' William said, crossing himself.

Longsword nodded. 'I need only your word, and I am

mightily relieved to hear you say so, for there are those that say you had a hand in it…'

'Because I stand high in the King's regard, no doubt,' William scoffed.

'Well,' shrugged Longsword, 'you know how these matters grow legs in the absence of the truth…' Longsword's voice again trailed off, but he made no move to leave the chamber.

'There is more that troubles you?' William asked.

Longsword sighed. 'Are we to take it that he is dead?'

'I do not know for certain,' William replied, recalling John's new policy. 'But if he is not yet dead he is not, I think, intended to live, and if he *is* allowed to live, he will do so blind and castrate…'

'You *know* this?' Longsword asked frowning, suddenly wary.

'No, as I have said,' William retorted testily, 'I do not *know* it; I merely guess it. John has as yet no legitimate issue; he is determined to retain Normandy and the Angevin lands – against my advice – and Arthur is, or was, a threat to him as long as he breathes.'

'So you comprehend that John is behind Arthur's disappearance?'

'I doubt *that* not at all, but whether he or another, or how, when and where, the destruction of the line of Geoffrey of Anjou is, or has been, actually accomplished, I am as anxious and as ignorant as the next man.'

Longsword nodded and held out his hand. 'I am right glad of that. I feared for a moment that His Grace's allusion to having raised you was to indicate you were an accomplice in all his machinations.'

'No,' William replied with a shake of his head. 'Nor was I flattered by such an insinuation.' He paused a moment, then went on, 'and if it troubles you that I cleave to John and do not slip the leash and lay my sword down at Philippe's feet, I will tell you, for you deserve to know and we cannot embark upon so desperate a campaign that now awaits us if you nurture suspicions about me and my loyalty. I do so because, in the first place I owe him fealty for most of my lands, especially those in Ireland, a loyalty I put above much else, but also those on the Welsh march and elsewhere in England...'

'And second...?

'And second, I see in England a brighter prospect for this House of Anjou, free at last of its curtailments and obligations to the House of Capet. Philippe grows over-weening in his manner and will wrest all his vassals' lands from them before he feels easy under his Crown. Better for John to let him have them, securing a large indemnity that would fill his own coffers, and withdraws to hold England in his own right...'

'You inferred that you had made some such proposal to him?' Longsword asked, interrupting.

'Aye, I have, and moreover, I suggested that he might yet retain some influence hereabouts by setting Arthur free under the condition that the Prince held Brittany as a fiefdom of John's, proof if it were needed that I would sooner have the young man alive than dead.'

'And John?'

'Thought me a madman, could not even consider the possibilities arising from my suggestion and all but lost his mind at the mere mention of Arthur's name.'

'From which you deduced the boy dead?'

William shrugged. 'What else was I to think? John is not the man to enjoy being reminded that he has destroyed a weapon useful in his possible diplomacy.'

Longsword nodded. 'Aye. Thank you for your candour. Now we must go our separate ways,' he said and as they parted William continued to be troubled by the brooding look in the eyes of his companion-in-arms.

For a long moment William stood alone in the Council chamber. He should himself make preparations for departure, but first he must dictate a letter to Isabelle and went in search of Thomas, his confidential clerk.

***

Amid the glittering chivalry of Normandy and England a High Mass was sung in Rouen cathedral next morning for the success of John's arms and afterwards the King rode out to speed Longsword and his men upon their way to the westward. William rode at his side, turning back into the city to review his own troops, massed under arms in an encampment beyond the eastern faubourgs.

John lingered, intent on an afternoon's hawking, which William privately deplored. While it gave him a free hand with the last of his preparations for war, it set an evil note to the King's leadership.

'The soldiers should see you, My Liege,' he expostulated.

'Have they not seen me enough?' John retorted sharply.

'They need to be imbued with a sense of readiness, of urgency,' William argued. 'They need to understand we are ready to move at a moment's notice…'

'Oh, fie,' replied John, summoning his falconer and looking up at the clear and near windless sky. 'Bring the peregrine tiercel,' he said, 'I have not flown him for a while and the day looks promising...'

'My Liege...' William expostulated.

'Get you gone Marshal,' John snapped, 'be about your business and may your chevauchée strike with its usual effectiveness.'

For a moment William regarded the King as he waited impatiently for the arrival of the peregrine. Was there a note of sarcasm in John's tone as to William's intention to employ the hit-and-run raid of his last campaign, or was he simply going to leave matters entirely in William's hands?

As the hooded bird arrived and took all of the King's attention William knew the answer to his unasked question. All was to be left to William and Longsword; if they failed John had scapegoats. 'My Liege,' he said curtly, by way of respectful farewell, tugging his horse's head around.

'You will sup with me this evening, Marshal, and we shall await news of Philippe's first move,' John called out after him, preening the slate grey plumage of the beautiful bird.

'As you wish, my Liege!' William shouted back, over his shoulder and without turning round.

CHAPTER FOURTEEN: PHILIPPE AUGUSTUS
1203 – 1204

Philippe's first move was swift and devastating. Not even William had guessed it, though he marvelled at its cleverness. It seemed the French King had learned something from his enemy, for Philippe, his army and siege-train, moved directly on Vaudreuil, by-passing Chateau Galliard and appeared before the place in such over-whelming force that the garrison threw open its gates without resistance. The circumstance had John grinding his teeth and muttering imprecations against treachery but William, less interested in matters of loyalty, realised that Philippe – whether or not he had secured his coup through treason or just sound strategy – had isolated Chateau Galliard and the Lionheart's great military complex of adjacent Les Anderlys.

'He has gained the whole left bank of the Seine, by God!' William growled at John de Earley, 'and stolen more than a mere march upon us.'

'I see the hand of William des Barres in this,' remarked De Earley.

'Maybe, but Philippe is no fool and we have taught him his business well, John, too well, I fear.'

'We must relieve Chateau Galliard,' De Earley responded, 'even though it is cut off.'

'Aye,' replied William, ruminating and rubbing his beard. 'And it will prove costly, I have no doubt.'

'Well, at least we have an objective,' added De Earley

in his cheerfully breezy manner, reposing an utter faith in William's military skill.

William considered the matter, visualising the lie of the land and sending word for Wolfscar to join him. When he had done so, the mercenary captain and William sat late into the night discussing a plan for the relief of Chateau Galliard.

***

'Is this the fellow?' William asked De Earley, looking at the matelot, who stared back with a matching curiosity. He looked as little like the mariners who had conveyed William and his retinue from Milford Haven to Ireland as a rabbit resembled a hare, reminding him more of the seaman he and poor Robert de Salignac had conversed with, on their return from the Holy Land.

'These men know their business, if not their place,' remarked De Earley, the man's lack of deference towards his master irritating the faithful knight.

'He will need to,' muttered William, turning to the matelot. 'I am told you are a good pilot for the Seine, and the chief among the barge-masters?'

'I am the Master-Pilot, Messieur,' the man answered bluntly, provoking a cough of outrage from De Earley, who growled something inaudible to William.

'How many barges can you muster, Master-Pilot?' William enquired.

'As many as your Lordship can pay for,' the matelot answered, eschewing any title.

'Thirty?'

'Forty if you wish it.'

'Forty then,' William turned and beckoned to his clerk, Thomas. 'This man will discuss terms. I require forty barges, well-manned and to be at my disposal for seven days. You will tell no-one of this until I tell you to gather them...er...' William struggled for the right phrase.

'You will want them alongside at the city quay to embark troops, I suppose.'

'I will,' agreed William, supressing a smile as De Earley fretted at the lack of respect the matelot appeared to be affording William. In fact William rather warmed to the man and his direct approach.

'At the new moon,' he persisted, stating the fact to show he guessed William's intentions.

'Indeed...'

'That will be in September...'

'And what if it is? Do you fear the gales customary at the fall of the leaf on the river?'

The Master-Pilot shrugged. 'No...' the man paused, as if considering something, then he said, 'no matter. The barges shall be at your disposal as you wish.'

'And the need for secrecy...?'

'I shall swear my fellow guild-members to that, have no fears.'

'Very well. Thomas here will settle the matter of money.'

The fellow spat on his hand and held it out to William. An outraged De Earley jumped forward and pulled the Master of the River away as William grinned at De Earley's action and the bewilderment on the Master-Pilot's face.

That evening William and Wolfscar sat at board with the King and afterwards withdrew into John's private chamber, the better not to let their plan leak out.

When he had heard what they had to say, John nodded agreement, asking only: 'And when do you intend this manoeuvre?'

'In the small hours of the night of the next new moon, Your Grace.'

'Very well,' the King responded, biting his finger-nails. 'That is what, ten days away?'

'Nine, Your Grace,' put in Wolfscar.'

That night it began to rain.

***

For six days it rained intermittently but heavily at times, the sky full of thick cloud, so that William considered the precaution of moving under the darkness of a new moon unnecessary. However, on the eve of the initiation of the operation the sky cleared, and the wisdom of the measure proved itself. That evening the King's army received its final instructions. William and Wolfscar were to lead a powerful mounted column by a roundabout route to reach the Seine near Chateau Galliard unobserved, much in the manner they had approached the French siege-lines before Arques. Meanwhile a second party of foot-soldiers and cross-bowmen were to embark in the barges and, working upstream past Vaudreuil in the darkness, to reach Anderlys shortly before dawn.

Two days before the new moon, on a crisp autumn morning, William's chivalry mounted up and rode out of the encampment and away from Rouen, disappearing into the countryside.

***

'Well?'

'There is no sign of them,' John de Earley said,

drawing rein and pulling his charger alongside William as, with Wolfscar, he waited at the head of his column in woodland near Les Andelys. It was still dark, but the September day was advancing fast and the lack of news from the river was disturbing. Everything turned upon the simultaneous attack of William's heavy, mounted chivalry and the water-borne contingent with its archers and foot-soldiers.

'May Hell's mouth swallow the bastards,' snarled Wolfscar, 'I smell ignominy in this mist...'

'There is a good deal of mist on the Seine,' added De Earley, ever optimistic, 'there is yet time.'

'Perhaps,' temporised William, his heart sinking in private agreement with Wolfscar to whom he now turned.

'What think you?' he asked.

'I am paid to fight,' Wolfscar replied shortly, 'though I would rather do so in better circumstances...'

'You could have no better company,' snapped De Earley, sensing the sneer in the mercenary's tone and jumping as always to William's defence.

'John!' snapped William. 'This is no time for divisions. Return to your post and let us know the moment you have word of the barges.'

Without a word De Earley spurred his destrier into a canter, leaving William and Wolfscar to sit their mounts in a pre-dawn silence broken only by the snicker, stamp and snort of horses, the creak of harness and a low murmuring among their waiting retinue. Above their heads the canopy of trees barely moved in the still air. After half an hour they heard again the thump of hooves and De Earley appeared, now a dark, shadowy figure in the twilight.

'The first barges are in sight!' he said, reining in.

'Very well,' responded William turning in his saddle and staring into the gloom, down the long line of mounted knights and men-at-arms. 'Pass the word,' he commanded, and heard the diminuendo of the spoken command as all grasped their reins more firmly, adjusted their buttocks in their saddles and readied their weapons.

'Pray God this is Arques all over again,' William said, crossing himself. Alongside him De Earley and Wolfscar did the same, De Earley whispering 'Amen,' then William ordered the column to advance.

Although the approach to Chateau Galliard was far longer than William's last such attack, just as at Arques they advanced under the distant but looming battlements and dongeon of the Lionheart's great castle high on its rock. And just as at Arques, the still air was full of the wood-smoke of the enemy's bivouac fires, but there the similarity ended. For if Philippe had been caught at Arques with his breech-clout round his ankles, at Chateau Galliard his sentinels were alert and his army had slept on their arms. As William's men deployed to attack, shouts of alarm went up and the great French encampment sprang to life. In an instant of comprehension William realised that Philippe had prepared for a surprise, that if he did not get his knights mounted, his chivalry stood shoulder-to-shoulder with his infantry, forming a wall of steel round his siege lines even as William's column closed with them.

What followed was a disaster for John's cause. Although few among William's force were killed, they were unable to get at the enemy, let alone break through the siege-lines. As for the showers of cross-bow quarrels that were supposed to have laid waste the enemy along the river's bank, William saw not a sign, though the broad bosom of the Seine was covered by a thick mist. Rather than an attack on two fronts, William's men found themselves under a heavy fire of bolts and arrows which did great execution among the horses and, after perhaps twenty minutes of almost futile wheeling about and shouting obscenities, Wolfscar withdrew his routiers and William followed suit with his mesnie and attached knights.

'Where in the name of Christ were your barges?' Wolfscar snarled at De Earley, reining in and removing his helmet once they had withdrawn into the forest again. All about them swirled the remnants of the bold column that had left the shelter of the trees two hours earlier, many with two men mounted up on a single horse, evidence of the damage they had suffered at French hands.

De Earley bit his lip. 'I don't know,' he admitted sheepishly, 'I swear to God I saw them...'

'Be quiet!' William commanded, and they all heard the faint thunder of horses and jingle of harness. 'They pursue us!' he added.

'They'd be damned fools not to!' Wolfscar retorted.

'We must split our force and take advantage of this mist before it clears,' William ordered quickly. 'Do you retire the way we came,' he turned to De Earley, 'John, get the mesnie to follow me.'

As Wolfscar turned about and shouted an order, William spurred his horse forward, turning to the west. For a few minutes he rode alone, then he heard his men catching up with him. It was now full daylight but the autumn sun was insufficiently warm to burn off the mist quickly and after an hour William ordered a halt. Jumping down from his horse he laid his fingers against the ground. There were neither vibration nor sounds of pursuit, only a puzzling and low but monotonously rhythmic thud-thud, coming from the direction of the Seine. William looked at De Earley.

'The barges,' he said shortly, jerking his head. Without a word and calling half a dozen of his own knights to him, De Earley set off to reconnoitre. While William waited for De Earley's report, he rode back down the column, still anxious about a French pursuit. It was here that he heard indistinct words, recognising De Earley's voice and that, he guessed, of the Pilot-Master of Rouen. When the voices ceased, so too did the rhythmic thudding and a few moments later De Earley rejoined William.

'I did see a barge,' De Earley said quickly, in an attempt to exonerate himself, 'but only one. The rest had been held back by the strong flow of the river...'

'The rain,' growled William, suddenly comprehending the effect of freshets in the river. 'The bastard did not take account of the effect of the heavy rainfall, by the Rood!'

'Aye, my Lord,' De Earley responded.

'And he could have warned us, but preferred to take our gold rather than lose the opportunity of getting his hands on it.'

'Aye, my Lord. He said he did send one barge on ahead, to warn us of their slow progress...'

'The one you saw and doubtless empty of bow-men to

speed its progress!'

De Earley said nothing, but hung his head in shame.

'My Lord Marshal!' William turned in his saddle as a knight of his mesnie rode up to the head of the column. 'I hear noises of pursuit!'

William lost not a moment. There was no point now in bringing on a fight that would only end in further humiliation and probably capture and the protracted agonies of ransom. He waved the column forward and headed downstream for Rouen.

***

William made his obeisance to the King and to the Queen. They had just come from Mass and the young woman looked pale and frightened, her small, round face almost haggard in the jumping flames of the flambeau in their sconces. 'The horses are ready, My Liege.'

John grunted. His eyes were heavy lidded, though whether from lack of sleep or an excess of wine the previous evening, William did not know. Nor, he found himself thinking, did he much care, though Queen Isabelle's plight touched him and as John drew his cloak about him and made for the steps, William offered his arm to her.

'The tower steps are slippery, Madam,' he remarked solicitously.

'My Lord...' she murmured timidly, her thanks implicit in her acceptance of his courtesy. When William and Isabelle of Angoulême reached the torch-lit courtyard, John was already mounted, nodding to his bodyguard to start the long journey, not down the Seine to Harfleur, but west to Barfleur. Above them stars glittered in the clear sky and William felt the tremor of the slender body at his side as Queen Isabelle confronted the prospect of the long and arduous ride. Assisting the Queen onto her side-saddle, William waited while she arranged her fur-lined mantle about her. It was cold, a frosty morning, the last of November, and the horses' breath wound about them in steamy wreaths.

Isabelle smiled her gratitude; she must be a stranger to kindness, William thought. 'God go with you, my Lady,' he said, quietly, stroking the warm neck of her palfrey.

'And you my Lord Pembroke.' They both crossed themselves and William swung into the saddle behind Isabelle, alongside the dozen close members of John's household and the remainder of the escort. As the Queen passed under the portcullis of the inner barbican, William took his leave of Peter de Préaux, in whose hands Rouen was left.

'I fear our Lord the King's absence may be a long one,' William said, leaning down from the saddle to clasp De Préaux's extended fist.

De Préaux nodded. He said nothing but his expression was bleak. Both men knew that Normandy was lost. Longsword's force had suffered reverses and the Bretons, under the banner of Prince Arthur's half-sister Alice, herself held in durance by John far away in Bristol, but led by Alice's father, Guy de Thouars, were already at Lisieux, *en route* towards at the western gates of Rouen. Though De Lacey continued to hold Chateau Galliard, Les Anderlys had fallen to Philippe, and all but a handful of other fortresses, including Verneuil on the southern border of Normandy, had been taken either by Philippe or De Thouars. Even now Philippe's war-host approached Rouen from the east and John's departure was nothing more than flight, conducted secretly in the pre-dawn darkness.

Just after curfew a week previously William had seen the baggage train off under the escort of Wolfscar, John de Earley and most of his own mesnie. After the affair before Chateau Galliard the two men made ill bed-fellows, but there was no helping it, for the wagons and carts contained all of John's treasure and no small amount of William's. Its quiet departure from the capital of Normandy was portentous, though John's standard continued to fly above the city and the Court continued to function as normal within the citadel.

William gave De Préaux one last, grim smile and put spurs to his horse. He was armed for war and rode his destrier, for fear of ambush and treason, treachery having been much talked about in the weeks that followed the retreat from Chateau Galliard. He was anxious to catch-up with John and his Queen as they left Rouen and had lingered alone only to sat farewell to the wretched De Préaux. In his departure, even William Marshal, Earl of Pembroke, had sent his standard on ahead, in the care of John de Earley and the heavy escort of the baggage train.

The King and his entourage moved swiftly westwards, heading first for Caen before making for Bayeux, where the pace slackened. The baggage train was now one day's ride ahead of them and, to William's ire, John ordered a break. The following morning they set off again and, on the evening of 4th December 1203, they arrived with the baggage at Barfleur where a score of vessels lay awaiting them.

The night was occupied in transferring the baggage

aboard ship and the following morning the King and Queen, their small Court and its military escort embarked for England. King John, who had long since earned the nick-name 'Lackland,' seemed now to embody that distinction, particularly among his own nobles who were personally stung by the creeping night flight from Rouen where most had left friends, lovers and families to starve under siege as the King abandoned his lands south of the Channel Sea.

***

They landed at Portsmouth from whence they proceeded to Winchester. Here John lingered for some weeks and here, one evening following Christmas, when he was playing chess with his confessor, a courier from Normandy arrived. After being ushered by William into John's presence the young knight, exhausted by his journey, had dropped to one knee, and awaited the King's pleasure, but John was intent on studying his game and, after an intolerable silence, moved his king's bishop. 'Check,' he said.

'My Liege,' prompted William, in an attempt to gain the King's attention. But John continued staring at the board as his confessor made to move a pawn, thought better of it and resumed his study of the chequered board. 'My Liege,' William repeated, 'here is one come from Rouen, with word from Peter de Préaux and who would...'

'Have colloquy with me...yes. I know...then let him speak.' John said, never lifting his eyes from the chess-board. The unfortunate knight looked from the King to William, who nodded for him to proceed.

'Your Grace, I am charged by my Lord of Préaux to

inform you that Rouen is invested.'

'De Préaux knows his duty,' the King said, as he assessed his confessor's decision to move his queen's rook, releasing his own king from bondage.

'Your Grace the city cannot hold out indefinitely...'

'If your master wishes my permission to capitulate upon terms, he does me dishonour.' John growled menacingly, sitting back with a vexed look at being interrupted in his game. 'Marshal, can you not deal with this matter?' he asked peevishly.

'My Liege, De Préaux has negotiated a thirty-day truce with King Philippe...' William began, having learned this from the courier.

'Well, then. Let him see to my affairs accordingly,' John turned away and again leant forward to study the chess-board.

'Our stocks of foodstuffs are running low, My Liege...' added the young knight, unsteady on his one, aching knee.

'Then let them starve!' John shouted rounding upon him. 'What in the name of Almighty God do you expect me to do about Rouen? Damn Rouen! Damn Chateau Galliard! Everywhere I see only treachery! Tell De Préaux his bollocks shall answer for his conduct! Tell him to hold out in my name; the campaigning season will open in two or three months' time... Now get out!'

'Come,' William murmured, touching the young man on the shoulder and leading him in search of food and a bed for the night. 'There will be no relief of Rouen,' he confided quietly. 'Tell your master to hold out as long as he can and then seeks terms...'

William found he could barely endure the look of

despair in the young knight's eyes. 'My Lord of Pembroke,' he said, half-sobbing with fatigue and profound disappointment, 'I never expected to hear such words from you.'

***

The spring of 1204 found William and Robert, Earl of Leicester, in Paris, at the Court of King Philippe II of France. They had been sent by John in the wake of the surrender of Chateau Galliard by De Lacey on the 6th March and the death, at Fontevrault, of the aged Queen Eleanor in April, to seek terms of a formal peace, but a peace which would buy time for John to prepare a new army, relieve Rouen and recover Normandy. Although William had little hope of the success of his embassy, and was only too aware of his advice to the King to relinquish all claims on his French lands, he was anxious about his estates at Longueville and his castles, which still remained in the hands of his castellans. Moreover, the news of Eleanor's death profoundly affected William, for it reminded him of his own mortality, a reminder that sat uncomfortably with his other preoccupations.

Philippe Augustus received the two English earls in private, rejecting outright King John's overtures for a treaty.

'I will hear no more of this matter of Normandy from my cousin of England,' he told the two emissaries as he bade them stand after delivering their charge. 'He has forfeit all, and his arms have failed him. The House of Anjou has lost Normandy and with the Duchy all else will crumble. Having been subject to the judgement of war, the matter is now passed beyond negotiation,'

Philippe said with an air of finality.

William felt the humiliation of the King's remarks. The King knew that having suffered at William's hands before Arques, he had trounced the Marshal under the ramparts of Chateau Galliard. William felt his cheeks burning; he was too old for this humbling, recalling the callow young man with the lank hair that he had last seen under the great elm at Gisors. The elm had been felled long ago and now King Philippe had risen to become a great King and William was obliged to submit. Then, sensing he had his quarry where he wanted them, Philippe smiled. 'However,' he said with an almost pleasant informality, 'both of you, my Lords, hold lands in Normandy and while some remain in the hands of your vassals, they now lie in my gift. You can no longer hold them under John, but my esteem for you persuades me to offer them in fief to me...' The King paused to let the import of his words sink in.

William's lands of Longueville were rich and through Isabelle he had acquired other properties, the manor of St Vaast-d-Equiqueville near Dieppe, the castles of Orbec and Meullers. If he could only hold them until his second son reached his majority, then the provision he could make for his family would secure them a bright future, whichever way the wind blew in England.

In the wake of John's futile gestures to retain power in Normandy many such accommodations were rumoured to be in the making, several Anglo-Norman barons sought to divide their patrimonies according to preference. William had no grounds to trust the French King, but he had less and less love for John, whose moods changed faster than the course run by a hunted hare, and whose policies verged now upon the fantastical. Besides, he himself had an affection for Normandy, the land of his growing-up, while Longueville and the rest he had acquired by his marriage to Isabelle de Clare and he was loath to let any of it go, for all his advice to John to relinquish Normandy. The former was a personal, familial matter, the latter based on political and military reality was the King's problem.

'Well, my Lords?' Philippe brought William back to reality with a jerk. It was clear that both he and Earl Robert had been caught-out by the French King's apparent proposition and it was equally clear that Philippe had enjoyed watching the two of them pondering their response.

'My Lord King,' Leicester began uncertainly, 'I know not what to say at this instant...' His voice trailed off and William, who could in that moment think of nothing to add, watched Philippe as he rubbed his clean-shaven chin and regarded the two discomfited and elderly men before him. It was clear that he was playing with them, but William shut his eyes to that; perhaps a compromise could be reached. He held his peace, sensing the offer would come from Philippe and that it would not be long in coming.

'My Lords,' Philippe said with a soothing reasonableness, 'should you choose to willingly surrender your rights to your Norman estates and order your castellans and seneschals to hand these places over peacefully, I should bind myself in writing to a restoration to each of you in exchange for your homage within one twelve-month of your signing such a charter. Besides this, I should require only that you each paid my treasury five-hundred silver marks.'

That evening the two men ate alone together to discuss Philippe's proposition. Being unable to read, anxious about the mention of a charter and unwilling to disclose this to Leicester, William put himself in the position of listening first to his colleague's opinion and then challenging it.

'How will you justify serving two masters?' he asked.

'We should not be the first, William. Why, do I not recall that you, yourself, refused Richard fealty for Ireland, arguing that your first obligation was to John as Lord of Leinster?'

'Aye, but Richard was King and John *his* vassal,' William countered.

'Do you think John able to dispense with your services? To you above all men he owes much. When he is reasonable he would surely see your point of view in preserving something for your sons.'

'When he is reasonable, perhaps...' William rose and began stalking up and down the chamber. It was clear that Leicester intended to fall-in with Philippe's plan, but William knew the motive behind the French King's offer, and said so. 'He would detach us from John if he could, and if he cannot, he would compromise us...'

'How long d'you think John is going to last without you in particular, eh?' Leicester asked impatiently. 'He stirs-up anger and rebellion wherever he goes.'

'And you would ride upon my back, is that it?' William retorted.

'How so?'

'Well, in my being indispensible, and in John therefore acceding to my serving two masters, you could too.'

Earl Robert shrugged. 'We must both make our way on the world, William, you and me. God knows but Queen Isabelle has yet to bring forth a boy…'

'John is young,' William snapped dismissively, 'and I am grey as a badger.' He sighed and called for more wine. 'Truth to tell, Robert, I have little appetite for any of this and sometimes long for an end to it all… Come, let us not fall out. That is what Philippe wants.'

'Let us sleep on the matter then.'

'Amen to that.'

The following morning both men broke their fast alone and then walked together by the Seine. By noon they had agreed to Philippe's proposal under a pledge of mutual support. William had come up with an argument that, far from an act of disloyalty, it might be turned to John's advantage to have two barons close to his enemy. Leicester had looked askance at this notion, but held his peace. William Marshal, Earl of Pembroke was clearly wrestling with his conscience.

Later that day they sent word by Philippe's Chamberlain that they sought a private audience with the King. But Philippe did not respond, not then, nor for a month. They were assured their message had been passed to Philippe, but that he was absent from his capital. They should, they were assured, avail themselves of the pleasures of Paris.

It was only after they heard that Peter de Préaux had thrown open the gates of Rouen to the Capetians on 24th June that a messenger arrived to summon them to the King's presence the following day.

'Well, my Lords, I am told that you desire to speak with me,' Philippe said, obviously in high good humour over the events at Rouen. Paris was full of lurid tales of the extremity to which the citizens had been reduced. Cats, dogs and rats had vanished from the streets and men and women were said to have devoured babies and eaten stewed leather.

'My Liege,' began Leicester with intended and pointed deference, 'my Lord of Pembroke and I accept your offer and are willing to set our names to such a charter as you may present us.'

'Very well,' said Philippe with a smile, then twisting their tails, asked William, 'You are at one with my Lord of Leicester?'

William swallowed hard. 'Yes, my Liege.'

And later, as William carefully inscribed the signature that his clerk Thomas had taught him, he could not get out of his head the look of cunning pleasure with which King Philippe had regarded him. He was never to forget it.

CHAPTER FIFTEEN: DOWNFALL 1204 - 1205

On their return to England, Leicester fell ill and it was Marshal alone who sought out the peripatetic Court of King John to lay before him the result of their embassy. The King lay at Nottingham, biting his nails as William reported Philippe's outright rejection of any thought of a peace treaty.

'I am dispossessed of my ancestral lands,' he murmured in that pitifully plaintive tone that William recalled hearing before. William held his peace until John stirred. 'There is something else?' the King asked.

'Aye, my Liege,' William confronted the King boldly, though with a thumping heart, preparing himself for an Angevin rage. 'My Liege, I have lands in Normandy, lands once held by Richard de Clare and acquired through my marriage to my wife, the Lady Isabelle...'

'And you wish to retain them.' John finished the sentence for him and stirred ominously again. He was no longer lolling in his customary fashion and had relinquished the stem of his goblet. Instead he had made his right fist into a tight ball.

'If it pleases my Liege Lord here in England,' William said, slowly in a speech he had deliberately rehearsed.

'And Robert of Breteuil, my Lord of Leicester, he too has lands in Normandy... what of him?'

'He is brought to bed with a serious distemper such that his life is feared for.'

'How very convenient,' remarked John sarcastically.

'And you compounded with Philippe, no doubt, to do *him* homage,' John went on, his tone of voice unremittingly derisive.

'In a twelve-month, if it pleases Your Grace, and upon a payment...'

'How much?'

'Five hundred silver marks.'

'Christ was betrayed for less...'

'There is no betrayal, my Liege...'

'No betrayal? How then is that? And do not address me as "my Liege" as I am clearly *not* your Liege!' John was peevish now, and dangerously so.

'Your Grace, I have precedent enough. After the surrender of Rouen, Peter de Préaux, who did you there honourable service, was by your consent allowed to retire to his English estates, leaving to his brother Jean the Norman lands once held by their father. Surely I might be allowed some similar compromise on behalf of mine own heirs.'

A look of astonishment crossed John's face. Then it hardened. 'In what way is that precedent for you, my Lord of Pembroke?' he asked coldly. 'Did you yourself not advise me to relinquish all my lands south of the Channel Sea? And now you require sanction to lick Philippe's arse like the dog I see you have become? By the Christ, I have raised you too high, Marshal...' John rose and thrust his face into William's, glaring up at the older man. 'And you have presumed too much!'

William's heart contracted as John turned aside and began a furious pacing of the chamber. At any moment he anticipated dismissal, in which case his cause was lost, perhaps irretrievably. He had nothing to lose now by standing his ground.

'Your Grace,' he said, 'King Philippe asks only that I do him homage, no oath of fealty was mentioned.'

John snarled dismissively at this as he turned on his heel again, struck by another thought. 'Philippe has *bought* you and Leicester, has he not?'

'No, Your Grace! Never!' William sensed his moment and grasped it. 'Never, my Liege. Have I ever once given you cause to doubt my loyalty until this moment? And now I come, not to conceal what I have done but to lay it before Your Grace in all openness and honesty.' He got no further as John cut in.

'You think me a fool, you think your age and your service to my family allows you such presumption...' William shook his head, but John continued, pacing up and down: 'I did not take your advice to relinquish my ancestral lands in exchange for an indemnity, but by the Rood I have thought often upon it. Better I had done than to be driven out at dead of night as I was.' John paused again and confronted the taller man. 'Do you know what conclusion I came to, Marshal, eh? And all upon *your* sage advice?' William shook his head. 'I perceive that the future has no room for such ambiguities that you seek. You are either for or against me, or for or against Philippe of France. Think on that, Marshal, and think not of your manor and brace of castles, but of your lands in the Welsh March and in Ireland...'

'For which I have ever done you full fealty, even in the teeth of the Lionheart, My Liege,' William snatched the advantage, though John's stale breath was hot on his face. John's eyes flickered and he turned away; William sensed a sudden change of mood.

John flung himself into his chair and grasped his wine, lifted it and drank deeply. After a long and pregnant moment of silence he expelled his breath and looked up at William. 'I fled, William, fled from my ancestral lands,' he said, his voice suddenly low, his eyes moist.

'My Lord King,' William said quietly, 'allow me to do homage to Philippe for my wife's lands in Normandy and I will swear to you upon the heirs of my body that, in any conflict, I shall cleave only to you and Your Grace's service as I have ever served your family.' William paused, then added what he considered his master-stroke, alluding to his reputation for military prowess. 'Think, My Liege, if Philippe thinks he has bought *me*, a man not unknown to him, then I might draw close to him to your advantage.'

The King frowned and stared at William. 'You would hold your homage to Philippe that lightly?' he asked after a pause.

William smiled wryly. 'My Liege, there is precedent enough for *that*. Even oaths of fealty have been cast lightly aside.'

John caught William's meaning; many had been the time he himself had broken an oath to his father, Henry Curtmantle, and his brother, Richard, Coeur-de-Lion. 'You would swear to act as you say, always, even unto death?' John asked, softening towards William.

'I would My Liege. Even unto death.'

John rubbed his chin then fell to unconsciously biting upon his finger-nails. Suddenly removing this hand from his mouth, he asked, 'but what of Leicester? What I give to you, I must give to him.'

Conscious that the King was about to change his mind

again, William pressed his case. 'The Lord Leicester is ill. Let us await God's will. Should he recover and come open-handed to Your Grace, then welcome him and reward him for his embassy. If not,' William shrugged, 'then this conversation can lie quiet between us.'

John thought for a moment then, looking at William, nodded. 'Very well, my Lord,' he said slowly, 'but should you betray me, you and the male heirs of your body shall suffer in every manner I can devise and order.'

Aware that he had been a most fortunate man, William made a deep obeisance and made to withdraw. As he did so, John added, his voice hard again, 'do you keep your word, or most assuredly I shall keep mine.'

***

'Was that wise, husband?' Isabelle asked as William told her of his audience with the King. Isabelle lay a-bed in their chamber at Chepstow Castle.

'Wise or not, it is done now,' replied William resignedly, slipping under the coverlets beside her. 'And Leicester is not expected to live, I hear.'

'Is that God's will? Isabelle asked.

'What else can it be, eh?'

'The Devil tempting my Lord's pride.'

'By Heaven and all I hope for, I would not wish such a thing upon Robert of Leicester. God forbid it! Surely you do not think that I…'

'I merely fear for you, William,' Isabelle replied, laying a hand upon his arm as he sat up in bed. 'God knows I pray for you and our boys, but I have no ruling of you. Your courage and stout heart may lead you astray from piety.'

William sighed. 'By the Rood, 'Belle, you sound like my old tutor Nicholas de Sarum.'

'Perhaps that is why God ordained that I became you wife. You forget sometimes, husband, that I am daughter of a King...'

William turned to her and smiled. 'That I do not, my love, but John does.' Then, attempting to change the subject, he remarked upon his pleasure at the betrothal of their eldest son, William, to the daughter of Baldwin of Béthune, an old friend of William's.

'Of that we are both glad,' Isabelle said wearily, composing herself for sleep.

But as Isabelle's breathing grew regular, William lay awake, troubled. He had not told his wife all that had occurred for there had been an encounter with another old acquaintance from his tourneying days, Robert de Meulan, Count of Aumale. In the collapse of Angevin power in France, De Meulan had lost almost everything and, in the name of friendship, had sought William's help. Fearful of losing Longueville, William had offered De Meulan money for his English manor of Sturminster.

'That is a harsh bargain, William...' De Meulan had said and William had noted the pathos in his old friend's eyes.

William, his head full of his most recent joust with the King, had hardened his heart and brushed De Meulan off. Now his conscience troubled him deeply; he had used De Meulan ill. Isabelle had just remarked upon his growing conceit. Now he recalled Geoffrey FitzPeter's advice not to over-reach himself, and the pride with which he had confronted his father in the hall of Hampstead Marshal after King Stephen had released him from his custody when he had hung a noose on the beam above his father's chair. Staring up into the darkness he rebuked himself, praying for Christian humility; God forbid that he should lose what he had gained through over-weening conceit.

It did little to console him that he had Sturminster passed to one of his household knights, for to compound his sin in dispossessing De Meulan of the manor, he had insisted that in granting the land to him in the first place, the King set aside the claim of two Countesses who disputed the grant. He knew that his intransigence in the matter had angered John, going as it did against the advice of others on the King's Council. He knew too that John had had an entry made by the clerks in the justice rolls; this act held the spectre of a dark threat over an illiterate man. Now, as he lay sleepless and troubled by his own folly, William could only see in his mind's eyes the reproach in the eyes of Robert de Meulan.

***

The rain fell in sheets as the war-host under the Earl of Pembroke trudged north-west, out of Carmarthen town and into Ceredigion. John De Earley led them with his own small mesnie, a van-guard with its out-riders to root-out any ambush set by the Welsh.

In the aftermath of his confrontation with the King, John had swung like a weather vane. Having lost Normandy, a rising tide of disfavour among his English barons made John preternaturally nervous of losing the loyalty of William. And if he disapproved of William's conduct over Sturminster, he nevertheless tried to placate William. In typical conduct that was both vacillating and cunning, John sought to buy William's complete loyalty by turning the tables upon him: if John must give-up Normandy, then William must relinquish Longueville and, at Winchester in early October, John had granted him in compensation the castles of Goodrich, in the east of the March, and Cilgerran in the far west. Whilst Goodrich lay in the gift of the King, Cilgerran did not, for although it had formerly been part of the Earldom of Pembroke, the Princes of Deheubarth had seized it seventy years earlier and held it ever since. Now, at the head of a force composed of William's own vassals and those who owed scutage, backed by a contingent found for him by the King, he marched to recover the lost fortress.

William had met the Princes of Gwynedd and Powys at Worcester in July and knew of the internal dissension among the Princes of Deheubarth, Maelgwyn ap Rhys having been engaged in civil strife with his nephews. With the year far advanced, William nevertheless brooked no delay, eager to make his compact with John and ease his troubled conscience. Besides, his failure to relieve Chateau Galliard had stung him and he needed some feat of arms to re-establish his reputation for prowess and recover the esteem of John in the face of a clique of the barons who, though no friends of the King, were happy enough to see the uppish 'Marshal' brought low.

As the host descended yet another hill, slipping and sliding on the wet track, William drew aside, out of the line of march, and allowed the troops to pass him as though in review. Whether mounted or not, most advanced with eyes downcast, shielding their faces from the driving rain, and they did not see William until they drew abreast of him. A ripple of recognition passed along the sodden column as men recognised the big man on his destrier. Although most marched in miserable silence, William heard the grumblers and the swearers, noting their sudden silence as they caught sight of him. At several points he rode a few yards with them before again pulling up, repeating the process over and over, until he had reached the rear, commanded by his nephew, John Marshal.

As he accompanied each detachment he spoke to them, encouraging them and promising them a short campaign and wine at the end of the day's march. A dry bed was beyond his powers to guarantee, but his words had some effect and John Marshal exchanged a grin nearly as wide as John de Earley's, when William fell in beside him and outlined his plan.

'This rain is excellent cover, then,' remarked John when he had heard all William had to say.

'Let us hope so. That and the darkness of this coming night.'

Few in the war-host slept that night although the rain eased in the small hours of the morning. Sent on ahead to reconnoitre, John de Earley reported the way open and so William roused his force and, long before the winter's dawn, marched on. Intent on surprise he knew he could push his men for two or three days before the vomiting sickness or hunger took hold of them.

Low cloud concealed their descent from the Prescelly Mountains and no-one reported their coming as they closed the castle on its rock between the Teifi and the Plysgog Rivers. In the last hour of their advance, William ordered the scaling ladders brought forward from the small train of light-weight siege engines and had them carried forward by the mounted men-at-arms.

'Get you up ahead, John,' he shouted at De Earley, urging his tired men forward in one last effort as they came in sight of their objective. Riding up and down the line, his sword drawn, William was a fury of activity and succeeded in galvanising most of his force, though a number had dropped by the wayside in the last hours of that gruelling march.

Those that stayed the course took heart on coming within sight of Cilgerran and William was obliged to ride hard to recover his position with the van as they ran and rode the last half-mile. Only then did the *teulu* of Maelgwyn see the approach of their doom, too late to offer more than a token resistance as the scaling ladders were flung up against the ramparts and a forlorn hope of the enemy stormed their defences, swiftly securing the barbican and throwing open the gates. As John de Earley's mesnie clattered under the archway and called upon the castellan to surrender they found themselves confronted with unarmed men, or men who wore neither mail nor hauberk and bore only a hurriedly snatched-up sword.

The outnumbered and surprised garrison capitulated quickly, calling for quarter which William, riding up at the head of his own mesnie, his great standard with its red lion rampant fluttering in the damp air, granted immediately.

'Tell your men to lay down their arms and we shall harm no-body,' he told the castellan, adding an invitation to dine that evening at his own board and of his own food, but at the behest of the victors.

Within two hours William's entire war-host was warming itself within the keep, laughing, eating and drinking at the expense of the Princes of Deheubarth, and extolling the brilliance of William Marshal, Earl of Pembroke, who had taken back what was rightfully his.

In the castellan's chamber William called for John de Earley, pen, ink and parchment. 'Write me two letters, John,' William said, beginning to dictate. The first was to King John, informing him that Cilgerran had fallen to his arms, the other was to Isabelle. Then he called John Marshal to him.

'My Lord,' complained his nephew ruefully, 'you left nothing but the pickings to me.'

'No, John, but you shall have the ruling of this place until the spring, for I must to the King. See that you send out a strong party to bring in those men who fell by the wayside. I would not have them taken by the resentful Welsh.' John nodded his understanding. 'I shall have you relieved in the spring,' William went on, 'when we have re-ordered our forces, I intend you to pass over into Ireland and ensure my fiefs are secure in Leinster. I shall have Thomas write to you in due course, but I tell you now in order that you may prepare such of our present force that owes myself allegiance. I must, perforce, return to the King what is his before myself crossing into Normandy. Do you write your report to the Lady Isabelle at Striguil...'

After William had left the chamber to carry out a survey of the castle, John looked at De Earley. 'The man exhausts me,' he said, wiping his brow as he poured a cup of wine.

De Earley grinned. 'That is his secret, my Lord

Marshal. Note his capacity for detail; the large and the small, nothing escape his notice,' he said admiringly.

'But Leinster...' John Marshal pulled a face, 'I hear Geoffrey FitzRobert does not enjoy his time there.'

'Maybe not,' De Earley remarked consolingly, 'but I hear his private fortune grows there.'

***

William reached the King's Court at Clere in Hampshire by mid-December, laying one of the keys of Cilgerran Castle symbolically at John's feet as he made his obeisance. William had brought Isabelle with him and it seemed, that Christmas, that John had forgiven him for his dubious conduct. As a sop to his conscience, William sent De Earley with a sum of money to De Meulan, who was now existing on royal charity alone.

In April 1205, with John's permission under the guise of a second embassy, William crossed over to France with letters of licence to King Philippe, who lay at Anet, once the scene of William's triumphs in the tourney. He presented the documents kneeling at the King's feet.

'You come alone this time, my Lord Pembroke,' Philippe observed, smiling slyly. 'I hear that God has called Robert of Leicester to account for his sins.' Philippe crossed himself. 'And may the Lord have mercy upon him.'

'Amen,' responded William, following the King's example.

'And the time of your oath-taking is upon us...'

'Aye, Your Grace.'

'Tomorrow,' said the King slowly, 'in the cathedral of Notre Dame, you shall do me fealty for your lands in France.'

William's heart missed a beat. There were others present in the King's chamber; two clerks wrote at a table, his Chamberlain stood with his rod of office close to the throne, An attendant baron or two idled further off, in nominal attendance upon their King; he could not challenge Philippe, yet he must do something to avoid the trap he suddenly realised the French King had laid for him and upon the brink of which he now teetered.

'I come humbly to do Your Grace *homage*,' William said with quiet but contradictory emphasis.

'You come to *obey*,' the King said, rising and dismissing William as he swept from the presence-chamber, the two barons falling in behind him. One of them looked back with a grin and William recognised Guillaume des Roches.

***

When he returned to England, William found the Court knew all about his humiliation at the feet of King Philippe Augustus and, in paying his respects to John, it was clear that John knew all about it too.

'By God's bones, my Lord of Pembroke, this time you have surpassed yourself in your arrogance!' John roared at him.

'My Lord King, I can tell you in all honestly that I have done nothing against you! What I did, may it please you, I did with your leave...'

'By my leave? D'you think me a fool? Then that I gave you a licence to swear fealty to the enemy of my house, and now that you can brush aside such an oath as mere homage? Eh?' John paused, cast about for a moment, then added: 'By the Christ, I gave you no such licence!'

William stood aghast. While the King was right in claiming he had given him no licence to swear fealty, he *had* given him permission to do Philippe homage for his French lands. Now John seemed to be denying even the existence of a limited authorisation. For a man who could neither read nor write much more than his name, William had no real idea of exactly what the King had given him. It seemed to William in that brief moment that his sins had found him out and that he had indeed far, far over-reached himself. Then John terminated the interview.

'Get out of my sight!' he snarled, 'and consider the fate of others; the times for serving two masters are past. Ask Robert of Meulan what befalls those who try it...' William hesitated, prompting John to roar: 'Get out before I call the guards to have you thrown out and the clerks to draw up an instrument of banishment.'

***

A few weeks later, in June, William was summoned to return to Court at Winchester where most of the barony of England had assembled. Unknown to him the King had for some months been assembling the ships and men for a major expeditionary force to sail across the Channel and recover the heartlands of the House of Anjou. Huge sums had been expended upon the hire of mercenaries and the chartering of ships, a fleet of which lay in Portsmouth Harbour. Now John mustered his chivalry to give his final orders, only to find a great number of the barons opposed to the expedition, fearing that in attempting to recover what he had lost, the King would lose what he had.

Thwarted at this late hour, after laying out

considerable sums in preparation, John was in no mood for debate. In a cold rage he resolved to command his vassal Lords, one by one, to serve him in France. He began with William, who demurred.

'My Liege, as you well know, I cannot fight for you in France being in that country King Philippe's man. Command me anywhere else and you shall find me…'

'Bollocks, my Lord!' John bawled. 'Utter bollocks! You are a traitor to my Crown, Marshal! My Lords,' John lowered his voice and addressed his nobles, pointing at William. 'Judge you not that this man is a traitor?' It was a masterly performance, an attempt to both coerce those who shared William's intention, if not his reason, calling upon those among them whom, John knew, were nursing a growing animus against William. There was a growl of agreement among the younger knights, particularly those envious of William who served in the King's household.

'Philippe of France has put you up to this, Marshal,' snarled John, but William interrupted him.

'No, my Lord King, Philippe of France has not put me up to this. Besides my inability to follow you into France, there is my opinion, and that is that such an expedition as you now propose is a monstrous folly…'

A murmur of agreement met this contention by William and, for a moment he thought that he might guide the debate into a sensible channel, but John's blood was up and he was intent on making William pay for all his recent sins, real and imagined.

'I am your King,' he snarled quietly enough, but his voice rose as he recited his titles. 'I am, besides, Duke of Normandy, Duke of Aquitaine, Count of Anjou, Maine,

Poitou! I am to be obeyed, not thwarted and checked like a dog.'

'Why then did you call us to your Council?' riposted William.

'To inform you of the service I required of you! Now your refusal exposes you as a traitor whose disloyalty is now become so notorious that in failing to banish you before, I shall now have you confined to await my pleasure! You are an instrument of France and by God you shall answer for it!'

William's temper rose with the heat of his blood. Whatever his shortcomings he was not a man to be so publicly humiliated and he flung down his challenge to the King in a voice of fury that roared out above the King's as he stepped forward, alone between the King and the assembled chivalry.

'Good my Lord King, answer it I shall and by my honour too!' He spun round, turning his back upon John. Raking the gathering of nobles, barons, and knights with a glare, he bellowed: 'I will meet any man in arms to settle this matter, to try in single combat whether I be a traitor or not! Any man!'

In the long silence that followed, the assembled chivalry looked at one another and seemed to shrink away from William, further isolating him. Instead of fear William was suddenly swept by a sensation of exhilaration such that he had not felt in years.

'Any man,' he repeated, almost mocking them, 'be he half my age...'

There was utter silence, though behind him John moved, biting his finger-nails and supressing a rage as not one of his nobles stepped forward to take this old man at his word. But William had not finished. Turning back to King but addressing the greater company he said, greatly daring, 'be alert to the King, lest what he thinks to do to me, he will later do to each and every one of you!'

The King flung his goblet across the chamber with a cry of strangled anger and quickly Baldwin of Béthune stepped forward in an attempt to end the unpleasant spectacle of so public a clash.

'My Liege,' he said, 'too many hot words have been here flung about without the coolness of thought. I beg you that good sense might prevail and that God's peace may reign among good Christians...'

A number of the barons muttered their 'Amens,' and although this was not universal, it took the heat out of the moment. John slumped in his seat and ground his teeth while John de Earley stepped forward and, taking William's arm, drew him through the crowd – which parted for them – and out of the presence-chamber.

'By the Christ, my Lord, but you will ruin us all yet,' murmured De Earley; he was not smiling.

Later, Archbishop Hubert FitzWalter, came to William who sat late at his board in company with a handful of his household knights, drinking deeply. 'I have persuaded His Grace to abandon his projected expedition, at least for the time being, and largely on the grounds of your sound military advice, my Lord of Pembroke. But you have this day given grave offence and I am to tell you that the King has withdrawn his favour from you.'

William sighed, but held his tongue, overwhelmed by a sense of shame and anger that he had been made a fool of by King Philippe, and – at a stroke – lost his reputation for loyalty. In his cups, his ambition had the taste of ashes and, even as the Archbishop had entered the room, he had conceived the idea of taking the cross. He would best serve his family by leaving Isabelle to manage his affairs and sail with such of his mesnie who would accompany him to Outremer, for he had an affiliation with the Knights Templars.

But John had other plans for him and FitzWalter was his mouth-piece.

'You are to deliver up your son William, my Lord,' Fitzwalter announced with a chilling finality, 'as a ward to His Grace the King.'

***

William placed his hand on the lad's shoulder as Isabelle stifled the urge to weep. The atmosphere in the couple's private chambers in Chepstow Castle was chilly with uncertainty. 'The King would keep you close to his person, Will,' he explained, trying to keep his voice unemotional, 'as I was kept close to Stephen during the Anarchy. This is a service you must render me for my sake and that of your mother, brother and all our family. Do you understand?'

'Aye, father.'

William said nothing more for a while but squeezed the lad's shoulder. After a moment he managed to add, 'you bear a proud name, Will, and the blood of Kings runs in your veins too, thanks to your mother.'

'What will become of you, father?'

'Me? Oh, I am ordered north, to meet and escort King William of Scotland to York where my Lord the King intends a conference.'

When the younger William had left them, Isabelle said coldly, 'I fear he will suffer the fate of Arthur of Brittany, husband.'

William rose. 'No, John would not do that.' He has yet some need of me though he pretends not and sends me upon this embassy to keep me from Court. Hubert FitzWalter has warned me that he will punish me by taking some of my lands, probably those in Sussex, but I am persuaded, both by FitzWalter and Ranulph of Chester, that he has need of me to hold the Welsh March and possibly England if he ventures into France next year.'

'By the Cross,' Isabelle said quietly, 'I hope you are right.' She paused but William knew her to be angry with him, still fearful for her first-born, yet unwilling to cause a deep rift between them. 'If anything happens to…'

'The lad is fifteen Isabelle. I was but five…' William broke off and Isabelle looked up, thinking her husband lost in recollection, but William had made a shrewd decision and suddenly changed the subject. 'If John *does* venture into France when the campaigning season opens, I shall send a powerful contingent of my men to serve him…'

'Is that all you can think of? Besides, you would appease him thus?'

'I would *serve* him thus,' said William shortly. 'As for myself, I am too old to go campaigning. I shall, when the moment is right and I can see how the land lies, seek his permission to go quietly into Ireland. And you 'Belle, shall come with me.'

Printed in Great Britain
by Amazon

82113802R00174

The King's Knight

RICHARD WOODMAN